CRIMSON REIGNS

BRENDAN NOBLE

For my family, who have made this series possible with their love, support, editing, and tolerance of my endless rants about the book.

Also by Brendan Noble
The Prism Files, Book One:
The Fractured Prism

Contents

Chapter 1

Drip. Drip. Drip. I had lost count of the number of water droplets that had seeped through the crack in the ceiling ages ago. The puddle in the middle of my prison cell reflected the sunlight sneaking through the window, the only way to follow the passage of time. The light came and went, the ceiling dripped and dripped, and I slowly lost my mind to boredom. *Why didn't they just kill me?*

There was nothing to do in that cold, cramped cell. In the corner, a camera watched my every move. Its little red light robbed me of my sleep every night. Poseidon told me once that your brain knows when you're being watched and puts you on alert, so you should never stare at your target.

Poseidon. He was the closest thing I ever had to a dad, and he was butchered by Razor: someone he trusted, who I trusted. I got my revenge, but that couldn't bring him back. I would never be able to bury him. The United People's Front will have already dumped his body into some remote pit with the others they'd slain. He was better than that. He was better than them. Despite his rough appearance, he always had a good heart. *Had.*

Razor, or should I say "Otto Preus," betrayed us all the night of Operation Blackout. If I hadn't stopped him, the UPF's cameras would still be up, spying on every part of peoples' lives. If he'd managed to kill me, I wouldn't have been able to save Julia and her family from Isaac and Wilhelm Preus. The Militia was all but destroyed because of him, slaughtered in the homes of those kind enough to open their doors to the desperate Reds trying to avoid being dragged off to the UPF camps, where they would inevitably be worked to death. *So many innocent people dead because of a political game.*

The Preus family wanted the throne, but instead, they got chaos. Wilhelm lost his eldest son, Isaac, when I shot him, and he would likely never see Otto again. I didn't feel bad. After killing the King and spoiling our chance at uniting against the People's Front, he deserved to suffer. He deserved every bullet I put in both he and Isaac's chests. Wilhelm deserved to live the rest of his life knowing that he would go down in history as a mass murdering villain. *Snake.*

I rubbed my left forearm. The pain from the burn had faded in time, but the scars remained. They were yet another reminder of Razor's betrayal and my failure to realize it sooner. We lost Southpaw and Bobcat when the UPF burned down that safe house the night I saved Julia. The saddest thing, though, was that they were now just two more names on a long list of deaths caused by that traitor. He wasn't dead —yet— because I showed him the mercy he refused to show so many helpless Reds. He would pay for his betrayal, though. If I couldn't make sure of it, Delaware would.

I swung my legs over the edge of my bed, if you could call it a bed, and groaned in pain. In high security solitary they gave us nothing more a slab of wood covered with a sheet to sleep on. It was better than the cold and wet stone floor but was not great for the bullet wound on my arm. It had slowly started to heal in the week and a half since Wilhelm shot me during the coup attempt, but without adequate treatment, the throbbing pain remained.

The UPF guards would be coming to collect me soon for my trial, where I would be sentenced to die for my crimes against "the collective." It didn't matter that I saved almost the entire royal family and nearly a hundred Whites. It didn't matter that the People's Front was complicit in the attempted royal coup and responsible for the death of the King. They desperately needed someone to blame, and I was an easy target. *Coyote's dead, but they can still kill Ivan.*

I thought years ago that I had come to terms with the inevitable ending of a life in the Militia. Maybe I had back then, but now, I had something, and someone, to live for. *I'm sorry Julia.* She had lost her dad already, and now I would be executed as she watched, unable to stop it.

I missed her more than anything. In that moment I would have given everything I had left to see her just one more time, but there was no way the UPF would let that happen. They needed me to be seen as a terrorist and a threat to the average person, not the hero who saved the princess and most of her family. Isaac had announced our relationship to the royals in the ballroom, but to the public, it was still nothing but a rumor. If people found any proof that our relationship was real, I would suddenly become relatable, human, and dangerous. Instead of killing the terrorist masquerading as Coyote, they would be killing the boyfriend of the pure and innocent Princess Julia.

I had heard nothing from outside the prison since they came

for me that night. They had dragged me away from Julia as she mourned over her father's body. I had yelled and fought to no avail as she watched me go, helpless to stop them. *The government must be destroying me in the news, but how are Julia and the rest of her family reacting? Are Delaware and Snapback out there working to get me out?* There was no way to know, stuffed in that stone and metal cell, isolated from the world.

The familiar noise of military boots on the stone floor echoed from the hall, growing closer as I knelt and put my hands behind my head. I still had the bruises from my multiple lessons on what happened when I resisted. *My fight is over now.*

Light flooded into the room as three guards flung open the steel door and started barking orders, "On the ground, now!"

I didn't move fast enough and received a swift kick in the chest, knocking the wind out of me and forcing me to struggle for air as I lay face-down on the ground.

A guard spat at my cheek and muttered as he cuffed me, "Terrorist piece of shit."

The biggest one yanked me to my feet and gave me a push to get me moving. My bare feet shuffled along the rough stone floor, each step feeling like a mile as I began my death march. My mind was numb. There was little to no hope left, and thinking about Julia, Delaware, and Poseidon just made me feel sad and alone. I couldn't afford to show that emotion as I faced the court. There was no way I'd let them have the satisfaction of knowing they got to me.

I was pulled from my trance as we reached the entrance of the prison and a roar of voices hit me at once. One of the guards opened the door into the frozen world, and I tried to comprehend the chaos that was unfolding outside. In the early morning light, UPF guardsmen were dressed in riot gear and trying to hold open a path for us to the armored van waiting ahead. Oranges and Reds were spread as far as I could see, pushing against the line of guards, the frigid wind carrying their calls for my freedom across the terrace.

The noise was overwhelming, and the guards looked worried as we approached the van. I saw the fear in the eyes of the Red Tags beyond the wall of riot police. They were all strangers, but they were risking their lives to fight for mine.

Suddenly, I noticed a familiar face, and my heart stopped. Poking her head between two guards on my left was Delaware. She smiled for a moment as our eyes met. Then, the lines of guards broke like a dam, and protestors flooded the aisle.

The world erupted into fighting and yelling, and I was grabbed and pulled towards my right. I was defenseless with my cuffed wrists, and a guard intercepted the Orange who was pulling me. In the resulting scuffle, I was knocked to the ground, and my head smacked into the pavement with a *crack* as I cried out in pain.

After what felt like an eternity of lying there, disoriented, I struggled to my feet and pushed my way towards the road. The protestors stood their ground, trying to stop the guards from closing in on me. I was nearly there when a series of shots rang throughout the terrace. *They won't let me get away...*

Around me, the first few bodies hit the pavement. Screams filled the air as I threw myself back onto the ground in desperation, hoping the bullets wouldn't hit me.

The sounds of gunfire and the thunder of the crowd running from the scene surrounded me as I lay there, frozen and wondering if I would die before even going to trial. After another minute, though, the shots and the screams faded. The guards barked orders to each other and to me, but my ears were still ringing, and I didn't understand what they were saying. One of them grabbed me and yanked me off the bloody pavement. I didn't resist. *They tried to save me, but they just delayed the inevitable.*

The guard pulled me quickly towards the van, and I had just enough time to see the carnage around me. Bodies were sprawled in every direction: Oranges and Reds gunned down like savages, their eyes wide in the terror of their final moments. The pavement was a pool of crimson. The smells and sights were awful. I wanted to vomit, but they'd starved me for days, and there was nothing in my stomach to throw up.

Where is Delaware? I couldn't see her anywhere, which was a good sign, but there was a sea of bodies. She could have been anywhere. I put a foot in the van and took one last look down the street, hoping to see her. The guards pushed me forward, but in that moment, I spotted her short frame in the distance, looking at me hopelessly. *Thank God. She's alive.*

This was a new, awakened UPF. A few months ago, there was no way they'd openly gun people down in the streets, even Reds. They used to act in the shadows, arresting people before executions, but with the Secretary of Intelligence's journal, Operation Blackout, the Preus' coup attempt, and everything that must have happened while I was in prison, they'd put their fist down.

A guard pushed my head down as I stepped into the black van.

My mind spun as he attached a chain to my cuffs, forced me onto the bench along the side, and threw a black hood over my head. The van lurched into gear, and we began the drive to the court-house.

Chapter 2

I *won't leave here alive.* Our footsteps echoed as the guards dragged me down a hall. With the hood, I had no idea where we were heading within the building. The air was warm, and I could hear the soft *ding* of an elevator.

I couldn't help but think about what had just happened. There were so many people on that terrace, so many people dead trying to help me. *Why die for a lost cause like me?* If they had killed Delaware, I don't know what I would have done or could have done. If I finished my life knowing my best friend died in a desperate attempt to save me...

We stopped for a few seconds before I heard the elevator door slide open in front of us. The guards pulled me onto the elevator, and I hummed along to the jazz until a sharp elbow was jabbed into my side. They kept a tight grip on my arms as the door opened, and we stepped into the room. For few moments, we just stood there in silence until a deep voice came from a few yards ahead. "Take off his hood."

Light flooded into my eyes, and I squinted, trying to identify the speaker.

The figure moved behind a desk and sat in a large leather chair. "Come, Ivan. Sit."

My eyes finally adjusted, and my heart stopped. *Bachton.*

The General Secretary of Northern Mississippi pointed to one of two chairs across from his desk. "I said *sit*."

The guards released me, and I hesitated before walking towards the chair, acting as if there was a trap along the path. *Why am I here?* I sat and held my cuffed hands uncomfortably behind my back. Bachton's eyes scanned me for a moment, waiting for me to say something, but I was both too shocked and too cynical to speak, so I just stared at him.

His purple tag and bald head shone in the sunlight spilling through the window as he leaned forward on his desk. "It truly is a pleasure to finally meet you, Ivan. Though, I never expected the *infamous* Coyote to just fall into our laps. Impressive, how you managed to hide in plain sight." A wry smile crept over his face.

I didn't respond.

He laughed. "You shocked us all when you managed to not only escape our trap but also stop the Preus' coup. Of course, though, the public will hear about our heroic rescue of the royal family from Coyote and his terrorists."

I shook my head. "I expected nothing more than a lie, but people will see through this one."

"Don't you see, Ivan? The truth is what I say it is. Everything else is the lie. The truth is controlled by the providers of information, history controlled by the victors, and politics controlled by those willing to play outside the rules. To the collective, you are nothing more than a conspiracy theorist wishing to blow up the glorious society that we have created."

I rolled my eyes. "There were a hundred people in that room, all influential and trusted. You can silence some Reds on the street, but you won't stop the royals from telling the truth. Killing me won't silence them."

Surprise crossed his face for a passing moment. "Very good, Ivan, but you miss the point. They can talk all they want, but people see what we want them to see, hear what we want them to hear. The royals are nothing but whispers of an old, dead regime. An old, dead regime that allowed for the creation of the system you seem to despise."

The last thing I wanted was for him to be right, but he had a point. There was little difference between the old, corrupt American monarchy and the shadow that existed in 2021, a hundred years after the end of the Third Civil War, when the old Kingdom of America was divided, and the socialist People's Front took control of Minnesota, Wisconsin, and Iowa, creating Northern Mississippi.

The monarchy still clung to whatever power they had, everyone else be damned. Even most of those who would have helped the Militia against the UPF cared about regaining the monarchy's hold on power, not about freeing the people. It was an uncomfortable compromise from the start, but I had worked for years outside of the system. Nothing had changed, but now, I saw hope in using the monarchy and its flaws for good.

I shifted uncomfortably in my seat, lacking a response to his prying. *He wants a reaction. Don't give him one.*

Bachton sighed and rubbed the bridge of his nose. *Poseidon used to do that when he was disappointed.* He spoke, "It is quite amazing how much I've learned about you in recent months. We wondered for so long about the man behind the Coyote mask and how he somehow made himself more important than El Capitan himself."

He was flattering me to get a response. It worked. "Someone has to be the vocal one. I made a good mouthpiece."

He smiled, content that he had provoked another response. "Yet, it was so much more than that. A shame. The hunt was fascinating, until Otto Preus handed over everything."

I clenched my fists, and my blood pressure rose as I thought about Razor's betrayal. He was my recruit, my friend, and he ruined everything. I had failed to spot the mole; Bachton knew it.

He raised an eyebrow, entertained yet again by my physical response. "Not only did you manage to piss us off, but you also angered the third most powerful royal family. You, Ivan, are *quite* the coalition builder. The Preus family came right to us after your little spat with Isaac ruined their agreement with King Timothy." He noticed my surprise. "You caused this, and I can't thank you enough. You even stopped that idiot Wilhelm from taking the throne for us."

I was speechless. What was their plan? Who did they want on the throne? Was King Timothy III's death my fault?

The General Secretary chuckled as my mouth hung open. "That Preus fool had actual ambition. That is not what the monarchy is for. You saved me from having to plan an assassination."

I furrowed my brow. "Why did you bring me here? To gloat before you take my head off?"

He sighed and sat back, causing the sunlight to reflect off his head and into my eyes. I squinted as he shook his head and responded, "Unfortunately, no." Reaching down, he opened a drawer, and pulled out a fancy sheet of parchment. His eyes scanned it before he set it on the desk and continued as he slid the parchment towards me. "In the absence of a monarch, the Royal Council has issued this decree. Read."

Tentatively, I leaned forward to read the parchment. The ice-blue seal of the Hughes family was emblazoned on the bottom, next to the white crown of the Royal Council. The General Secretary's eyes analyzed me as I read, shocked. It was a brief account of the events following Operation Blackout, detailing how I saved most of the Hughes family and the other royals. They were vouching for me.

I was overwhelmed, and my heart stopped as I reached the bottom of the letter: *As a servant, owned and overseen by the royal Hughes family, Ivan falls under the jurisdiction of royal law and the judgement of the Royal Council. Therefore, the Royal Council, on behalf of the request of Queen Vera Hughes and her daughters, does issue this pardon of Ivan 181375 for any and all crimes committed as of the time of this declaration. We request he be released immediately and returned Hughes family service under the terms of the Treaty of Minneapolis.*

My head spun. *I'm not going to die.* Queen Vera had requested my release, but why? She had to know that this would damage her family's reputation ahead of the crucial vote for a new monarch. It put them in danger. The public saw me as a terrorist, nothing more, and they hated me for it. Now, that rage would be pointed at the Hughes family, at Julia.

Bachton folded his hands together as I slumped back in my chair. I'd spent the last week and a half awaiting my trial and death sentence. Now, I had a whole new set of challenges, none of which I was prepared for. My release would create yet another crack in royal political life, one that the man in front of me would surely take advantage of.

The Queen was right. I'm nothing but a pawn. She was far too skilled at maneuvering within the political world to take a risk like that for no reason. Whatever her play was, though, I couldn't see it.

"I had hoped to see you dead for quite some time, but it appears that your princess has convinced the Queen to save your life." He sighed. "Unfortunately, my hands are tied. Violating the Treaty of Minneapolis would end the peace we've held for so long with the royals, so I will honor the Royal Council's request. I do so look forward to seeing what problems you cause for the monarchy next."

I clenched my fists behind my back and cocked my head to the side. "Sad, you won't be able to see any of it. How're your cameras? I heard they caught a virus."

He let out a single, obnoxious laugh. "You are correct. Somehow, even with our intel, your little mission did quite a lot of damage to our systems. But fear not, we will have them back soon. Besides, your little Militia is destroyed, and the royals are weak and divided. You have accomplished nothing, Ivan. To the collective, you are nothing but a nuisance."

"And you're a mass murderer," I snapped and then hesitated. "Now, can I take the fancy piece of paper and go, or you got something in the other drawer?"

He ignored my sarcastic remark and stood. "I have a country to run. While you insist on destroying everything you touch, some of us must ensure that we keep on moving forward." He gestured to the elevator. "My men will show you out, and, one last time, I'd like to thank you for your valuable services for the collective." *Bastard.*

I stood, stared into his eyes for a moment, and shuffled towards the elevator. As I approached the guards, I looked at one of them. "I'm a free man now. Please remove the cuffs."

He scoffed and pushed me onto the elevator. I stumbled into the wall and leaned against it, taking a deep breath as a black bag was, yet again, thrown over my head. This time, though, I was going home.

Chapter 3

There are different cages in life. Some are physical, others are built by our mind's imagination, and even more are beyond our knowledge. Death is the most obvious one. It's unavoidable, yet I had been handed the key. For some reason, God or fate or whatever decided that I got to live on while innocent people died around me every day. Queen Vera should never have pushed for my pardon, and Bachton should not have allowed me to walk away, alive and free. Yet, my freedom sat in front of me in ink, stamped with an official seal.

I was not free, though. Not really. I had been handed the key to one cage but had stepped into another. This one was different. There were no sharp objects trying to kill me, no bars holding me in. Instead, it was hard to tell that there was a cage at all. It was a large open space, stretching as far as I could see, a mirage. A cage of glass makes you feel free, until everything shatters around you.

After our van had taken a few turns, one of the guards removed the bag from over my head. I didn't understand the need for it in the first place; the van had no windows. I still had no idea what building we had been in, though it was obviously in downtown Minneapolis. *What were they trying to hide?*

I sighed and spun my cramped wrists within the cuffs. Everything hurt, from my head to my heart. I didn't know why, but I was going home. It was home, in a way. The palace held the girl I loved. The Enclave would always occupy a part of my heart, but it was gone now. I assumed that after the raids, the Reds I'd seen outside the jail were those left, scattered among the various neighborhoods north of the river. The police hadn't taken them yet, but they were next.

I remembered what Bachton had said. He was keeping me alive partially because he thought I was useful. I was over my head in the political game, just treading water after diving into the deep end. That recklessness had almost killed me and everyone I cared about. I had pushed too hard, and everything we'd worked for, everything we'd suffered for, had been for nothing. Operation Blackout took out the UPF's cameras for now, but there was no legitimate threat to their power that could exploit that weakness.

I leaned my head back against the wall of the van, feeling each bump in the road on my skull. Of all my evasions of death, today had been the biggest. Nothing was just about me anymore, unlike in the past. Sure, the Militia would have mourned the loss of Coyote, but there was always another lieutenant to step into the role, always another Red willing to die for the cause. Now, everything I did meddled with the fragile balance of power in Northern Mississippi, each step causing another crack in its foundations. I was allowed to move into the royal world again, but I wasn't sure if that was a good thing.

The van rolled to a stop as the driver bickered with someone. *Must be the royal gates.* I doubted that the royals wanted UPF goons anywhere near the palace after their support of the Preus' coup attempt. The whole situation was ready to explode. All it needed was a fuse. *Bachton hopes that's me.*

The first time I'd entered through those golden gates, I was a hero, the savior of the princess. Even if I didn't receive the welcome of one from most of the palace occupants, the Hughes family had been grateful for what I'd done. Now, I was no stranger, though I did not expect a warm welcome from many in the palace. A Red entering the royal territory as a hero was controversial enough. A Red with a history in the Militia —entering in chains— was unacceptable for the Whites.

As I heard the gates screech open, those thoughts faded, and my heart raced. I could see Julia again. *My princess.* After all the chaos of the past few weeks, all I wanted to do was hold her forever. I laughed quietly to myself as I thought about how much I had missed the smell of her wintergreen perfume and that rebellious smile she only wore around me.

Julia had lost so much. She'd mourned the loss of her dad for the last week and a half without me, and on top of that, she'd surely seen me torn apart on the news while I awaited my execution. If her mom and the Council hadn't saved me, she would have lost the two most important men in her life. She of all people didn't deserve that.

The guard across from me glared at me as he said, "Wipe that smirk off your face, you scum. Just because the General Secretary agreed to let you go doesn't mean you can't be touched."

I looked down, still smiling to myself before looking back up to the guard. I asked, curious, "Why do you do this? You heard what he said, how he lies to people for power. How do you sleep at night knowing that's the man you support every day?"

The guard looked across to his colleague before responding to me, "You wouldn't understand. I have a kid, a family. All of this, it might not be perfect, but I've heard the stories about before, when *they* were in charge." He nodded his head towards what I assumed was the palace. "We have food, a home, and safety. Things run smoothly when you terrorists aren't bombing factories and destroying our cameras."

I shook my head. "I don't think *you* understand the state that we live in. It must be nice, living comfortably as a Green. Hell, I'd settle for a last name."

The guard to my left barked, "That's enough!"

I lowered my head and stared at the ground in front of me. *These guards, even if they hate me, are people* too. They'd chosen a different path, one that I thought was wrong, but I didn't see evil in them. At least most of them had souls, unlike the heartless beast that had sat in front of me less than an hour before. My fight was not with them, even if our roles meant we stood on opposing ends of the battlefield. They wanted a good life for the ones they loved, just like me.

The brakes rattled as we came to a stop. The angrier guard yanked me to my feet as the other slid open the side door, and I stepped out into the light. Waiting for me on the snowy steps was Michael, a Blue butler and Queen Vera's right-hand man. He looked almost happy to see me, as a grin crept over his face. His pompous voice hid any excitement, though. "Welcome, Ivan. Queen Vera is waiting for you in the throne room. Guards, please remove the restraints."

The angry one huffed and unlocked my cuffs. The guard winced as he released me, like someone had punched him in the gut. It felt good, having UPF guards to escort me to freedom when they'd rather kill me.

I rubbed my irritated wrists, happy to finally have use of my hands again. "Good to see you too, Michael, or should I say, 'sir.'"

Michael sighed, disappointed in me as always. "Follow me."

My bare toes froze as I followed him towards the entrance, my feet molding into the snow with each step as the air sent a familiar shiver down my spine. I would soon be warm, fed, and actually clothed. *The palace has spoiled me already...*

Michael maintained his perfect posture and poise as we continued through the Great Hall. Repairs were underway to fix the damage from the Preus' coup, but bullet holes remained. The damage continued through the hallways towards the throne room. *You can't destroy what you want to rule.*

I shuddered as I thought about what the ballroom must look like after that night, and I had no desire to return anytime soon. In my mind, I could still picture the King's large body slumped onto the ground, one bullet in his brain as a crimson halo pooled around his head. Nothing could change my failure to save him.

Every night, I saw the same image of Isaac holding a gun to Julia's head, and every night I pulled the trigger again and again. Even now, I felt the rage boiling inside of me. Julia was mine to protect, and he had threatened her in more ways than one. I would never regret that kill. *Burn in hell, Isaac.*

We reached the doors to the throne room, and I studied the great lion stretched proudly across their face. The Hughes family had held the throne since the creation of Northern Mississippi. Was that era about to end? That question would have to wait for later, though, as the doors slid open, and Michael motioned with his head for me to follow.

The world outside was snow; the throne room inside was ice. The ice-blue carpet and decorative banners of the Hughes family still hung as the country awaited the election of a new monarch. My return to this room was as uncertain as my initial entrance no more than four months ago. Before, I wondered about King Timothy's intentions, now I wondered about his widow's.

Queen Vera sat on the throne, studying me as I entered. Since she was born in Russia, she could not be elected queen herself, but I could tell she was enjoying the throne while she could. She wore black in mourning for her husband. I felt sorry for her, but I'm not sure how sorry she actually was. As I approached, her face was expressionless, exposing nothing. With Timothy III dead, her favorite daughter, Natasha, could finally take the throne. She had cared for her husband, but he was not the puppet that she wanted him to be.

On either side of her stood the princesses, also dressed in black for their dad. As I walked, Julia's eyes met mine, and we traded smiles. It took everything I had not to sprint across the room and hug her. Despite her excitement, though, her eyes looked tired. She had been through so much, and I hadn't been there. She was trying to hold her graceful front, but I knew her too well. This had been an awful week and a half for her, yet she was still trying to be brave.

Next to her, Alexandria smiled softly, and I nodded to her. It was abnormal for her to be so modest and formal, as she wore the same simple dress as her sisters, and her usual rebellious demeanor was replaced with sorrow. Between the disgusting attack on her and the loss of her father, she obviously felt the weight of it all. Alex was one to normally disguise it with a dismissive attitude, but this was too much. She deserved better; they all did.

Natasha and Helena stood to their mother's left with poise and dignity, as always. They had been trained by Vera to hide their emotions in public, and that was exactly what they did. Natasha couldn't let feelings get in the way of her election to the throne. Now was a time for focus.

I smiled at Julia one last time before kneeling in front of the throne and looking up at Vera. "Your highness, m'ladies, I am forever in your debt. You saved my life."

Vera responded, her ever so slight Russian accent creeping into her voice, "And you, Ivan, saved ours. I shudder when I ponder what could have occurred if you had not arrived."

Natasha stepped forward and spoke, her voice pristine like fine china. "You acted bravely. Count Wilhelm and Baron Isaac would have taken all of our lives if you had not stopped them. Thank you, Ivan." She stepped back, as if returning to an assigned position.

I could only nod and look down in response. I appreciated the gratitude, but it was hard to know what was genuine and what was for show. My gut told me that everything so far had been the latter.

Vera sat up straighter in the throne. While her stature was much less intimidating than that of her husband, it was hard to not feel humbled when kneeling in front of the throne. "Natasha is correct. We are all incredibly grateful for what you did for us that evening, regardless of your *activities* beforehand. The pardon is simply an expression of that gratitude on the part of both our family and the Royal Council. While this may put us in a... difficult... situation, we feel that it is a just reward for your bravery."

It may have been flattery, but it was working, and I felt a sense of pride about that night for the first time. Before, there had been guilt about what I had failed to do, but they had reminded me what would have happened if I had not been there. "Thank you, your highness, but Jonah and the other servants were the true heroes. The events of that night were partly my fault. It was my mess to try and fix. They risked their lives, but they held no blame for the coup. That was heroic."

The Queen's eyes wandered in thought for a moment before she responded, "That is humble of you, Ivan, but you are correct. The coup was partially the result of your altercation with Isaac. The Preus family has despised us for nearly a century, and you expedited their timeline. This plot must have taken years to plan, and without the marriage to position themselves for power, they became desperate. I told you what would happen if the engagement fell apart, Ivan, and we suffered because of it."

I bit my cheek and looked down. She had a point.

She continued more with pride, "As for the servants, they have been rewarded for their bravery. Jonah has begun his service as the new chief of security for the palace, and the servants have each been given a sizable bonus. The guards that we lost have been buried in a new section of the royal graveyard, recognizing their sacrifice for us all."

Those guards had mocked and sneered at me for months, but when I saw their bodies scattered throughout the palace, I felt nothing but sorrow and shock. The Preus family and their mercenaries had committed mass murder; there was no way to forget their atrocities.

I tried to smile through the twinge in my heart that I felt, but it wasn't very convincing. "I'm glad. Though, I'm sure Jonah will be smug about being my new boss." I glanced at Julia, and she rolled her eyes as she often did when I made silly, sarcastic deflections.

Vera's eyes narrowed, not entertained by the humor. "He will do a fine job. Though, security shall be more of a concern following the aforementioned events. We are all targets, especially once the public hears of your release. While we have released a public statement of our accounts of the events, the People's Front will use this against us. Now, more than ever, we must be united." She looked to her daughters. "This family is under assault from every side. I need to know, Ivan, do your loyalties lie with us? Have you truly put your past life behind you?"

I looked down, hesitant, before making eye contact with Julia. *Coyote is dead. Time to move forward. You promised her. You owe her that.* I spoke to her instead of the Queen, "You have my loyalty. Coyote is gone, forever." It almost hurt to finally admit it. There was no turning back. While my goal was still to destroy the Prism, things were different now, complex.

Julia smiled at me, her eyes thankful. I knew how much that meant to her, and I could only hope it was the truth.

Chapter 4

The meeting with Vera felt like it lasted an eternity. Eventually, though, it came to an end, and after the others had left the room, Julia and I rushed towards each other, meeting in a hug. For a moment, things felt right with the world again. Somehow, we'd both survived the coup and its aftermath. I thought I'd never see her again, and I held her in that embrace for a long time, shaking with excitement. "You didn't think you were getting rid of me that easy, did you?"

Her arms pulled me tighter to her. "I missed you so much."

I smiled, even though she couldn't see it. "I missed you too, more than anything."

We released each other from the hug, and her ice-blue eyes shone as she spoke, "I thought you were going to die."

I put my hands on her waist and kissed her quickly. "Remember, I said I'm not going anywhere."

She bit her lip and stepped back. "Not in the throne room." *Always one for perception.* She nodded towards the door. "Come."

I accompanied her out of the throne room. In that moment, I was so happy to see her that it didn't matter to me what the royals thought of us. All I wanted was for it to be just her and me together, not worrying about the rest of our terrible world for just a few minutes.

The guards raised an eyebrow at me following Julia as she

flowed through the halls, but they said nothing. They'd obviously heard the stories of what Isaac had said about us in the ballroom. I assumed everyone had.

When we reached her room, she flung the door shut, wrapped her arms around me, and kissed me. The hesitant princess was gone. Her joy to see me seemed to replace her caution as she pulled me closer. She pulled at my shirt as she looked into my eyes and laughed. "The orange outfit is quite the look on you."

I smiled and gave her a peck on the lips. "Probably still better than what I was wearing when we met."

She smirked. "The one-sleeved jacket was a *unique* touch."

"Sorry I didn't come prepared for our first date."

She laughed and pulled me towards the bed. "You count that as our first date?"

I followed and kissed her again. "It's either that or our trip to the Enclave. Your pick."

She took her shoes off and flopped onto the bed as a sarcastic tone jabbed into her voice. "If I remember correctly, I almost died both of those nights."

I laughed and lay down next to her. "What can I say? I like to keep things exciting."

"I would prefer our relationship be more than one of us almost dying consistently." Pulling my shirt up a little to reveal the scars on my abs and side, she ran her finger along the stab wound from the night we met. My heart raced. It still felt weird to be so vulnerable with her.

I covered her hand and laughed meekly. "Hey, some of the times we both almost died."

She rolled her eyes and pecked my cheek. "I love you."

"I love you too, my princess." I pulled her closer to me and kissed her for a long time. A rare joy calmed my heart when I was with her, and there was nowhere else I would have rather been. Even if we only had a few minutes to be alone, those were my favorite moments.

When we separated, she smiled at me, and I took a deep breath, content. I loved that we could face the world together and joke about our crazy relationship at the same time. We were a couple and a team.

We lied next to each other, and for a few moments, neither of us spoke. I felt her soft breaths through my chest, and I shut my eyes, enjoying the rest while I could. After a couple minutes, I broke the silence. "How are you feeling after everything?"

Shifting, she took a deep breath, and I felt her body stiffen in my arms. When she eventually responded, the laughter was gone from her voice, and I could hear the sorrow creeping in. "It has been hard for all of us. We've hardly left the palace." *She's avoiding talking about her own feelings.*

"I know the feeling. This morning was the first time I'd been outside since the coup."

She pulled my arm from around her and slid her legs over the side of the bed. "When they dragged you away, I felt so lost. If it hadn't been for Alex… She was the only company I've had. Mother has been too busy posturing Natasha for the election, and Helena won't speak to me now that she knows about us."

I sat up and tried to move next to her along the edge of the bed, but she stood and paced over to the desk. Her arms were crossed.

26

Why won't you be open with me? I stood and shuffled to the center of the room, thinking of how to get her to talk. "I think we have both been trapped inside for too long." I nodded towards the door. "C'mon, let's go for a walk."

She sighed before squeezing a smile through her shell. "You know me too well."

I laughed. "It's my job."

She grinned. "Which job?"

"Both of them."

She ignored my stupid joke and pointed to her bathroom. "I had some of your clothes brought over. Your coat should be with them."

I bowed, said, "Thank you, m'lady," and slid to the bathroom, quickly changing out of my prison scrubs and into real clothing. It felt freeing just to take those itchy orange clothes off. Part of me still wanted my old Militia stuff back, but the fancy bodyguard outfit would have to do.

Julia had her coat on already when I was finished, and she led the way through the palace and out the back doors. As I followed, I couldn't help but think there was a serious reason for her defensiveness. It was rare for her to avoid telling me how she felt.

We stepped out into the frigid winter day and began down the main path through the garden. Its colors were gone, covered with a blanket of white. Our breaths came as puffs of fog, and with each step, the snow crunched beneath our feet as we strode towards the lake.

I looked at Julia, the trees of the forest behind her. She looked tired. I thought about the look she had on her face when I appeared the night of the coup, how she managed to disarm Isaac, and how I saw her heart break when that fatal gunshot echoed through the ballroom. She had been so courageous when our lives were at stake, no longer that damsel in distress I saved on a street corner in St. Paul. Julia was strong enough to hold Isaac at gunpoint, but I was glad she didn't pull the trigger. There are some lines that can only be crossed once.

I touched her arm, and we stopped in front of her dad's statue. It seemed to glare down at us as I spoke, "I'm sorry I wasn't there. I'm sorry I couldn't save him."

She glanced up at the statue of Timothy III before back at me, her eyes full of concern. "No, Ivan. You can't blame yourself for what they did. If it wasn't for you, my whole family would be dead."

In one night, Julia's life had come crashing down around her, bursting the royal bubble. Now, she saw the world for what it really was: dark and dangerous. Our trip to the Enclave had been a taste of what could happen, but nothing could have prepared her for the awful sights and sounds that she saw in that ballroom. I wanted to ensure she was aware of those dangers but also protect her from them. It wasn't about me, though. We lived in a complex web of intertwined alliances and conflicts. I was just another piece in the puzzle, not the master, and that was hard to accept.

I tried to force a smile. "You dodged the question before. How are *you*? Trust me, it's okay."

A tear ran down her cheek, and she hesitated. "I feel like someone ripped my heart out and then shoved it in backwards."

I looked towards the frozen lake, thinking for a moment before speaking, "I'm so sorry, for all of this."

She looked away from me. "The last few weeks have been awful. I thought you were going to die, Ivan. The look I saw on your face when Isaac threatened me... You gave up Coyote, revealed everything you've ever done to the world." More tears filled her eyes as she hesitated and returned her eyes to mine. "I... I never meant for that to happen when I asked you to give him up. You were willing to die for me. You almost died because of me."

"I'd do it again a hundred times, even if it meant actually dying. There was no way that I'd let that bastard kill you. The Militia is all but destroyed, Julia. You and Delaware are all that I have left." I smiled and cocked my head to the side. "Besides, it is my job to keep you safe, especially from your mass murdering ex."

Life returned to her eyes as she tried to hold back a grin. "He is *not* my ex." She shuddered, and I met her in a hug. When we released each other, she walked to one of the plants and ran her fingers through the snow. "You know the tragic thing about white? It is so pure, the combination of every color reflected into your eye, but mix it with something or remove one color, even slightly, and it loses its purity. The snow is beautiful until it meshes with dirt and mud, a cloud so tender until it darkens, a white shirt so clean before it's stained in crimson..."

Two images clashed in my mind. One came from my concussion nightmare, when I held Julia's lifeless and bloody body in my white blazer, the other, from the night of the coup, as the blood from Timothy III's wound seeped down his head and dripped onto his shirt. That second moment had stained her memory too.

She continued, her voice still hushed but her eyes alight as she turned towards me, "We're all born White, uncolored. We're all born human, full of every physical and spiritual element that creates us. It's this world that destroys that purity. They force a color onto us, and then we're incomplete, lost without the souls they've stripped away…"

Clearly, this had been weighing on her mind. She was right in a profound way, but I didn't know how to respond. I'd never really thought about what it would be like without the Prism, everyone being "White," unfiltered. Would we still be so divided without it, or was something else tearing us apart? I could only smile at her in response.

She gave a small smile. "What?"

I chuckled. "I thought you studied science, not philosophy."

She laughed hesitantly. *At least I can still make her laugh.*

When she spoke again she looked down at the snow melting along the tips of her fingers. "It's not philosophy, it's the physics of light. For some reason, the Front believes that they can control people like variables in an equation. We don't work like that. We are like water: fluid, changing, and adaptive. Freeze it into a solid, and it becomes brittle, breakable, and difficult to put back together. That's what they've done to people: frozen them into the form they desire. It all shatters in the end. We have souls, we have minds, we have hearts. No amount of indoctrination can change that. No Prism can change that."

I thought for a moment, remembering the world I'd come from, how peoples' lives were controlled by their color. It didn't have to be that way.

She met me in another hug. "How do we go on after this?"

"Like we always have. We will make the best of it and try to fix things so tragedies like this won't happen again."

She stepped back, and I could tell she was trying to smile, but her face exposed her doubt. "We can't just ignore what happened."

"Of course not, but we have to live on. You're the bravest person I know: a princess willing to go to the Enclave, willing to risk everything to help fight the Prism, and when Isaac put a gun to your head, you took it from him and held it to his. Your dad didn't deserve what happened to him, no one who died that night did, but you can make him proud. *You* are Princess Julia Hughes, *you* are the one who can mend this fractured country, and *you* should be the first elected queen of Northern Mississippi, not Natasha."

I shocked myself a bit with that statement. I hadn't planned it, and the words had just slipped out, but it was the truth. Northern Mississippi needed a new monarch, and it had to be her, or we would be doomed. Natasha would be weak, her mother's puppet, unable to stand up to the constant threats to the country and her family. While Vera was no friend to the UPF after they turned a blind eye to the coup, she had no desire to challenge them for power.

The other obvious contender, at least before nominations were announced, was the vulture, Duke Richard Bilgram. That slave trading bastard was too much of a coward to attempt a coup himself, but he had been building a coalition and waiting for the Hughes family to show signs of weakness. This election was his chance.

Julia was not ready for my suggestion, and her eyes filled with fear. "I don't want to think about that right now, Ivan. This is a time for mourning, not political intrigue."

I crossed my arms. "Of course, mourning your dad's death is important, but everything you just said made it obvious that you belong on the throne, Julia. There's no better way to avenge him than to take his place and fix this broken country. If Natasha or the Duke takes the throne, everything, *everything* we have done has been for nothing. I need you to do this. The country needs you to do this."

"Enough, Ivan! I said I don't want to think about this right now, and do *not* tell me what I need to do. My whole life, everyone has made my decisions for me. Please, do not be like them."

That stung, but she was right. I needed to give her time. The election wasn't for a couple of months anyway. Something was stopping her from committing, though. I didn't know if it was fear of her mom, the position, or something else.

I bit my cheek and dropped my arms, conceding for now. "You're right. I'm sorry. This has just all been so crazy. When I woke up this morning I expected to be executed. Then, I was taken to meet with Bachton and shown the Royal Council's pardon before coming here. It's all happened so fast. The election can wait."

She glanced up at her dad's statue before pacing down one of the paths. I followed as she spoke, her brows still furrowed but her eyes curious, "You met with the General Secretary? What happened?"

I sighed. "On my way out of the jail, Delaware had a crowd of

Reds storm the guards and try to help me break away. The guards gunned them down in the street with no hesitation…"

Her eyes widened in shock, and she covered her mouth. "No… Ivan, that's awful. And Delaware? Is she…"

I closed my eyes for a second. All I saw were the bodies scattered across the terrace. When I opened them again, I could only look at the forest in the distance. "Delaware got away, but they didn't need to die. They didn't know about the pardon."

She stepped in front of me, forcing me to look at her. "Ivan, you couldn't have known, and even if you did, you had no way to communicate with Delaware. This is the government's fault for overreacting. Those people died trying to save you because you're a hero to them."

I ignored her compliment. *I'm no hero.* "The guards threw a bag over my head and escorted me through some building. Bachton told me that all of this is my fault, that I led Isaac and Wilhelm straight into his arms. Apparently, they didn't even want Wilhelm to take the throne. The UPF just wants chaos in the monarchy. They would have assassinated him if he had been successful."

Julia fiddled with her ring. "He was trying to mess with your head."

I scoffed. "He *thanked* me. Some hero." I knew that Bachton was playing games, but it didn't matter. He had planted a seed of doubt in my mind.

She pursed her thin lips and glided towards the pier. "He believes that your presence will further destabilize the monarchy."

I sighed and followed. "Is he right?"

We'd reached the edge of the pier, and Julia knelt, touching the sheet of ice covering the water. "I don't think he realizes how many problems you can cause him. He sees you as a rogue, as Coyote. Bachton knows what you can do in the dark, but I have seen what you can do in the light."

She stood and walked back towards me. The soft wind blew her hair as she walked, and as much crap as we had been though, I still couldn't help but feel happy to be back with her. When she reached me, she slid her hands into mine and looked into my eyes. "You're a hero to me, Ivan. You're a hero to Jonah, to Alex, to the Reds, to the people you saved that night. People are fickle, and it's going to be difficult. Everyone has mixed feelings about you now, but I believe in you. Together, we can prove to the royals that you can play the game without stirring up trouble."

I smiled wryly. "I can try." *But can I actually do it?*

She nodded. "I hope *we* can." She took a deep breath, and her voice became stern. "We can talk about the crown later, but those discussions won't be possible if you cause too much controversy. Everything you do is still attached to me, remember that."

I nodded, and we stood in silence for a minute, just looking at each other. I would have done anything to make her happier, but I didn't know how. Eventually, I broke the silence again. "It's good to be home."

She smiled before biting her lip and failing to hold back the tide of sadness that hit her face. She looked over the lake before meeting my eyes. "I know why he sent you back today..."

I shook my head, confused.

"Today is father's funeral."

Chapter 5

The limousine winded through the streets of St. Paul, following the hearse on the parade-like drive through the city as we looped our way back towards Minneapolis. A solemn crowd lined every inch of the sidewalks, a sea of black coats and hats. They had lost their king. Timothy III may have been passive by my standards, but he had been well respected by the people. Even if the position had become little more than a figurehead, they wept for him.

I looked at Julia seated next to me, clutching Alexandria's hand for support. Her dad died having fought for nothing, yet he received a grand parade and tens of thousands of people paying their respects. Poseidon died a hero. Where was his parade? I didn't even get the bury him. *Why would the world start being fair now?*

My eyes met Julia's for a moment, and I tried to give her a small smile as I whispered, "You doing okay?"

She bit her lip and looked down. When she raised her eyes to me again, they were full of tears. There was no need for words. *Of course she isn't okay.*

Vera looked across the limo at us, her face skeptical. She had not mentioned our relationship, but it was an obvious elephant in the room, or limo, as I returned to my position as Julia's bodyguard. I still had no idea why she called for my pardon. Was it a reward for saving them, a gesture of love towards her daughter, a way to stain Julia's chances at the throne, or something else?

Helena held a tight grip on her mother's hand. She was only fifteen and had already lost her dad. I respected her strength at such a young age, holding herself together on a day like that. In this broken country, she was caught in the middle of conflicts much bigger than she could understand as Vera used her as another pawn in the game. Someday, Helena would be quite the political force. For now, though, she simply tried to avoid letting her sorrow show, playing a difficult role for a teenager.

The drive dragged on as we watched the crowds pass by. It had already felt like an eternity, and we weren't even in Minneapolis yet. The funeral procession was obviously in no rush, and the silence made things worse as nothing could distract us from Timothy III's final farewell. It was tradition, though, for the people to see the procession through the Twin Cities.

I looked to Natasha, seated across from us. In that moment, she was not the opposition or the presumptive heir. She was a girl who had lost her dad. Even with her resilience, she picked at her cuticles anxiously as she peered out the window. All eyes were on her now, and her father's shadow was gone. It was time for her to step forward if she wanted to claim the throne. That pressure was an obvious weight on her shoulders; I had never seen her this nervous before, not that I saw much of Natasha at all.

I touched my tag for a moment. Julia was right about the General Secretary's timing. With the whole country watching, the UPF's most wanted terrorist would be entering with the royal family. The Royal Council had released their explanation of my pardon, but I doubted that it would be enough. Fear is a greater motivator than the truth far too often. Instead of the event being a remembrance of the beloved King Timothy III, it would be stained by my presence.

We had just passed the train tracks on West 7th Street when I noticed the flags lining the fences along the curb: a black background with a crimson-outlined upside-down Prism, split down the middle, and three stars. *The Fracture.*

The anti-Prism political group had made waves in recent months, and with the near death of the Militia, they were the last real force left among the lower colors. Julia had noticed the flags too and was studying my reaction. I whispered to her, "How have they reacted to everything?"

"Not well. With the Front's work camps and the raids, many have lost faith. Some are calling for war."

I shook my head. "They would never win." So much blood had already been shed with no real change, we needed a different approach.

I wanted to feel proud that I'd made a mark, but the country didn't need another martyr, another war. It needed a leader to show them another way. I'd spent so many years trying to fix things, but things weren't any better. If anything, they were worse. The UPF crackdowns, the safe house massacres, the Reds slaughtered in front of the prison, it was all because of what I'd done. We had been a thorn in their side, so they cut off the whole vine.

I looked at her as I leaned forward and gave an unconvincing smile. "It's going to alri…"

A blast of searing heat hit me. I flew to the side, landing roughly on the pavement and scraping my arms and knees. *What the hell just happened?* I sputtered and coughed as I tried to clear debris from my eyes.

My vision slowly recovered. Around me, I could see nothing but smoke and the wreckage of the limo. Screams came from every direction. Sirens blared in the distance. I crawled along the pavement, calling out for Julia blindly as smoke burned my eyes. My heart pounded, my body ached, and my head spun. *Who did this?*

Ahead of me came a cry, "Ivan! Ivan!"

I struggled to my feet, ignoring the pain in my legs as I limped towards the voice. "Julia! I'm coming!" The smoke was beginning to clear and Julia was on her feet when I reached her. Her dress was badly ripped, and she was covered in cuts, but she was alive. I grabbed her shoulders and looked into her panicked eyes. "Are you ok?"

She scanned the wreckage around us, looking for her family. "Don't worry about me! Where are they? Who did this?"

I followed her gaze and spoke shakily, "I'll look for them, stay behind me and stay low. Whoever did this could still be out there. We'll find your family."

We shuffled through the wreckage, coughing as smoke filled our lung. A few yards away, we found Alexandria huddled along with Natasha, both in shock, but both okay. Natasha looked at me, her eyes lost. "Find mother! Find Helena!"

I nodded, trying to look reassuring, but I wasn't in a much better state. The world had lost its mind. Someone had bombed the convoy, and I could do nothing to stop it. I pushed towards the other side of the street, shouting for Vera and Helena as the sirens closed in. In my search, I turned over what used to be the door to reveal the burned bodies of the chauffeur and the bodyguard who was in the passenger seat. *Two more lost in service of the crown.* The blast had come from the front of the limo; they never stood a chance.

I kept climbing through the debris until I heard shouts ahead. Vera was huddled near the fence, crying for help. I ran towards her. "Your highness! Are you..."

The Queen looked up at me like a wounded animal. In Vera's arms was Helena. Her body was limp, and half of her face had been charred from the heat. Crimson covered her mother's fur coat, and she wasn't moving. *No...*

Julia cried out from behind me and rushed to them, cradling her sister and trying to comfort her mom. As Natasha and Alexandria followed Julia to their mom, I could only stand in shock. I felt my fingernails dig into my skin as I clenched my fist. *The piece of shit who did this is going to pay.*

Vera and Natasha were lucky to have survived, we all were. Instead of the wanted terrorist, the bomb had killed innocent Helena. She didn't deserve this. She was too young to be a part of any of this chaos, yet there she lay, murdered by forces far bigger than herself. To assassinate the King for the throne was cowardly, to kill a young girl in cold blood was demonic. *This family has suffered enough. This country has suffered enough.*

I scanned the scene, panicked and uncertain what to do. The

world seemed frozen in time. My breaths were quick and inconsistent. *What do I do?* Royal guardsmen from the convoy were sprinting towards us while others searched the crowd for the bomber. A crater filled the center of the road as burning piles of car parts lay scattered across the pavement. From the look of the scene, the blast had come from the front of the limo, right where Vera and Helena had been sitting. My shock and sadness were replaced with a rush of adrenaline. I wanted to yell, to run, to kill the bastard that did this.

As I watched the crowds, something caught my eye: A young man, not much older than me, had slid a bandana over his face and slipped down a back alley nearby. The guardsmen were pushing the opposite direction, through the main roads. My instincts took over, and without thinking, I was over the fence and in hot pursuit.

The pain in my knees stabbed at me as I hit the pavement, but I ran through it. All that mattered now was catching the masked man. My brain wasn't working. Instead, I was driven forward by a rage that burned through my body. As I reached the alley, I spotted his footprints in the snow and followed them to a metal door at the back of a building. It was unlocked.

Slowly, I crept inside and entered a large, dark warehouse. With the quick transition back to my old role, they hadn't given me my weapons back yet, so I was unarmed. If he had a gun, I would be in serious trouble.

I crept along what seemed like shelves, moving as quietly as possible. With the lack of light, I couldn't see him anywhere. *Where are you, you bastard?* Suddenly, a shuffle came from nearby. I threw my weight into the shelf and pushed, knocking it over with a *crash.* A yelp came from the other side, and I leapt towards the noise.

My hand made contact with a piece of fabric, and I pulled with everything I had, yanking the man out from underneath the boxes, but he fought back. For a few seconds, we struggled on the floor, wrestling for a dominant position. There was no skill in the fight, just the unrelenting hatred that filled my heart as I drove my fist into his face over and over until he gave up his fight.

In the dim light creeping through the windows, I saw the uncovered part of his face. His eyes were full of rage, and his red dog tag earring shone in the light. The second of relief ended, though, as he flung his fist at me and tried to force me off of him. I was too quick for him, using his momentum against him and firing an elbow into his face. He was stunned, and I pinned him to the floor before punching him just above the ear. He groaned as I yanked the black bandana from his face. *No...*

Looking up at me was an ex-militia member, Cockroach. He smirked. "The Coyote's still got his bite. Or should I say *Ivan*?"

I gripped his jacket and shook him forcefully. I wanted to kill him more than anything as I growled at him, "Did you do it?"

His smirk grew. "It's been three years and that's the welcome I get? Don't want to catch up? Fine. Let me go, and I'll talk."

I yelled again, "Did you do it?"

He chuckled. "C'mon. I won't tell you anything if you don't get off me."

I punched him in the face one more time for good measure and stood, spitting next to his head. "Piece of shit."

He raised his arm towards me and waited. "What? Not going to help an old friend up? What kind of manners they teaching you in that fancy palace of yours?"

I scoffed and crossed my arms. "Talk."

Cockroach pushed himself to his feet with a groan. "You've been working on your ground game. Used to be your weak spot."

I stepped towards him and snarled, "Answer the damn question."

He laughed sarcastically. "Well, even if you covered that spot, now you have five, well four, of them out there." He pointed back towards the road.

Sorrow mixed with anger as my voice cracked. "Helena was just a girl, *Roach*."

He shook his head in disappointment. "You thought you'd never see me again, didn't you?"

I spat in his face. "I *hoped*."

He laughed and stepped closer, so his face was just an inch away from mine. "Hades gave me the nickname for a reason."

I pushed him away. "You deserve it."

Pacing over to the fallen shelf, he bent down and looked through one of the boxes. "You used to be fun. You know that? When did you become a hard-ass?"

I let out a yell of frustration before ranting at him, "When innocent people started mysteriously dying on your missions. When the people I cared about started dying because of maniacs like you. Did you plant the bomb?"

He sighed. "What bomb?"

I grabbed his jacket as my voice shook. "Talk."

The other end of the warehouse opened, and a dozen armed Reds, dressed exactly like Cockroach, entered. One of them laughed. "Who you got here, Roach? Is that the Coyote?"

Cockroach grinned at his comrades before wagging his finger at me. "Tsk, tsk. I expected better of you, Ivan." I released him, and he smirked as he paced. "You should have known that they'd sweep the road ahead of time for bombs, but they couldn't thoroughly secure *all* the buildings. A good old-fashioned RPG did the trick, hidden beneath some old floor boards for me to retrieve when the time was right."

My whole face was on fire. "You're a coward."

He just laughed. "Insult me all you want. You're the one who betrayed us all, who works with the enemy." He grabbed my jacket and pointed to the ice-blue Hughes family pin. "You know, the royals who abandoned us all to the Prism while they sit in their mansions and palaces drinking tea and laughing at us little people?" He released me and straightened his jacket. "Regardless, 'Princess' Helena was not the target, Queen Vera was. That bitch has her hands in everything. You have no idea who you're working with."

I pointed at his chest. "You're the one murdering children!"

He cocked his head to the side. "The Militia is gone, Ivan. You failed. We're with the Fracture, and soon, we'll control the whole movement. It's time for the Reds to run the show, don't you think? We've been oppressed for so many years, but now is our time. Thanks for taking the cameras out by the way. We couldn't have done it without you."

I was speechless. The exact group that was supposed to be our hope among the people had turned their back on us. Cockroach was not someone I could trust at his word, but if they could pull off an attack like that, they had a lot of resources at their disposal.

He made a circular motion with his pointer finger and whistled to his comrades. "For old time's sake, Ivan, I'll let you live, but you should think about your choices. You abandoned Coyote, but you don't have to abandon us." With that, he turned and walked out the other entrance as the others followed behind, keeping their guns trained on me. I could do nothing but stand there, useless, before sprinting back to the crash.

Emergency teams were loading the royal family into ambulances when I arrived. Jonah was surveying the scene and directing royal guardsmen on their search. His eyes lit up when he saw me. "Ivan! Where were you?"

I responded frantically, pointing to where I came from, "The bombers. They went that way." He followed my finger as I panted, wincing as I tried to catch my breath. My ribs felt like they were stabbing into my lungs. "I had one of them, but he lured me into a trap. They ran out of the south side of a warehouse down that alley. They're... ack... they're all in black with bandanas. I would have radioed in but mine is somewhere in the wreckage."

He shook his head in shock before springing to action and relaying orders over his radio as I described the attackers to him. "All units reroute to Vandalia Street south of the scene. A squad of black clad men clad with bandanas were spotted fleeing from a warehouse nearby. They are armed and dangerous. Engage with caution. Chief out." He flashed me a look as he clipped his radio back onto his belt. "Why'd they let you go?"

I looked towards Julia, who was on a stretcher being loaded into the back of an ambulance. "I think they wanted me to see them. Their leader's name is Jackson 719220, but I know him better as Cockroach. He was kicked out of the Militia a few years ago for attacking civilians. Looks like he found a group that accepts him now." I nodded my head towards the Fracture flags.

"Since when is the Fracture turning to terrorism?"

"This is a new, radical faction within the group. Who knows how big they are?"

He groaned. "This is not how I wanted to start my job as security chief. Thanks for the help, Ivan. Go, be with Julia. She was wondering where you ran off to. We'll talk later."

I nodded. "Will do. It's good to see you again, Jonah. Wish it was under better circumstances." I hopped the barrier fence and ran to Julia. A paramedic was holding an oxygen mask over her face. He looked dismissively at me, but Julia nodded to him, signaling that I was okay. He handed me the mask and moved away.

Julia did not seem ready to talk. Her eyes were foggy, lost. I just sat alongside her, holding her hand in mine. I hadn't come to grips yet with what had happened: the explosion, Helena, Cockroach, the Fracture, none of it. Instead of laying its king to rest in peace, the country would now mourn the loss of the sweet youngest princess, taken from this cruel world far too soon.

The attack was unforgivable. Things were bad enough already with just the UPF killing innocent people. Now, we had an actual terrorist group threatening even the royals. I would need to find out how large Cockroach's faction was, but for now, my concern was with the royal family.

Vera refused to leave the fence-line and still cradled Helena's body in her arms. Paramedics tried to give her oxygen and bandage her serious burns, but she pushed them away as she wept. *There must be no worse feeling in the world.* My heart broke for her. In a matter of weeks, she'd lost both her husband and youngest daughter. Vera had her faults, but she didn't deserve to see her child die. Her daughters were all she had left in the world.

My eyes swept through the carnage laid out before me. The fires had been extinguished, and all that remained were charred limousine parts, chunks of concrete, and the endless snowfall. There were no more crowds, no more cameras, no more flowers for the fallen king. Like everywhere else in that fractured world, there was just pain and loss.

Chapter 6

I looked out into the lifeless Minnesota winter as Julia slept in the hospital bed. It felt weird being the visitor instead of the patient for once. Julia had been there for me on my second visit to this hospital, when I was knocked unconscious by Isaac's cheap shot with a rock. It was my turn to be there for her. The first time I'd been in the Royal Hospital had been less than five months before, but it felt like a lifetime ago. My world had fallen apart and been put back together multiple times since then. I didn't know what to think or what to believe anymore.

None of us had seen the attack coming. Even with my minor fears about the Fracture's more radical members, I never would have expected them to do something like that. Some members of the group had been asking for Julia's autograph just a month ago, now their most militant faction almost killed her. Cockroach didn't understand who he was messing with. Even if he was right about Vera being part of the corruption, launching a RPG at a limo full of her family was asking for collateral damage. He knew the daughters could die, and he didn't care.

Julia and I had been lucky. The RPG had struck the opposite end of the limo, so we were further from the blast. Still, she was beat up and badly bruised. The doctors had wrapped her up to protect her bruised ribs, fixed up the minor burns on her face, and demanded that she rest.

Natasha and Alexandria were in similar shape and resting in nearby rooms. Vera, meanwhile, had been badly burned across her back, neck, and face and was in surgery to try fix the damage. They said she'd be okay, but Helena had been next to her. She was lucky to be alive.

I'd refused any serious medical treatment besides burn treatment and the bandaging of some of the cuts I'd received. My ribs still hurt from the explosion during Operation Blackout, and my arm ached from where Wilhelm's bullet had struck me, but I was not the priority. The last thing I wanted to do was leave Julia's side.

As I sat there, waiting, the TV in the room blared the recap of the events. "The funeral procession for King Timothy III was disrupted today when a terrorist launched a projectile at the vehicle carrying the royal family. On your screen, you can see footage of the procession and the aftermath." I looked away. I couldn't stand to look at the wreckage again, not yet. *Shit.*

I'd seen a lot in my life, but today had been too much, even for me. Even as I looked away, the TV droned on. "Princess Helena Hughes has been reported dead at the scene. Queen Vera Hughes and the other princesses have been escorted to the Royal Hospital for treatment of various injuries, but they are all believed to be in stable condition. Two other royal servants were killed in the attack as well. As of now, neither the government nor the royal guard have released any information of the perpetrators, though the video clearly shows that a projectile was fired from a nearby building."

I shut my eyes and lay across the bench, trying to forget the scenes from the day. An RPG attack by the Fracture and a mass shooting by the UPF. Both were terrible tragedies. One killed an innocent teenager and nearly killed the woman I loved, while the other slaughtered dozens of Reds. One received a massive amount of news coverage, the other was never spoken of again.

The TV blared on, "In other news, the infamous Militia lieutenant, Ivan 181375, also known as the Coyote, has been pardoned by the Royal Council on behalf of Queen Vera. The United People's Front government has condemned the move, and a spokesperson stated quote, 'If the royals want to pardon terrorists, it is just more proof as to why the People's Front needs to lead this country.' While the royal pardon contradicts the government's report that Militia members, including Coyote, took the family hostage, there is little evidence to support their claim, and General Secretary Bachton has questioned the real reason behind the pardon. Ivan 181375 was also present at the scene of today's terrorist attack, and investigators are looking into any potential links he may have to the incident."

I grabbed the remote and flicked off the TV. "Go to hell." Julia shifted and groaned. I stood and walked to her side. "How are you feeling?"

Furrowing her brows, she replied, "Terrible."

I held her hand, trying to reassure her. "I'm so sorry."

"They killed her..." Her hand shook in mine.

"I'm going to make them pay. I promise."

Her hand tightened, and she spoke softly but intently, "Ivan, right now I don't need revenge. I need you."

I looked from our hands to her face. Her eyes were now open, like daggers of ice sending a chill down my spine. She was serious, but I knew the royal guardsmen would never catch Cockroach without my help. He had earned his nickname for a reason. "What if I told you I know who did this?"

"Is that why you ran off?"

Her fingers twitched as I ran my thumb along them. "I noticed someone suspicious and ran after him. I caught him in a warehouse down a back alley and wrestled him to the ground. When I took off his bandana, it was Cockroach, an ex-Militia member."

"That's an... interesting codename. Why was he ex?"

I groaned. "Civilians died during his missions too often, and he showed no remorse. We kicked him out a few years ago. Should have done it sooner. Anyway, he taunted me before his goons came out of hiding to surround me. Cockroach admitted to the attack, though, he said your mom was the only target. He claimed that I was working with the enemy and that your mom is corrupt. Apparently, he's become a leader in the most radical faction of the Fracture, and it's growing."

Her eyes grew wide. "What have I done?"

"This isn't your fault. These aren't the same people that supported you before. Today showed they have no morals. With the Militia all but gone, looks like they're recruiting the worst of the Reds."

She laid her head back against the pillow and stared into the ceiling. "Where did we go wrong? Is this all because of my family's history, or did we make it worse?"

"I don't know, honestly. At times it feels like everything is down to us, at others it feels like the world couldn't care less what we do. There are so many big players in this game. It's impossible to know what everyone will do, or even who they all are."

She shut her eyes. "The balance of power is so fragile. Each step forward we take risks shattering the whole thing."

"Another civil war is the last thing we need."

She sniffled as tears ran down her cheeks. "This world has enough suffering already."

I kissed her hand softly. "She was a good sister and princess."

"All she wanted was to not screw up, to make Mother proud, to make all of us proud. She was too young to see Mother's games. If any teenager was innocent, it was her."

I broke down and started crying. I couldn't tell if it was sadness, rage, or a mixture of the two. Twenty-one years as a Red and so many years in the Enclave had numbed me to so much pain and suffering. Some things, though, pierce the strongest callouses. "I'm so sorry. I don't know what else to say."

She opened her eyes again and looked at me. "You don't need to say anything, but I do."

"What?"

Her face filled with determination. "I know what I have to do now. I need to end this. I need to be the queen."

I squeezed her hand. "Why now?"

She shook as she spoke, "I see the evil in this world now, and I know Natasha cannot mend our country's wounds. The attack... The Fracture was created because of me, and I have to try and fix what I've broken. No one else can. I don't even know if I can, but I couldn't forgive myself if I didn't try."

"This isn't your fault, Julia. This isn't the Fracture that you inspired, and there was no way for us to know what would happen." I sighed. "Why were you so hesitant?"

More tears streamed down her face, and I grabbed the tissues for her from across the room. She blew her nose before responding, "This will tear apart my family. Mother and Natasha will never forgive me for stealing the crown from them, and I don't want the crown. I've always wanted to do my duty as a princess, but being queen means having real power. How could I ever be qualified to rule just because of who my parents are?"

I shook my head. "You're not qualified to rule because of your parents. You need to rule because you're the only White that understands the people beyond the royal walls and what we go through every day. Natasha thinks she deserves it because she was born first, but that's exactly why she can't be queen."

She took a deep breath. "Promise me you will keep this quiet. I want to avoid politics until after Helena and father's funeral, and the last thing we need is mother discovering our plan before we're ready." I smiled, and she sighed. "Yes, you can tell Delaware."

I kissed her forehead. "I promise I will respect the mourning time, but, for now, you need to rest."

She gripped my hand. "Please don't leave."

I smiled. "Wouldn't dream of it."

Chapter 7

The second attempt at the funeral happened without the procession and the crowds. While there were still nearly a thousand people in the auditorium, it felt more solemn and appropriate. This was not to be about the show. It was about a family that had lost a father and a daughter in quick succession and without warning; for a rare, brief moment, the broken country seemed to mourn together. It didn't matter if we were Red, Purple, or White, we cried along with the Hughes family. For one day, Northern Mississippi turned black in solidarity.

The days since the attack had been extraordinarily difficult for all of us, and even after they'd each been released from the hospital, the royal family stayed mostly confined to their rooms. No one in the palace slept. We couldn't, even if we tried. King Timothy's death had been a blow, but Helena's tore at our souls. They didn't deserve it, but the royals finally saw what the Reds experienced every day: suffering, conflict, and death. It haunted them.

I provided what comfort I could for Julia. We were excited to be back together, but Helena's loss hit her hard. We spent time walking through the snow covered forest behind the palace, talking about anything and everything to keep her mind at bay. I just listened to her flowing voice, hearing far too many details about the dramas she watched, delving into the worlds of her favorite books, and laughing with her about gossip and family stories.

Despite all the hurt and trials we'd faced, it felt like the first time we were a real couple, just talking about life. I learned more about the girl I loved just listening to her talk about her passions than I had for the months we'd known each other. We'd only been together just over a month before Operation Blackout and the coup, and in that time, we spent so much time focusing on the Militia and the Prism, stealing away the few intimate moments we had, and worrying about our relationship being discovered. Now that we were partially in the open, at least among the royals that believed Isaac, our relationship could grow out of the shadows and into the light.

We were surprised that Vera and most royals were tolerating us for now. Many were perhaps just waiting for the right opportunity to use it to their advantage, while others had gained an element of respect for me after the coup. I still had to prove that I could hold my own in the royal world, but it felt good to be recognized by some Whites for risking my life for them. Vera, on the other hand, definitely had plans in mind. I just couldn't figure out what yet.

When I wasn't with Julia, I worked with Jonah to identify the attackers and coordinate some type of counter-strategy. With a depleted guard pool and the Fracture being far outside the royal territory, it would be difficult to do much in response. We needed more allies, and after some serious debate, Jonah agreed to have me contact the remnants of the Militia behind Vera's back. Even with the Militia in shambles, we needed their connections among the Reds if we were going to figure out how deep the radicals' roots ran within the Fracture. Without my old radio, I still hadn't managed to get in contact with Delaware since the prison terrace massacre, but we would need her help to run some missions in Fracture territory.

Now that they knew about Coyote, many servants avoided me even more than before. Others, though, looked at me with a sense of respect after the coup. I understood how they felt; I was as split about my actions as they were. There was so much uncertainty on what had been the right decisions to make, but I couldn't get bogged down in the past. The present had enough threats for me to worry about.

The loss of her dad and sister had lit a spark in Julia's heart. With her eyes now open to the darkness beyond the royal walls, she saw that Natasha could not mend the immense wound that plagued Northern Mississippi. While Julia wasn't sure if she could either, she couldn't forgive herself is she didn't try. The alternative was sitting back and watching, helpless, as the country shattered around her.

No one besides the two of us knew about her plan to run for queen, but that would soon change as the nomination ceremony loomed in the near future. The funeral and mourning of her sister came first, though. She despised political discussions during that period but understood the gravity of the situation.

During the funeral, I stood in the front corner of the auditorium. Next to the stage, I was close enough to keep an eye on Julia and far enough way to be out of the spotlight. Rumors still flew outside of the royalty about our relationship, and there would be a prime moment to officially reveal it, but now was not it.

The room was full but lifeless. The dim lighting washed the visitors' faces, making them look like zombies. The elites of Northern Mississippi and beyond had traveled to pay their respects or at least appear in front of the cameras. The General Secretary himself was even there with his Cabinet, their deep purple tags muted by the lights. *They're the real zombies.* They made their way to the front and spoke quickly with the royal family.

There were fake smiles and pleasantries all around, though Vera's eyes met Bachton's in a momentary duel. Bachton then directed his glare towards me for only moment. He smiled, as if I was right where he wanted me. In response, I covered one eye with my hand for just a second. *You're blind.*

As Bachton made his way through the crowd, Julia's eyes met mine, and I shrugged. *What is she thinking right now?* The smallest of smiles appeared on her face before she regained her poise and shot me a look to behave. She always hated my stupid jokes, but they brought out her cute smile even in the worst of times.

I may have not been in the spotlight, but eyes were still on me. Julia was always aware of public perception, and now that she was determined to be queen, that radar was on overdrive. Everything about her would be questioned, especially me. The least I could do was not make that explanation more difficult for her.

A shiver ran down my spine as Duke Richard Bilgram and his wife, Ilana, greeted the royal family next. I'd hated the Duke ever since that first party, when he smacked me in front of the royals and Purples. All I could do was glare as he stared down Natasha in a long handshake before moving on to Alex. Natasha looked out of her element, and with her broken arm, she appeared even frailer compared to her counterpart's commanding presence. *If it was just the two of them in the race, he'd beat her.*

The nomination process had not officially begun yet, but everyone knew the two of them would be the top contenders. Bilgram knew the game, how to wheel and deal to win crucial votes among the royals, and Natasha's reliance on passive formalities would not be enough. The Whites wanted a strong, stable monarchy after the UPF dared to turn a blind eye to the attacks against the crown, and Bilgram held a bold demeanor that many felt would bring back confidence in the monarchy. They were wrong, though. He was nothing more than a vulture, picking on the weak. When met with real force of any kind, he would crumble and flee.

When he greeted Julia, she handled him with confidence. I was too far away to hear what she said, but she even managed to make him laugh. *How does she do that?*

Soon, the final visitors took their seats as the funeral began with a pseudo-sermon from a well-known underground pastor. With the banishment of religion under UPF law, it was an awkward arrangement. The monarchy still held its roots in Christianity, but its members could only de-facto follow its teachings.

I'd had little exposure to religion in my life, and the small amount I knew came from reading pieces of an old Bible that we had stored in the small Militia library in the Enclave. It was in some type of older English, though, so I didn't understand much of it.

When the pastor finished, Vera began her walk to the podium. Though the side of her face and head had been burned badly in the blast, she had recovered well from her injuries and surgeries to correct the damage. With much of her hair singed, she'd cut it short and wore a hat to cover as much as she could.

She reached the podium, and an eerie silence filled the auditorium as our hearts simultaneously stopped. The audience's tears began before she even spoke, and when she did, it was firm and direct. "This world can be cruel. The best of us can be taken from this life at any moment, leaving us to pick up the pieces. Timothy was a stern but fair man. He loved his country and his family, and he loved his daughters more than anything in this world. I will never forget the look he had in his eyes when they made him proud."

She paused and bit her lip, trying to hold back her emotions. After a few seconds, she had recovered and pushed on. "My husband was killed by envy, by greed. A weak, cowardly man took him from me, from us all."

At that last sentence, Vera paused and looked directly at Bachton before continuing. "Helena was too young, too perfect for this world. She cared deeply for her sisters, for her friends within royalty and beyond. She wanted this world to be a better place for all of us. Everything she did was to be the best princess, best daughter, and best sister she could be. I... I cannot express how much I loved her, how large the hole in my heart is now that she's gone. A mother should never have to bury her child."

She paused as emotion overwhelmed her, and her voice cracked as she struggled to finish her speech. "There is too much hatred in this world. A monster killed an innocent child because of that hatred." She turned her head towards me. "We will make it right for her. Her beautiful life will not be in vain." Turning her head back the crowd, she finished firmly, "My daughter will not be forgotten, and she will be avenged."

We all held our breath as she stepped from the podium and back towards the front row. The audience didn't know how to respond as tears flowed down their shocked faces. Julia and my eyes met as we had the same thought. *She just declared war.* This was why she was tolerating our relationship. *She wants revenge for Helena's death, and she wants me to do it.* Vera knew what she was doing. The whole country was watching, and she had drawn the line in the sand. The Hughes family was not to be trifled with. Her husband had allowed his enemies to plot against him, she would not.

As she returned to her seat, each of the princesses spoke in age order. Natasha rose first and nervously held the cast on her broken arm on her way to the podium. She gave a short, sweet, and boring speech about her father and sister, reading from a piece of paper far more than actually speaking.

After Natasha returned to her seat, Alex rose. Like her mom, she'd received a large burn on the side of her head. Hers had not been fixed so easily by the surgery, though, and grotesque scarring remained. Instead of covering it up, she'd shaved her hair on that side, exposing the scar. It was the most badass haircut I'd ever seen, and it shocked many in the crowd as she approached the podium. Her speech was surprisingly emotional as her normally controlled, rebellious demeanor was replaced by that of a lost daughter, trying to find her way. She had never been close with her father or Helena, but I never realized how much it hurt her as she spoke of the regrets she had for mocking her sister's properness and shadowing of various royals, for the nights she went out instead of spending time with her father or playing with her youngest sister.

My heart broke for Alex as I understood her struggle. She felt lost in the broken world in which we lived, plagued by past choices in a world that didn't quite get us. While she never felt like she belonged in her family, I'd never had one. Besides Julia, the only member of the family who bothered to have a relationship with her, Alex was alone. When she returned to her seat, she shared an impassioned hug with her younger sister.

After releasing Alex, Julia took a deep breath and winced from her badly bruised ribs before heading towards the podium. She'd been burned from the blast as well but not as seriously as Alex or Vera. Out of solidarity with Alex, though, she'd gone with her to get her own new hairstyle, an asymmetrical bob. It surprised me at first, as I'd never seen her with shorter hair, but while Alex's haircut was rebellious, Julia's was stunning. It allowed her to mourn with her sister, reveal her small rebellious side, and maintain her public perception at the same time; a perfect combination for her.

All eyes were on her as she approached the podium and unfurled her handwritten speech. She took a long look at the audience, gazed over to me, smiled solemnly, and spoke to the crowd, "Many of us in this world live relatively comfortable lives in our own little bubbles. We see the world that we want to see behind our walls and our guards. We believe ourselves immune to the pain and suffering outside of our personal bubbles. Suddenly, though, we find that our bubble is more fragile than we thought, and when it breaks, we are showered in a rain of shards that cut us to our core."

She paused for emphasis and pursed her lips before continuing. "I had my eyes opened to life outside our bubble a couple of months ago, and I found myself eternally grateful for the easy and safe life that I found myself living. For the first time, I saw the hurt and the loss of so many of our neighbors in the Twin Cities, saw the pain that we've all ignored as we go on with our lives each and every day."

The audience stirred restlessly. She had hit a sore spot among many, and Bachton glared up at her as he straightened his tie. It was abnormal for a princess to so openly criticize the way the elites lived to their faces and on live television. Julia knew the world would be watching, and she was taking full advantage of it. I was as shocked as the rest of the audience, though, as she had not spoken to me about her speech. She'd wanted it to be a surprise.

Julia's gaze scanned the audience for a moment before she continued. "Two weeks ago, that bubble burst for many of us in this room when Isaac and Wilhelm Preus murdered so many of the people that we loved and cherished before selfishly assassinating my father with a gunshot to the head."

She hesitated before speaking again, "My father died because one family believed that a crown and power is more important than human life. He was a man who loved his daughters, even when we dared to disobey him. He taught us each and every day to do what we believed was right. He did everything he could to protect his family, and he deserved better."

She looked down at her speech and took a shaky breath. Her voice became strained as she pushed through her emotions. "My little sister was the most innocent person that I've ever met. She looked up to me as an example, as a role-model. I still remember the times when she would walk behind me, step by step, imitating my posture and demeanor, trying to be the princess she was expected to be. She wanted to make us proud, to be a real princess instead of a girl too young to fully understand the royal world."

She bit her lip, and as she looked towards the casket to her left, her voice cracked. "I can tell you now, little Helena, you will always be a better princess and role-model than I could ever be. You were taken from this world by hatred, but you will be remembered with the pure love you showed us every day. I miss you, little sister."

As she finished and looked towards me. A tear streaked down my face as I tried to give her a reassuring smile. It was a beautiful eulogy, and Julia's passion and desire to protect life was one of the most amazing things about her. She felt the pain and suffering of the world as if it were her own, and she shared that feeling with everyone in the room and beyond. Confident, yet emotional, she spoke as an impassioned leader, daring the elites of the country to do better and trying to open their eyes. As I watched the audience's looks of awe when she glided back towards her seat, only one thought crossed my mind. *All hail the queen.*

Chapter 8

"Delaware? Come in Delaware."

There was nothing but static for a few seconds before her excited voice crackled over my newly acquired earpiece radio. "Coyote! I mean, Ivan!"

I laughed. "You can call me whatever you want, Del, though the news hasn't quite figured out that Coyote is gone."

"No, they haven't. They make it sound like you were the mass murderer instead of stopping him." She paused for a moment. "How's freedom feel?"

I sighed and leaned my head back on the stone wall of my tiny palace bedroom. "I wasn't even in jail for two weeks and people are already attacking the royal family. Couldn't you keep the Reds under control for a couple of weeks without me?"

She laughed before sorrow crept into her voice. "It's difficult when everyone is dead or carted off to those damn camps, but we've got a small group of refugees from the Enclave together. We've been switching between abandoned buildings on the eastside, dodging the patrols, but I think we've found a home in Payne-Phalen. Sorry we couldn't break you out. Those dicks killed so many people…"

I closed my eyes and pictured the terrace again. I wished I could forget it, but it was stained into my memory. "We'll make sure they pay, Del. They've taken so many lives. I promise, we'll make them pay."

There was no reply for a moment before she sighed. "Husky, Napoleon, and Switchblade are the only other lieutenants left after the safehouse massacres and traps, if you don't count Snapback. Husky and Switch have rounded up as many survivors as they can in Des Moines, but with just Napoleon in Milwaukee, we're in rough shape over there."

"Sounds like we're in rough shape everywhere. Any intel from the camps?"

Her voice crackled. "We're trying to infiltrate as many of them as we can, but they're locked up tight. I'll let you know if we hear anything."

"Del, you're in charge now. Keep me informed, but I'm not giving the orders anymore. I told Poseidon before Operation Blackout, and he agreed with me. It's your turn. I can't be a lieutenant anymore. I'm still here for you, and we're still on the same team, but Coyote is gone." There was no response. "Del?"

There was another pause before she responded, "Ivan... I'm only eighteen."

I laughed. "Yeah, but you'll be nineteen in a couple months."

"Aw. You remembered."

"Yup, and I'm giving you a promotion as an early birthday gift. Congratulations. Greens and Blues get cars, Reds get rebel groups."

She sighed. "You really think I can do it? With the Fracture recruiting so many people, I'm not sure we can do much."

"What if you had the help of the royal guard?"

"What?"

I chuckled. "The chief of the royal guard is a friend of mine. He is willing to work with the Militia if it means getting the bastards that killed Helena."

"Do you guys have any leads on who did it?"

"Cockroach."

She hesitated. "I feel like I remember him."

I sighed. "Roach was kicked out of the Militia for being a civilian-butchering psychopath a few months after you joined. Apparently, he's leading the radicals within the Fracture now. He launched the RPG."

"Shit. Okay. I'll see what we can learn." She paused. "How's Julia?"

I sat up and moved to the edge of the bed. "She missed me, and this has been rough on her."

"I bet."

"And she is running for queen."

Excitement flooded into her voice again. "What? Really? Maybe there is some hope in this hellscape."

I laughed. "I'm excited too, but please keep it quiet. We need to be careful. Vera will not be happy that she's running against Natasha, not to mention the Duke."

"Okay, roger that, but once that goes public, a lot of Reds and Oranges around here are gonna be real happy."

There was a knock at my door. "I gotta go, Del. We'll talk more soon. Let me know if you hear anything." I tapped the earpiece to switch back to my guard duty channel.

Michael was at the door, and I bowed to greet him. "Sir Michael, what brings you to my humble abode?"

He winced as if I had slapped him in the face. "Queen Vera requests your presence in the parlor immediately."

I nodded. "How's your day going, Michael?"

He forced an uncomfortable smile. "Fine. Please come with me."

As he led me down the hall, I placed a hand on his shoulder. "I'm serious. With everything that has happened, people are worried about the royals, but you were as close with Helena as anyone. I doubt anyone has asked about you."

Michael was silent as we passed through the Great Hall and nodded at the guards. When we entered a side hall, he spoke quietly, "I appreciate the concern, Ivan. Princess Helena was dear to me. She made this grey place a little bit brighter for us all, and it was a tragedy what happened to her. I do hope you manage to catch the perpetrator." He finished as we reached the parlor, and he gestured for me to enter. "Do be soft with her. The Queen suffers."

I nodded. "Thank you, Michael, and I will do everything I can to make them pay."

He turned sharply and walked off towards whatever needed butlering next. I never understood him completely, but he was a person too, even if he actually followed the rules.

I opened the door and entered into the parlor to find the entire royal family, plus Natasha's husband, Benjamin von Heusbarn. I was a little stunned but took a seat next to Julia on one of the couches. We smiled at each other before turning our attention to Vera, who stood in front of the lit fire place. *Did I just get invited to a family meeting?*

I'd always liked the parlor. It felt warm and homey in a palace that was often cold and oppressive. It was obvious, though, that Vera meant business. If this was strategy-related, I would have thought Jonah would be there to discuss his intel on the Fracture.

Vera's eyes studied me for moment before she began. "Now that everyone has arrived, we can begin." She paced behind Natasha and Benjamin's couch, running her fingers along the back. "It is quite obvious that things will have to change after recent events." She paused between the two couches. "We must work to restore confidence in our family, to reassure the people that our family is still *the* royal family. Richard Bilgram's coalition cannot be allowed to shake us with only one week until the nominating convention. We have labored for years to ensure Natasha's eventual election, and now, we must ensure those efforts are brought to fruition."

Benjamin nodded. "On that note, I have put together a plan of action stretching from today until the election. Each of us have our roles to finish this work."

He looked at his wife, who did nothing but maintain her little smile and say, "Precisely."

With the lack of input from Natasha, Benjamin hesitated before continuing, "Each of us must work within our circles. Alex, we would appreciate if you could connect Natasha with many of the younger royals who have recently reached voting age. They are a group that are unlikely to support the Duke, and we should use that to our advantage."

Alex grunted and shrugged. "Fine."

"Your enthusiasm is appreciated." He looked at Julia. "Julia, it is undeniable that you have a draw among the people, and I believe we can use that, in addition to your connections within the royalty, to assist Natasha."

Julia nodded, but her eyes remained down at her feet. "Of course."

Turning to me, Benjamin continued, "Now, Ivan…"

I cut him off, "Don't cause a distraction. Understood."

"Well… Effectively, yes."

His eyes looked full of fear, as if I would shoot him next. I realized that this was the first real conversation I'd ever had with him. He saw me as just another Red.

Shrugging, I replied, "I will try to stay out of trouble."

Throughout the conversation, Julia had been spinning her family ring in her hand. As Vera began to speak, again, about the campaign, Alex noticed her sister's nervousness and deflected the conversation. "How are we going to handle the security concerns when we travel into the city after all of this? I mean, Ivan and Jonah are great, but they can't stop a RPG."

Vera was taken aback that Alex bothered to contribute to the conversation so much so that she didn't seem to care about the change of topic. Julia looked relieved, but she was going to have to explain herself to Alex.

Vera stepped towards our couch and looked down at her middle daughter. "That is precisely why all visits outside of royal territory are to be restricted to official business only."

Alex shot to her feet, coming face to face with Vera. "You can't do that!"

Her mother stared her down. "It's something we should have

done a long time ago, but your father was unwilling to see the threats we faced. You can live without your parties and flings for now. It would do you some good."

Alex's icy eyes narrowed. "What are you going to do, lock me in my room and marry me off to some rich man who thinks I'm cute so you can get Natasha the crown you can't have for yourself?"

Someone needed to say it.

Julia popped to her feet to tear them apart. "We can work something out to keep everyone safe while not locking us in a prison. Mother, you know how important it is to me to visit the children and finish the orphanage, and Alex's *socializing* downtown brings an important connectedness that ensures we remain relevant with the people. What kind of message would it send if we closed ourselves off to the world?"

Alex was still fuming as her mother took a step back and considered Julia's statements. Vera obviously had a point. She had just lost her husband and youngest daughter and was worried about losing another. Controlling her daughters, though, would only further split the family.

Vera turned back towards the fire, pacing slowly. "I'm sorry you are concerned, but until we can ensure your safety, this is what must be done. The guards will be informed of this new protocol, and on official trips there will be heightened security." She paused and spun on one foot back towards Alex and Julia.

Alex flopped onto the couch and crossed her arms while Julia sat more gracefully, though I could feel her anxiety through her diplomatic mask. Vera cared about her daughters' safety above all else, but there was another reason she was asserting her authority. *She must be worried about Julia's public appearances threatening Natasha's standing.*

Natasha crossed her legs and looked condescendingly at her sisters. "Of course, this is the best decision for us. Who knows where those Fracture thugs will strike again? Mother is just being cautious, Alex. Besides, it would be splendid to see you around the palace more often."

Alex muttered under her breath, "Speak for yourself."

Natasha's eyes narrowed. "What was that?"

Alex faked a smile. "Maybe I could take up gardening in the middle of January."

Julia cut in. "Natasha, some of us like to interact with the community outside of the royal territory, to connect with them. We can't just live in fear our whole lives."

Natasha cocked her head to the side. "Interesting you say that, since so many of us have lived in fear ever since you brought a violent Red into our home. He's been here for only a few months, and in that time, we've lost father and Helena."

I raised my arms in a sarcastic faux surrender. "If you don't want me here, I can go. I'm sorry I risked my life to stop two homicidal maniacs from killing you all and ran down the man who killed Helena. It must be my fault it all happened, right? I'm just a low-life Red after all."

Vera raised her arms. "That's enough!" We all stopped, shocked at the uncharacteristic force in her voice. "My decision has been made. I expect you to follow my instructions, and I am sure that each of you will play your part to ensure Natasha is

70

elected."

We stared each other down before Julia stood. "If that is all, we should be going. We have a lot to do before the nominations." *Always the diplomat.*

Vera nodded. "Yes, we will talk more later." She shot me a look out of the side of her eye. "Please act with discretion."

I bowed before following Julia and Alex out of the parlor and towards Julia's room. The sisters quickly flew down the hall and up the stairs.

Once we reached the room and closed the door, Alex screamed in a fit of rage and threw herself onto one of the couches. Julia paced anxiously and ran her fingers through her hair while I sat across from Alex and pondered the situation.

Vera must have suspected something was up with Julia. The security concerns were real, but this power play had to be for something more. Did she know that Julia planned on running? If so, Vera would have already begun turning electors against her. We needed a plan of action before it was too late. That started with identifying potential allies.

I slid over to the desk and grabbed a sheet of paper as Alex began ranting, "I can't believe she's doing this! I can't be locked in this damn palace the rest of my life. Mom thinks she can manipulate us to serve her, like we're her puppets. She almost ruined your life with Isaac. I will *not* be married off to some inbred in order to maintain 'family unity.' Family unity my ass."

I couldn't help but laugh as I began writing names: Julia's close friends, reformers, minor royals who respected her dad, those at odds with Vera or Natasha, and those who despised Bilgram's slave trading. The list was substantial, considering the circumstances and the fact I was both awful at names and not familiar with all the minor royals yet.

Alex sat up. "What's so funny that?"

I smiled at her. "Don't worry. All we have to do is get your arranged fiancé to hit me over the head with a rock. Problem solved."

She bit her cheek, trying to hold in a smile. "You're funny Red. You know what? Jules should just be the frickin' queen instead of Natasha. She could shut up mom then." *Glad to see we're on the same page.*

Julia joined me on the couch. Her hair was disheveled, and I held in a laugh. Whenever she was ever thrown off her plan, pacing and destroying her perfectly done hairstyles tended to help her think things through. It was ridiculously attractive for some reason. She looked at me and then her sister. "Alex, I need to tell you something..."

Alex swung her legs back to the floor and leaned forward. "Anything."

Julia smiled and took a deep breath. "I believe that I need to be the queen, and not just to shut mother up, though she could use a bit of humility."

Alex practically flew over the coffee table and hugged her sister, knocking my list of names onto the floor. "I knew something was up with you! You have no idea how happy I am to hear that. I was *not* looking forward to schmoozing for Natasha."

Julia held her sister on her lap and laughed. "So, you're saying you'll schmooze for me?"

Alex raised her arms excitedly. "Hell yes!"

I could only laugh as this all unfolded. The two sisters were hilarious together, and I loved to see Julia's comfortable openness with her. "Hey, Alex, if you don't mind, you're stealing my girlfriend."

She laughed and stood, straightening out her jeans and blouse. "She was mine way before she was yours, Red. She may be *your* girlfriend, but she is *my* queen."

I chuckled and grabbed the sheet of names from off the floor. "If we want my beautiful princess to become the queen, we need to work the voters and gather up support before Vera can turn them against us."

Julia looked quickly at the list. "That's a good start." She paused for a moment, and I could see the gears spinning in her head. "We can schedule some meetings and flatter them, make them feel important, that's all most of these minor royals need."

I smiled and put my arm around her. "Then it's a good thing you're charming. I'll help where I can, but most of the royals hate me."

Alex strode over to the drinks table. "I will work my network as well. You'd be surprised how many friends I have around here. Plus, I know everyone's secrets. Did you know that Lord Patterson…"

Julia laughed and raised her hand. "We can swap our gossip later. Both of you will be able to work circles that Natasha and the Duke cannot. If we're careful, we can do this."

Alex grabbed the glasses on the table. "Of course we can. This calls for a toast! Jules, where's that awful champagne you have hidden?"

Julia groaned sarcastically and pushed herself off the coach. She strode over to the desk and opened a compartment hidden underneath, pulling out the bottle. She held it, cradling it like a model would in a magazine. "I would claim I was saving this, but Alex is right. We didn't finish it because it tastes terrible."

Alex was ecstatic. "Didn't stop us from drinking half the bottle!"

Julia blushed in embarrassment as I laughed and jumped to my feet. "Sounds perfect for a celebration."

Julia shook her head and handed the bottle to her sister, who began pouring the liquid into the glasses. She distributed the glasses among us and raised hers. "A toast, to my sister. A woman of poise, dignity, and the future queen!"

I raised my glass, shouted, "Here, here," and smiled at Julia. "To a princess who inspires children, holds mass murdering ex-fiancés at gunpoint, fractures the Prism, and will be the hottest queen in history."

Alex cheered, and Julia laughed. "Ivan!"

I winked at her. "That's not how toasts work, your highness."

She rolled her eyes and raised her glass. "To my rebel sister and terrorist boyfriend who always find ways to get me in trouble and push me to do wonderful things that I couldn't do without them."

I clinked her glass. "That's the spirit!"

Alex raised hers. "Well, alcohol is alcohol."

Julia laughed. "That is so not true."

We drank, and I cringed as the excessively sweet liquid rolled across my tongue. Julia's face looked like she had just sucked on a lemon.

Alexandria slapped her glass down on the table. "Next time, I bring the drinks."

Julia laughed as I wrapped my arm around her. "How dare you insult your queen's taste."

Alex raised her eyebrows at me and noticed how we were holding each other. "Well, at least she seems better at picking guys than champagne. Now, you two make-out or something. I have *work* to do." She slid towards the door.

Julia pursed her lips before calling after her, "Please don't cause too much trouble, Alex."

She smiled back. "Trouble? No, I'm just going to blackmail people about their affairs in exchange for votes. You two have fun, but it's too soon for little princes and princesses."

Julia's eyes shot a glare at her sister, who laughed and flew through the door. She looked into my eyes. "What did you think of your first family meeting?"

I kissed her before responding, "So, I'm part of the 'family' now?"

She ran her hand through my hair. "Basically. Besides, I'm glad you could be there. Even if there's tension, I love my family, and if we're serious about this, I want you to get to know them better. Things like this, with Alex, mean the world to me. It's impressive that you're a back-alley guy who never had a family and can work your way through royal family drama."

We swayed back and forth as if we were dancing to soundless music. "Natasha doesn't seem very keen to get to know me better."

She smiled softly. "It'll take time with her. I doubt she'll ever be your biggest fan, but she hasn't spoken to you much. She's scared. We all were when you came through those gates."

"You didn't seem phased by me."

She bit her lip. "Obviously, you had just saved my life, but I didn't know what to think of the cute Red hero from the Enclave at first. You were mysterious, but I felt like I could trust you, and you opened up to me."

I chuckled and kissed her again, slower this time. "And you were willing to see my world, try to understand me. You cannot know how much that meant to me, how much that means to me."

She looked at me, her eyes searching. "I still can't believe I'm doing this, that we're doing this. I never wanted to be queen, and even now, I don't know if I want to be queen, but I have this feeling in my heart that I have to do this, for Helena, for father, for everyone whom we've lost. You were right."

I kissed her forehead and shrugged. "I usually am."

She chuckled and raised her eyebrows. "Wow, so humble too."

I laughed, and we fell onto the couch.

Chapter 9

In the days ahead of the nomination ceremony, Jonah and I coordinated with Delaware to plan a small operation. Our goals were to assess the strength of the radical militant faction of the Fracture and identify its leaders beyond Cockroach.

Delaware and I were to attend a Fracture meeting and ask around for information. Her intel said that it was apparently rare for these large, official meetings to occur, so we knew something big was happening. It was likely related to the attack against the funeral procession, and we were more than curious on how the organization as a whole would react.

I was a well-known face in the Twin Cities, and Delaware was known in enough circles, so we both wore a hood and the Fracture's black bandanas. With the dark lighting in the warehouse near the western end of St. Paul, that would be enough to hide our identities.

Julia wasn't excited about my part in the mission, but she understood the importance. Now that I was working with Jonah and the royal guard, my work would be done as Ivan, not Coyote. Besides, she wanted to take down her sister's killers more than any of us, and this is how it had to be done. A Blue guard would have stuck out like a sore thumb.

Before we left, Julia kissed me on the cheek and whispered, "Come back to me."

I kissed her back and said, "I always will, my princess," before heading to meet Delaware.

Delaware and I agreed to meet up at our old rendezvous point in the Enclave. It was my first time back since the UPF began dragging people to the work camps, and my heart sunk at the sights. While the area had been the slums before, it had life. We had constantly been working to improve our way of life in spite of the government and higher colors leaving us to rot across the Mississippi River. Now, it felt like I'd entered a post-apocalyptic nightmare. There wasn't a soul to be seen. The snow-covered streets were empty, the poor and desperate people selling random goods were gone, and the Militia patrols had vanished. *My home is gone.*

The Enclave was dead, yet as I looked across the river, I saw a bustling St. Paul. People went about their days acting like nothing had happened. We'd increased awareness in the past months, but people cared only about their lives. It was too easy to turn a blind eye to a low-life Red being dragged off, never to be seen again.

Delaware rushed towards me as I reached the rendezvous point and tackled me in a hug. "We thought you were going to die."

I laughed. "Yeah, so did I, but either you or Julia would kill me if I did, so here I am. How's Snapback?"

She turned, and we walked towards one of the old cars the Militia had stored away. "He's good... We're good." She smiled with just the right side of her mouth. "I don't know how I'd be able to do this if he hadn't been there the past couple of weeks. He's stepped up and helped support me a ton. I'm sure a lot of the work is to keep his mind off Blitzkrieg, but he is healing emotionally, slowly. It's hard for him to talk about."

I climbed into the driver's seat of the car and hotwired the engine as Delaware slid into the passenger's seat. "It's been hard for all of us. We were betrayed by a friend and so many people died because of it. Makes it hard to know what's true anymore and who we can trust. It's like every step is a trap."

She chuckled. "That was deep for you. Sounds like you've been hanging out with your princess too much."

We drove into the West 7th neighborhood of St. Paul. While the east-side and the Enclave had always been the worst parts of the city, in the past month, many of the Reds fleeing the police raids had organized the area into the home base for the Fracture. The meeting would be nearby the warehouse where I had my encounter with Cockroach. I didn't know if he'd be there that night, but if he was, I would have to watch my back. If anyone would recognize me, it would be him.

The old warehouse was on its last leg. We could hear the creaking boards before we even made it past the guards checking peoples' tags. The rule was clear: Reds only. While the Militia almost never turned down a potential ally, the Fracture seemed to be taking on a purist Red mindset, and that worried me as much as the UPF's tyrannical policies. Accepting the Prism's classification as some type of reverse superiority instead of rejecting it completely would do nothing but lead to another civil war.

We passed by the guards with no issue and entered into the dim warehouse. The ground floor was filled with talking Reds and a few pre-Prism Blacks, all dressed in raggedy black coats like ours. These were my people, but I felt separated from them now. It felt like I was in limbo, caught between two completely different worlds that were rapidly changing.

I touched my hand to my ear, activating my earpiece, and whispered, "Jonah, we're in. I'll keep you updated."

"Roger. Stick to the plan, Ivan. The last thing we need is for them to catch our scent. Jonah out."

Delaware nodded to me, and we split up, taking positions at different parts of the warehouse to eavesdrop on any potentially informative conversations. As I leaned against one wall and scanned the room, a woman stepped out onto the metal balcony overseeing the ground floor. Two men flanked her: Cockroach in his black bandana and a massive guy in a black hockey mask.

I was confused. Before I was arrested, a vocal, but reasonable, Red named Tyrone 423001 had been the official head of the Fracture. We had never met in person, but he had been a friend of the Militia. He had been working to expand the Fracture's reach among all of the lower colors. *What happened?*

The crowd quieted quickly as the woman raised her arms and proclaimed, "Today, crimson reigns!"

The crowd roared with their arms raised, "Crimson reigns!"

This is a frickin' cult.

The woman smiled and leaned forward against the metal railing. "Welcome, friends and comrades, to the Fracture. I know that this meeting has come quickly, but I have good news for you all."

The crowd clamored and hollered, and she raised her arms to quiet them. "While we failed to kill the Russian puppet-master, we hit her where it counts. 'Princess' Helena's death has awakened this country, and they're finally ready to listen to our demands, ready to understand the pain that they've caused us for so many years."

As the crowd cheered I radioed to Delaware. "You hearing this?"

"This is bad. When did Tyrone lose control to this psycho?"

"I don't know, Del. Be careful. These aren't our friends anymore. They could destroy everything we've accomplished."

Jonah cut in over the radio. "Any ID on the woman speaking?"

I responded, "Not yet. I'll let you know if we find anything out."

The woman paced along the balcony, projecting her voice fiercely across the warehouse. "We are the ones who keep this country running. We are the ones who control this country's fate. We are the forgotten. We are the workers the socialists left behind, because we were too unruly, too disloyal for their precious Prism. Well who gives a shit what they think?" The Reds in the crowd shook their heads. "Not me. Not any of us. Want to know what I think?"

The crowd shouted in response, "Yeah!"

"I think that the Prism is upside down, that *they* should be *our* slaves. Let's see how they like it. Let's see how much the precious little Whites, Purples, and Blues like starving in the factories, in the mines, on the farms. There must be a bloodletting. Crimson must reign for the toxins to be purged from this city and this country."

Delaware came in over the comms as the crowd roared again. "That's all we needed. The radicals have taken over. Let's get out of here."

"No, we need to know what they're planning next. I can't risk them killing more innocent people."

"You mean, like Julia?"

She was right, but I ignored her sarcasm and crept through the crowd, moving closer to the balcony. I needed to figure out who this woman was and how she took power.

I was shaken by the enthusiasm of the crowd. So many of these people had once looked to the Militia to provide hope, but when we failed, they must have seen this radicalism as the only option left. This wasn't just about protecting Julia or her family anymore.

The woman continued as I walked, but I stopped as a group's side conversation caught my ear. A lanky Red boy was talking: "...but he's an Orange. What's wrong with him? The UPF kicks his ass just as much as ours."

A bulkier Red crossed his arms. "Even the Oranges have ignored us. I didn't see them shooting at those bastards as they dragged our families off to die. No, they shut up and hope they don't become us."

The lanky one shook his head. "But he..."

The third, shorter guy stepped towards him. "Ya don't like Max's plans? We can make sure ya end up like Tyrone."

The bulkier one laughed and made a slicing motion across his neck with his finger. "His head rolled for a long time when Roach cut it off."

Shit.

As the kid backed into the wall, the shorter guy continued forward and pulled a curved knife. "Ya either with us or against us.

Red or dead."

I stepped into the center of the circle, blocking him from the boy. "We're all together here guys. They've killed enough of us. We can't afford to kill each other."

The short one stepped towards me, knife raised, but with the height difference, it was hardly menacing. He was at least a foot shorter than me, and if he attacked, I had enough knives to kill him multiple times before he knew what happened. I scanned the room. It was too loud and dim for anyone to notice what was going on. With Max drawing everyone's attention, not many people were facing us anyway. That'd change quickly if things got ugly, though.

Shorty clenched his jaw. "Who the hell do you think ya are?"

I pulled a knife from my sleeve and spun it around my finger, its black blade dancing in the darkness as I mocked his accent. "I'm just a friendly neighborhood Red. Now, ya gonna leave my pal over here alone, or am I gonna have to report ya to Max?"

Shorty looked at the bulky one before regaining his grit. "She don't know ya."

I smirked. "Oh, believe me. She knows who I am." I took a step forward. "Shall I wave her down?"

He shot a glance towards the balcony before pocketing his knife and scrunching his nose. "Watch ya back or there'll be a knife in it."

I winked at him. "Right back at ya."

The two of them turned away and shuffled through the crowd.

Delaware's voice cut through the noise in my ear. "Saving another princess?"

"Shut up. We got her name at least." I turned towards the kid, who had slid down the wall in fear, and reached down to him. "C'mon. Not all of us are dicks."

He hoisted himself up with his nonexistent muscles. "Thanks. I, uh, I didn't realize how crazy things had got. Name's Oliver."

As Max continued her speech, I crossed my arms and looked away from Oliver, purposely avoiding having to state my name. "Me neither. Last time I'd checked, Tyrone was in charge."

"Don't talk about him around here. They say he was too nice to the upper colors. He was accused of 'working with the enemy.' Max and her goons took him and his friends out after everything went bad with the Militia."

I nodded my head towards the balcony. "I know Cockroach. Who's the guy with the creepy mask?"

He followed my gaze. "Nobody knows his real name. They call him the Mountain, because, I mean, just look at him. They say he broke a cop's back with his bare hands."

"Huh. Thanks. Any idea where Max came from? I've been around. Never heard of her."

He shrugged. "I dunno. She kinda just showed up one day and was all critical of how we were doing things. It was quiet, until..." He lowered his head.

I patted him on the shoulder. "I was a friend of Tyrone's. He was a good guy."

He looked back up at me with wounded eyes and whispered frantically, "It wasn't just him. There were others. The Oranges, his friends. If you knew him, you gotta get out..."

A light interrupted him. We turned to see cockroach shining a flashlight towards us as Max smiled. "Well, if it isn't the Coyote himself."

I whispered to Oliver, "Get out of here while you can."

He scurried into the crowd, avoiding the flashlight's beam as Max continued. "Since when did Princess Julia's boyfriend spend time among his fellow Reds?"

My mind raced for a way out of the situation. I was likely surrounded by armed men and women, and the nearest exit was at least twenty meters away. *Cunningness it is.* I smiled and held out my arms, pretending to stretch my back. "Oh, you know. I just wanted to see what turned a principled reform movement into a terrorist organization that kills innocent children. Stuff like that." I whispered to Delaware through the earpiece, "Get out of here. I'll figure it out."

I could almost hear her roll her eyes. "Should have stuck to the plan."

Jonah cut in. "You need evac? It's technically not our jurisdiction, but I can make it happen."

I didn't have time to respond as Max laughed and stared down at me. "When did you forget who you were, Ivan? You once fought for change, for our survival. You were willing to throw all of that away for a girl? Pathetic."

Rage boiled inside of me as I swept my arm towards the crowd. "None of this is fighting for change. You want to abuse the Prism for your benefit. You just want power. Don't you get that you're reinforcing the problem? I'm no monarchist, Max, but I sure as hell don't support mass murder. You're everything you claim to be fighting against. I fought for change, to end all this shit, but it didn't work. There's another way, a way that doesn't involve blowing up buildings and killing teenage girls. You just have to open your eyes."

She scoffed. "Is that what your lovely princess told you? All the royals have ever done is fight for their own power. You're naïve to think that will change now."

I narrowed my eyes. "I'd rather have hope than be heartless. Now, you gonna kill me or what, because people a lot tougher than you have tried before."

Max smiled and nodded her head towards someone. "No. I want you to crawl back to your princess on your knees and tell her about everything you saw here tonight. Tell her and her family that they will not be exempt from our vengeance. We'll come for them, and then we'll come for you, after you watch them suffer for the pain they've caused. You'll die last."

I opened my mouth to respond, but something knocked me hard in the back of the head. Falling forward, my face smacked on the ground. I was only out for a few seconds, but when I woke up, I was bound by my wrists and being thrown in a trunk. *Well, that could have gone better.*

Chapter 10

Everything hurt when they dumped me on a street corner in the north-west corner of St. Paul, confused and disoriented. Once I radioed in, Jonah sent someone to pick me up, and I changed before my walk of shame to Julia's room. She was reluctant to allow me to run missions in the new role, even with Coyote gone, and this was not going to help my case.

Jonah was waiting in the room with Julia. He stood at attention near the desk as she sat on one of the couches, her fingers intertwined in front of her. I smiled as I entered. "Hey beautiful."

She half-smiled and nodded towards the couch across from her. "Sit, Ivan." I did as she said before she continued, "How did the mission go?"

"Really well. We got a lot of useful information. I think their leader, Max, really likes me."

Jonah raised his eyebrows. "Well, she did let you live."

"Yeah, I don't think it's a great sign that my enemies keep seeing advantages in not killing me."

Julia crossed her legs at the knee. "You said this would be low-risk."

I shrugged. "If they actually tried to kill me, I would have been fine. A couple hundred poorly trained Reds are no match for me. Besides, a lot of those people love me, even if they won't admit it. There's more doubters in that crowd than she thinks."

"And what about Helena?" She looked worried at what I might say.

"Well, she showed no regret for accidentally killing her. Actually, she bragged about it. It was disgusting. She said that she would kill you and your family, making me watch, because I 'betrayed the Reds.'"

Jonah crossed his arms. "What do you know about Max? The Mountain?"

I shook my head. "You know as much as I do. I've never heard of either of them before. Besides Cockroach, it's like these guys came out of thin air. They killed Tyrone, his friends, and any higher colors part of the organization."

Eyes wide, Julia replied, "That's horrible."

Jonah sighed. "I thought dealing with the UPF and Bilgram was enough, but this? Our hands are tied too. There's not much we can do outside of royal territory under the agreements in the treaty. The only good news is that Delaware made it out fine and can work to limit the Fracture's influence among the Reds."

I lay down and stared up at the ceiling. "We need to rebuild the Militia. Without it, there's not much of an alternative for those willing to fight. We also need to show them that the monarchy isn't their enemy, even if it's just the better of two poor governments."

Julia laughed. "Appreciate the confidence." I looked at her and narrowed my eyes, asking her if Jonah knew. "Jonah knows I'm running."

Jonah smiled. I nodded and responded, "Glad to have you on the team, but Julia, you're not queen yet. The monarchy has not exactly been a positive thing, and I don't think it's the solution long-term, but we need *something* to build on. If you can restore some confidence in it, that will go a long way."

Groaning, Julia stared at the ceiling. "Even if I can restore some confidence in the monarchy, the election is months away. We can't just sit back and do nothing."

I cocked my head to the side. "Who said we do nothing?" She raised an eyebrow as I continued. "The Militia lost a lot of people, but there's still so many friendly Oranges who are rejected by the Fracture. There's also the Reds in the camps. If we can figure a way to connect with them, and maybe save some of them, the Militia will cripple the Fracture's support. Make the Militia strong again and we'll have an army outside the royal territory. Plus, if you can become queen, we can return to my original plan before all of this happened."

The room was silent for a moment as Julia pursed her lips in thought before saying, "That is a lot of 'ifs.' We need to take this one step at the time and address everything we can right now. We can't have a real plan with so many moving parts."

"It can't hurt to stay focused on the end goal."

She smiled. "Of course, but there is more than one goal, Ivan. Things are complicated right now. We can't rush into this."

Jonah nodded. "I agree. We need to focus on what we can control, and I think each of us can take lead on an area." Julia and I nodded, and he continued. "I can use my guard network to see if the UPF has any information we can use against the Fracture. I'll also see if we can learn anything about Vera and Natasha's plans."

A smile crossed Julia's face. "Good. Thank you, Jonah. I will focus on building a coalition to compete with Natasha and the Duke. With my mom barring me from non-official travel outside of royal territory, I'm not sure how much I can do to connect with Oranges and Yellows besides the underground social media networks."

Sitting back, I replied, "You're doing great with that already. I'll coordinate with Delaware to try and use the Militia to our advantage. There's got to be some people out there willing to help us. We just need to find them. The UPF is watching me, though. Even with their cameras down, I need to be careful with physical meetings."

Jonah nodded. "I'll see what I can do about getting Delaware some resources, weapons, whatever she needs. The UPF won't search any of our delivery vehicles, but they'll obviously keep an eye on them."

I thought for a second. "Julia, any chance we can use your orphanage to smuggle that stuff? It worked with the Reds, and it was one of the only places the UPF didn't hit on the raids. There's a good chance we can fly under the radar there."

"I don't want the orphanage to get caught up in all of this. It was fine before, but it is going to open soon. I can't put those kids in danger." Her eyes pled with me.

"If we don't use the orphanage, there's a bigger chance we get caught. Then we'll have bigger issues to worry about than whether the kids get to stay at the orphanage."

Her eyebrows furrowed, and her voice was stern. "I am not using children as shields, Ivan. The difference between us and them is our hearts. Don't forget that."

She had a point. We never would have forgiven ourselves if those kids got hurt because of our smuggling. Was it worth the risk, though? If the smugglers got caught, the Militia would be weak. They were scavenging now for what they could, but they were on the run and not receiving rations. It was Julia's orphanage, though, so it wasn't my call regardless of what I thought. "Fine. We will figure out another way to make sure the supplies reach them."

"Thank you, Ivan." She looked to Jonah. "Is that all?"

He nodded. "I believe so, m'lady."

She smiled at him. "Thank you, Jonah." He bowed swiftly and exited the room, and Julia's eyes studied me.

I groaned in pain and moved to the edge of the couch, meeting her gaze before dropping my eyes. "I'm sorry. I know you hate all this."

She pursed her lips before speaking softly, "Jonah told me what you did for that boy. He said that's what drew the attention to you."

Was it? I didn't have time to think about how Max noticed me in the moment. If we'd made enough of a scene for Cockroach to take notice, that would have made sense. We'd known each other for years, so he had probably expected me to do something like that.

I stood and sauntered over to Julia's couch and slumped down next to her, laying my head against hers. "They could have killed him."

She nuzzled her head against mine. "I know, my love, and that's why I'm okay with this now."

"Since when?"

Her fingers interlocked with mine as she spoke, "You're not hiding behind a mask anymore. You're fighting *for* something and not hiding it. You defended that boy, even though it jeopardized your life, and... after Helena, I'm starting to understand."

"Why is that any different from what I did as Coyote? I was working with what I had, what I could fight for. I was fighting for everybody I saw suffering around me every day. The mask was to protect my life when I was trying to save other people. You're right that I'm out of the shadows now, but I don't see much of a difference."

She sighed and looked towards the door. "I see a change in you, even if you don't. Instead of just fighting the darkness, you're also defending the light. You're more diplomatic, and I'm amazed how quickly you've picked up on the palace's intricacies. You've sacrificed so much for my family already and continue to do so. You defend those who can't defend themselves. I love you, Ivan, and I couldn't be doing this, any of it, without you. I'm just trying to say that I'm so grateful for you and for how much you've done for me. What have I given you in return?"

I laughed. "The pardon was appreciated. I like not dying."

"But even that was mother, not me. You gave up your life with the Militia, lost your secret identity, almost died..."

I stopped her in her tracks with a swift kiss. "And I got you." She blushed. "Plus, you went on TV, confronted a general, endured public attacks, and now you are running for queen because you were willing to listen and have your eyes opened to the world beyond the royal gates. This isn't a competition about who gives more in our relationship. Besides, if you become queen, our relationship won't matter. We both know a monarch can only marry a royal."

She smiled and raised an eyebrow. "You're talking about marriage already?"

I laughed. "No, but we need to face reality."

She looked at me, defiant. "If I become queen, I can change the law."

I shut my eyes and leaned back. "That's a dangerous assumption." It was crazy enough to think about Julia being queen, but the fact that she could only marry a royal had been stuck in the back of my mind. My stomach did flips thinking about her with someone else. It got even worse when I thought about the alternative: me becoming a royal sometime in the future.

We sat in silence for a minute, the soft, unending *tick tock* of the clock filling the room. The glass cage surrounded us, deceiving us with the idea of freedom yet again as we remained trapped. She laid her head on my shoulder and whispered, "Why is the world against us?"

I ran my hand along her head, with my eyes still shut. "When darkness is in control it snuffs out the tiniest of light."

Her mind was hard at work, trying to figure out a plan. "What if we made you a royal?"

I scoffed. "It's rare enough for a favored Purple or Blue to be elevated to royalty, but me?" She laughed. "What?"

"I believe we've broken quite a few traditions already. Why would this be any different? They already know we are together."

Sorrow filled my heart as I tried to find the words to respond. "Julia, I love you more than anything in this stupid world, but I can't ask you to do that. Princesses have flings all the time, so they'll tolerate this for now, but the second I'm made a royal, it becomes serious to people." I shuddered thinking about becoming one of the Whites. I despised so many of them, and I knew they'd never accept me.

She pulled on my jacket, forcing me to open my eyes and look at her. "Ivan, you have sacrificed yourself for me, for my family, for so many people. I will not sacrifice you. I will be the queen, and if you're willing, you will be my king." *King?*

I didn't know how to respond to that, so I just smiled and joked, "Just know that whenever I propose, I can't afford many shiny rocks."

She laughed. "Ivan!"

I kissed her and pulled her in close. "What happened to the cautious girl I saved on that street corner?"

She kissed me in response. "That girl has seen more in the last five months than in the rest of her life. This decision is not one I take lightly, Ivan. I love you, and I want to spend the rest of my life with you. When the time comes, I need you by my side when I'm on the throne. Together, we can show the country that a stupid tag means nothing." *This is so freakin' fast.*

"I love you too, but we don't need to make major life decisions tonight. It's time for you to sleep." I wrapped her in my arms and carried her to her bed. "You have a lot of schmoozing to do tomorrow, and I am exhausted. It's been a long day, and my head is killing me."

She laughed as I pulled the covers over her. "We are insane, are we not?"

I kissed her forehead. "We're mental."

Chapter 11

In what world am I qualified to be the king? Can I really let her take that risk for me? I'd managed to squash those questions before last night, but now they ruled my mind. As I stood guard during Julia's meetings with various minor royals, I couldn't focus on the give and takes occurring in the room. I'd faced death multiple times, but this felt so much worse. The royal world was still all so new to me and everything was moving so fast. It made my head spin just thinking about it.

"Ivan." What if the royals try to overthrow her? "Ivan." How can I possibly prove myself to that extent? "Ivan." How can I possibly deserve her as a wife when the time comes? "Ivan!"

Shaking myself out of the daze, I saw Julia standing in front of me as she gestured to the royals next to her. I stood at attention. "Yes, m'lady."

She gave me a concerned look for a moment before her princess mask returned to its normal place. "We are finished. Please escort me back to the car."

I apologized with my eyes before bowing. "Yes, of course, m'lady."

She smiled to the royals and curtsied. "Thank you, Lord Meier and Lady Ella, for your time. It has been an honor. I do look forward to seeing you at Saturday's nomination ceremony."

The man, whose hair perfectly matched his poorly-fitted grey suit, bowed. "Please, the honor has been all ours, your highness. No one from the royal family has ever visited our Rhinelander villa. It truly has been a pleasure, my dear." Lord Meier then turned towards me, and I froze in shock as he rose a shaky finger towards me. "Are you the boy that they say saved the royal family from Count Wilhelm?"

I looked towards Julia, asking silently if it was okay to respond. She smiled with half of her mouth and nodded. I turned my head back towards Lord Meier. "I did what I could sir, but the true heroes were the servants who rushed into the ballroom. I just bought them time."

He smiled, showing his sloppily held dentures, and nodded. "You're a good boy then." He nodded towards Julia. "Take care of her. This one is our only hope."

I nodded. "I will, sir."

Julia curtsied again and followed me back out of the villa towards the car. I put on her peacoat and shivered as we headed back into the northern Wisconsin tundra. The Twin Cities were freezing in January but were nothing compared to this eternal winter. I get why nobody ever visits.

Our long day had consisted of meetings with strategically chosen royals throughout eastern Minnesota and rural Wisconsin. While none of the most powerful names resided out there, these royals were important votes if Julia would stand any chance. As Lord Meier implied, most of these Whites had been ignored for years if not decades. The fact that Julia was willing to brave the storm to visit them when no one else would must have meant the world to them. Even among the royalty, not everyone felt respected.

Besides just making her look good, there were two more crucial reasons we went on the road. First, Vera was watching Julia's every move in the palace, worrying about her plans for the crown. These meetings, which Julia had pitched to her mother as outreach for the family away from the threats of the cities, provided perfect cover for her to rally support ahead of the nominations in three days. So far, she had earned the backing of every family she'd met with, and even if they were minor royals, it was a great start.

The second reason we were on the road was to scout out one of the UPF's so-called "work cities" that the UPF had thrown so many of the Reds into. We both wanted to see one with our own eyes to get a better grasp of the situation and possibly provide some intel to Delaware. We weren't optimistic about being able to save them with the current state of the Militia, but we needed to regain the faith of the Reds before they fell into the Fracture's hands or were killed by the UPF. I had been reluctant to allow Julia to scout the camp with me. She insisted, though, and I lost the fight.

This meeting with Lord Meier had been crucial to our plan, as he was one of the only royals alive who had met King Timothy I, II, and III. He may have been from a remote part of Wisconsin that no king had ever visited, but Franz Meier knew everyone and was well respected. In the last hour, her charm and determination had gone a long way in a short time; Julia had convinced him to not only support her bid for queen, but also be the one to nominate her. The legitimacy of the nominating royal was crucial. Having a well-connected backer would go a long way towards Julia's candidacy being taken seriously.

When we reached the sleek black SUV, I opened the door for her before sliding in behind her. She ran her fingers through her hair, still getting used to the new style. "Everything alright, Ivan? What was that in there?"

I gazed out into the sea of white. "Yeah, I just got lost in thought for a minute."

She pushed harder. "You seem to be doing that a lot today. Something is wrong."

I crossed my arms. "Don't worry about it. There's a lot going on right now, and I'm just trying to wrap my head around it."

Her eyes analyzed me, concerned. "I didn't mean to be forceful. I understand. The past couple of weeks have been crazy for me too, but we can't get distracted. These people will look for any reason to doubt me, to doubt us."

I sighed. "Understood." Why can't I just be honest with her?

Her eyes narrowed. "We're in this together, right?"

I took a deep breath, trying to calm my nerves. She is not the enemy. She's doing this for you. I forced a smile and met her eyes. "Always."

We hit a bump and Julia pursed her lips before looking out the window. "Good, because our last meeting is the most important one yet. Franz gets us the nomination, but it is Countess Alanna Lorenz who is the key to proving that we can win. She is known for accepting only the best, and that includes monarchs. Her family is notorious for choosing to not cast their votes instead of supporting a monarch they didn't like. My father, grandfather, and great-grandfather all failed to receive their family's votes. Rumor has it, the last monarch their family supported was King Abraham Lincoln during the old Kingdom of America."

I laid my head back against the seat rest. "Who?"

Her energy level spiked and her raised voice made me jump. "You don't know who Abraham Lincoln was?"

I shook my head. "I know he was one of America's kings, but the Militia didn't have that many history books. The ones we had only really talked about the Revolutionary War and First Civil War."

"He saved the Kingdom of America from collapse, ended slavery, and won the Second Civil War. The monarchy was falling apart, but he tried to reform it and started moving towards a republic. If it wasn't for him, the country would have fallen apart sixty years sooner." She groaned, distraught. "If only he had more time. Maybe he could have fixed things."

"What happened?"

She sighed. "He was assassinated. It's sad. He was probably the only good king that America ever had, and his reign was the shortest." She looked back out the window.

I followed her gaze. "We can't change history, though. It's not like we can go back and tell Washington that the British knew about his plan to cross the Delaware."

"I always wonder what could have happened if he had lived to help create the new government. Just imagine: The First Civil War may have never happened. Maybe Jefferson could have lived."

How far you can fall so quickly. Thomas Jefferson was went from a hero as the writer of the Declaration of Independence to a defeated outcast when he led the rebellion against John Adams, Alexander Hamilton, and others' creation of an American monarchy less than a decade after the end of the Revolutionary War. Jefferson was eventually executed, while other leaders such as James Madison and Benjamin Franklin fled west.

Julia pondered for a moment before speaking, "We can only change the world that was left for us."

I smiled and wrapped my arm around her shoulder. "At least I know that Queen Julia's reign will be remembered as the era that saved Northern Mississippi."

She smiled softly and kissed my cheek before her eyes filled with concern. "How do you know? Doesn't every monarch believe that?"

I laughed. "If every monarch, general secretary, and prime minister actually cared about their country, things would be so much different. You don't even want the crown but are doing so out of duty. Most people do it for power and status, nothing more. No offense to your ancestors, but the bar is really low. If you can make the monarchy look like a legitimate force instead of a reality show, you will have done more than all the Timothies combined. You may like reality shows, but let's save the country from this one."

She chuckled. "How do you know so much about all of this? You told me that Poseidon had to teach you how to read."

"He did, using the few books that were around: history books, ones from before the war. The Militia tried to hold onto everything they could when the UPF started burning 'anti-collective' books after the war. We had some of the only copies left in the country of anything resembling what actually happened."

She yawned. "And the only other copies are in the palace library. Seems that we're two of the few people to have actually learned real history."

We sat in silence for a while, her head resting on my shoulder. I felt bad for her, feeling each bump in the road as she tried to relax for just a moment. It had been a long day. She deserved a break. We didn't have long until we would reach Alanna Lorenz's family mansion, but she needed every second she had to get her energy back ahead of the meeting. While she played the art of the diplomacy, I just had to stand in the corner and not cause distractions.

I watched the snow-covered hills fly by as we drove. The SUV charged through the wicked wind, and I was amazed that we were still able to drive through the storm. We hadn't seen another car on the road for most of the trip. If Julia was going to form a coalition, though, it needed to start now, whether the skies were clear or not.

Driving through northern Wisconsin was a whole new world to me. I'd never stepped foot outside of Minnesota in my life as the movement of Reds had always been highly restricted, leaving us isolated from the rest of the country. Our trip back out to the River Falls orphanage to save Delaware and others a few years ago had been risky, but no matter where we were going, it was always difficult for Reds to get out of the city. I was only exempt from the travel restrictions because of Julia.

At times, it felt like St. Paul and Minneapolis were all there was to the world. In the same way that I had opened Julia's eyes to life within the Enclave and the worst parts of St. Paul, she was now opening my eyes to life beyond. Much of Northern Mississippi's population had been forced into the cities in a mass industrial effort, but life persisted outside the city streets.

Every so often on that day's travels, we would pass by a town in the distance. From what I'd heard, life was not much different in those towns. Reds were still enslaved on farms or in factories, and color still meant more than humanity. They were away from the UPF's twin hearts, but the veins pumped their poisonous ideas to even these far-reaching villages.

This upcoming meeting was important, but I was anxious for it to be over before it had even begun. I needed to see the camps with my own eyes. Countess Alanna's mansion in Woodruff was just half an hour north of the Harshaw camp. The sun hovered at the horizon. Night was coming, and when it did, we'd figure out what had happened to so many Reds.

For now, though, we were pulling into Woodruff, and I ran my hand along Julia's head. "We're almost there, hun."

She took a long, deep breath, and her poise returned to its place as the chauffeur parked in front of the mansion. I slid out of the car and held the door for Julia as she stepped into the storm. As she gazed at the dated mansion, I tried to guard her from the blowing snow, but her ice-blue peacoat was quickly coated in yet another layer of white. Her cheeks were flushed pink from the cold as a disgruntled butler guided us into the mansion.

Inside, the butler took Julia's coat, exposing her formal dress and blazer. She was here to impress, and that meant ensuring she appeared as official as possible. The last thing she needed was to seem too young to be considered for queen, even if she was the youngest remaining princess. The butler then led us through a series of hallways and back into a conference room. Countess Alanna was waiting with her two daughters and three sons, none of which had earned a significant name for themselves. According to what Julia had told me, their mom led the way, and rumors had swirled for a long time that the Lorentz family would struggle to stay relevant once she was gone.

Julia remained standing at the head of the wooden rectangular table, opposite of Alanna, and flashed a smile. The children bowed and curtsied before taking their seats while Alanna simply nodded her head. "Welcome, Princess Julia. Few have ever made their way to us this deep in the winter."

Julia curtsied as Alanna took a seat. "The honor is all mine, Countess. I am quite enjoying the beautiful power of your region's weather. The white snow covers everything." She smiled jokingly. "I never thought I would see heavier snowfall than in Minneapolis."

Alanna nodded and held an open hand towards the seat at the end of the table. "Indeed. Please, take a seat. I am sure your journey has been an arduous one."

Julia sat and crossed her legs at the knee. "I have had a wonderful time meeting with many of our respected royals throughout the day, but I will admit that it has been quite a long journey."

The countess raised an eyebrow. "Of course, though your father obviously did not feel that we were worth the trip."

Julia didn't miss a beat. "That is true, but I am not my father. He did not understand the importance of the royalty outside of the Twin Cities. He did not understand that being a monarch is about the people you must lead, no matter where they reside. I hope that you will not blame me for the sins of my father when you consider the request that I have for you this evening."

"And what, exactly, is that?" Alanna's eyes narrowed.

Julia smiled sweetly. "I believe that, if we are going to mend the divides that are tearing this country apart, I must become queen, and I would be honored to have your support." She paused a before scanning the rest of the family. "All of your support."

The eldest son let out a laugh. "Why would we do that?"

"That is why I am here today, to address any concerns that you may have." Julia looked delighted at the challenge. "I hope that I can convince you to support my bid, but first, I would like to hear what you believe the monarchy could be doing better, for you and for the country."

Alanna spoke again, "Your willingness to come to us is a good first step, but it is impossible to know what is an empty gesture and what is genuine, especially during an election. Our family does not give its support lightly." Julia nodded, and Alanna continued, "We need assurances that our business will be protected from the Front's attempts to steal it from us. Your father and grandfather simply allowed the socialists to take what they wanted from us and so many others. We're one of the few legal private companies left."

"Of course, your cranberry and dairy farms will be protected. As I believe I have shown in recent months, I have no intentions of backing down to the People's Front."

Alanna nodded along with her children and then paused. When she spoke, it was oddly hesitant compared to her previously confident demeanor. "I do have one more sensitive request as well."

"Anything."

The countess took a deep breath. "As I am sure you are aware, the Front has constructed one of their work cities nearby. In the process, they seized quite a bit of our land, and our workers are no longer willing to work in the area."

Julia's eyes filled with genuine concern. "I am so sorry to hear that. What specifically is causing your workers grief?"

Alanna looked over to her older daughter, who shifted uncomfortably before speaking, "The smell is awful. Our Yellow and Orange Tag workers have also expressed concern about the safety of some of the Red Tags within the work zone."

This had my attention now. If the camp was drawing the attention of nearby royals, then it must have been bad. Very few Whites bothered to care about non-royals. Though the Lorenz family had a reputation for being stubborn, they were far less elitists than most royals. What do they want done with it?

Julia leaned forward. "I share their concern. How can I help?"

Alanna spoke again, "We need you to push for the work city to be disbanded. Neither us nor the residents want it, and with our fears about the Reds within, we cannot tolerate its presence any longer."

This was good news for the first time in what felt like forever.

The Lorenz family not only wanted to get rid of the camp, but they were willing to back Julia if she wanted to as well. It was a dream come true and more political backing to potentially free the Reds.

If Julia was as excited I was, she did a good job disguising it as she replied, "It is part of my plan to work for the complete dissolution of the work cities, so I believe we are on the same page here."

Relief flooded the family's faces and Alanna smiled for the first time. "I am happy to hear it. We have been impressed by your calls for reform. It is past time for us to fix our broken monarchy." She looked at her children's faces. "I believe I speak for my family when I say that you have our complete support, and we will make it known at Saturday's convention."

Julia beamed. "I am humbled to have all of your support. We truly can accomplish great things together, and this will not be my last time visiting your beautiful home."

Alanna stood, and the rest of the table followed. "May your journey home be as smooth as possible, your highness."

Julia curtsied. "That is very much appreciated Alanna." She turned to me and smiled. "Let's return to the car before this storm buries us, shall we?"

I bowed, "Of course, m'lady," and led her back into the stormy night.

Chapter 12

The Lorenz family was right about the smell. It penetrated everything for over a mile around the camp. I quickly doubted whether bringing Julia along was a good idea, not that I had a choice. For the sake of our relationship, I gave up on my last-minute protests. *Remember, she doesn't want to do this. She doesn't want to do any of this. She needs to.*

The storm raged on, but this would be our only shot. We had left the trustworthy chauffeur a mile back and proceeded the rest of the way on foot. The risk of detection would be too high if we drove any closer. The last thing the UPF wanted was people actually being able to see what was happening inside the camps.

I peered through my binoculars, trying to get a glimpse of something, anything, but the wind continuously blew snow through my vision. "We need to get closer." I looked towards Julia, wrapped up in a much larger coat and fuzzy hat now that the meetings were done. "You doing okay?"

Her eyes were solid ice, focused squarely on the camp in the distance. "I will be fine."

She was lying, but I knew calling her out on it wouldn't fix anything, so I pushed through the snow towards the tree line. In the search lights from the towers, I could begin to see the camp's makeshift buildings. While the UPF claimed the camps were "work cities," Harshaw wasn't even a city. They had cleared out a section of trees near the biggest field they could find and, from the looks of it, forced the Reds to build these structures.

I peered through my binoculars again, trying to get a better look at the buildings. They were shoddily built wooden structures covered in tarps: definitely not enough to protect against the freezing temperatures. Lines of barbed wire surrounded the camp, and tall search towers were topped by snipers. *Keep an eye on them.*

Julia lowered her binoculars. "They're going to freeze to death in there. We need to do something."

I kept scanning the camp. "What can we do? There's got to be hundreds of guards in there."

"When I am queen, we will free them, Ivan. I promise, even if it requires the royal military."

Before I could respond, I noticed guards beginning to scramble all over the place near the center of the camp. "Something's happening."

We winced as the first shots rang from the center of the camp. I covered Julia instinctively before looking towards where they came from. My heart dropped. *Firing squad.*

I kept her head down as she fought against me, trying to get a look. "What is it? Ivan?"

My heart was caught in my throat, and I couldn't bring myself to respond as I watched the second group take their positions. The Reds were clothed in nothing more than ripped jeans and a T-shirt. If those squads didn't get to them first, the cold would. *That could have been me.*

Julia continued to fight. "Ivan, let me see." She broke free and turned just as the next volley shot through the Reds' skulls. All we could do was watch in horror. *May they rest in the peace they lacked in this life.*

Coyote would have tried to storm the camp. Coyote would have snuck out everyone he could have, risking his life and potentially accomplishing nothing. I still felt the urge to do the reckless, but with Julia beside me, I knew we needed a better plan. We would do everything we could to break them out of this hell-hole. To-night was not the night, though. A former rebel lieutenant and a princess were not exactly a well-suited rescue squad. We needed the Militia's manpower and the royal guard's resources if we were going to break the Reds out of not only this camp but the others as well.

Julia cried out as she watched the guards drag the bodies into a pile and pour gasoline over them. I quickly covered her mouth as a search light swung towards the trees, followed by a sniper's barrel. I looked into her eyes and held a finger to my lips as we shuffled behind a row of trees. We'd seen enough.

The watchtowers' lights swung towards us as the guards shouted. I covered Julia as a sniper's bullet whizzed over our heads. "We need to go, now!" I pulled her to her feet and we started back towards the car as barks echoed across the field. *Dogs. Shit.* Julia was struggling through the snow, so I grabbed her arm and pulled her along. "Those dogs will catch us if we don't hurry."

We trudged our way through the deep snow and back towards the car. There was no way to cover our tracks, and the dogs would be gaining ground on us if we didn't hurry. The storm was only getting worse. Each step was another battle against the raging wind, and it was impossible to know how close we were to the car with such little visibility. We could only push on as the shouts and barking dogs closed in.

My face burned from the cold when I approached the end of the forest. Suddenly, I heard a cry from behind me, and I looked back to see Julia face-down in the snow. *We don't have time for this!*

I tried to help her to her feet, but she cried out it pain. Without thinking, I picked her up in my arms and pushed back towards the road. Adrenaline drove me forward as I groaned and fought forward into the blinding snow. Behind me, the barking had become deafening. *We're not going to make it.*

The car had to be close, but when we reached the tree line, it was nowhere to be seen. *Whose idea was it to bring a black car?* I pushed towards the road and looked down at Julia for a moment. "We're going to be okay."

She couldn't bring herself to respond. It didn't matter. We were about to die on the side of the road in the middle of nowhere in Wisconsin, and talking was just another distraction. All I could do was break into the closest thing to a run I could muster while carrying her in a desperate search for the car.

As we reached the edge of the road, the first shots rang out and bullets peppered holes in the snow around us. Julia flinched in my arms with each one, and I did everything I could to shield her from the bullets. *She has to live.*

The SUV appeared ahead, and I shouted, hoping that the chauffeur would pull closer. My legs screamed with every step, but I refused to give in as the bullets rained around us. I hauled Julia into the back seat of the SUV, but as I tried to get in, a sharp pain shot through my left arm.

Julia's eyes filled with terror as I looked down to see a massive dog's jaw biting into my forearm. I cried out in pain and kicked, trying to dislodge the beast. It growled and shook its head back and forth, sending pain shooting through my arm. In my panic, I couldn't think about anything but survival, and I threw everything I had into one last kick. The force knocked me into the car as the dog released me for just a moment.

Stunned and disoriented, I flung the door shut and yelled for the chauffeur to drive as the dog looked ready to lunge again. As the car sped away, the bullets sounded like a hail storm against the side of the car. *How are we going to explain this to Vera?*

Julia sat silent as I gripped my arm, likely shocked from the incident. The dog had ripped away most of the fabric from my jacket's forearm, exposing my old burn scar and the jagged marks where its teeth had gripped me. I was bleeding everywhere. I ripped the fabric that was left and used it as gauze, trying to stop as much of the blood as possible, but it wasn't going to be enough. *They should just reserve a bed for me at the hospital at this rate.*

I laid my head back against the headrest, disoriented, and looked out the window. Smoke was rising from the camp in the distance. They were burning the bodies. *How many have they killed? How many are left to save?* It was impossible to know. As much as the UPF needed the Reds to prop up their failed economic system, having too many of us was a burden to the collective in their eyes.

Bachton will pay for this. He'll regret letting me live.

Julia groaned in pain as she tried to help cover my arm. Both of us were a mess, but we were alive. We'd seen the camps, and I understood now why they would do anything to keep them a secret. With that many guards, saving the Reds would be nearly impossible, but we had to find a way.

I weakly gripped her shaky hand as I closed my eyes, "What have we gotten ourselves into?"

Chapter 13

Explaining away Julia's twisted ankle would have been simple, but my dog bite and the armor-plated SUV riddled with bullet holes were highly suspect. We knew we would hear about it once I was stitched up at the hospital. A destroyed $250,000 SUV and a princess almost dying were not two things Vera would take lightly.

She did not take them lightly at all, and we were enduring her wrath in the living room upstairs. She paced back and forth in front of the fireplace, ranting about our irresponsibility, "Do you know what would have happened to our family if we lost another? We are barely holding onto power, and there would have been mass chaos if you'd been killed. And you, Ivan." She turned towards me and pointed her finger. "What kind of bodyguard lets a princess go anywhere near a place like that? You are her… boyfriend for Christ's sake!" She looked ready to vomit when she said "boyfriend." I took a little satisfaction out of that.

I was standing at attention at the end of the couch and hung my head. "I take full responsibility for the events of last night, your highness."

Julia interjected, "No, Ivan, this was my fault. He did not want to let me go, but when I insisted, he came along to protect me." She held her chin up. "I *needed* to see what was in that camp, mother. It was far worse than I could have imagined."

Vera hesitated. "Go on."

Julia took a deep breath. "We saw the buildings they lived in. It is even worse than the Enclave. They have nothing but tarps thrown over some wooden poles. The Reds are going to freeze to death. That is not all of it either. We saw the guards executing dozens of them via firing squad and burning their bodies." She trembled.

The Queen furrowed her brow. "That is concerning, indeed. Natasha and I will have to address this with the Front as soon as possible."

You mean Julia... I was still entertained by Vera's confidence in Natasha. *Is she really this naïve, or are we being played?*

Julia narrowed her eyes at her mother. "Please tell me you don't believe the Front is unaware of this? Asking politely for them to cease the operation of the camps will accomplish nothing, Mother. We must convince the Council to act before more Reds are killed."

"As I said, Natasha and I will address this. Do not think that just because your father is gone that you can suddenly play head of state."

Julia rose, placing her weight on her good ankle as she shot an icy-glare at her mother. "If that is all..."

Oh, she's pissed.

Vera sighed and stepped closer, analyzing her daughter's face. "How did your *other* meetings go?"

Julia held her chin high. "Well. They appreciated a member of the royal family visiting them, especially under such conditions. I believe that *we* have their support."

Vera nodded and looked out the window towards the gardens. "Splendid. Thank you for enduring that uncomfortable journey. Wisconsin will be key in securing victory over Bilgram's traitors." Julia simply nodded. "Very well. You may go, but I would like to speak with Ivan, alone."

Julia's took a deep breath and raised an eyebrow at me. I just shrugged, and she hobbled out of the room. *Please come back...* Vera gestured for me to sit, and I did, reluctantly.

She sat on one of the other couches, looking sternly at me. "You must understand my concern regarding your actions with my daughter. This family has been shaken enough without you making it worse."

I cocked my head to the side. "Making it worse? I saved your lives, in case you forgot."

Narrowing her eyes, she responded, "That likely would not have occurred if you hadn't foiled our agreement with the Preus family. Now, we are more vulnerable than ever, and your relationship with Julia makes that worse. I have tolerated your relationship for her emotional support after the loss of her father and now Helena, but its continuance will only further erode the people's confidence in our family. It must end."

I exploded and was on my feet, fists clenched by my side. "What did you expect, for this to be a fling? Did you think the low-life Red in *your* palace would eventually get bored and leave? Did you think Julia would eventually get over me, over us?" Any sense of restraint was gone. My brain was off. This was pure emotion as I continued to berate her, "What do you think we are? There's a reason I gave up everything I had to protect her and her family, *your* family. For my entire life, I've questioned every moment if what I was doing was right. With her, I know what I am doing, what I *need* to do, and nothing will stop me from doing that: not the UPF, not the Fracture, and not you."

She sprung to her feet, meeting me face to face in a rage. "You have put my daughter and my family in danger too many times. I will not let you tear this family apart. You understand me? You believe that you know everything after a few months among royalty, but Ivan, you know absolutely nothing."

I glared into her eyes. "I don't have to tear your family apart. You've done a fantastic job of doing that yourself. And guess what? I know a lot. I know that you're desperate to get Natasha on the throne, because you've always wanted it for yourself. I also know that you care deeply for your daughters, that they really do mean the world to you, and that you would do anything to protect them. You'd do anything to avenge Helena, you'd do anything to rein in Alex, and you'd do anything to not lose Julia. You can't do any of that without me. *You* need me, your highness. Whether you like it or not, if you kick me out, your family falls apart permanently, and you never get the sweet revenge you so desperately need on the Fracture."

My face was on fire, and my heart raced. Vera's rage was replaced with a moment of fear. She stepped back into the couch and stumbled before catching herself again. She appeared lost for words. *Time to go.*

I held my head high before bowing. "Your highness, I will take my leave." With that, I stormed out of the room, leaving the Queen gaping behind me. I'd take the little victory over her. None of what I had said was planned, but I meant every word I said from start to finish. She needed to hear the problems she'd caused and why she needed me. I had caught her in her own trap, and it felt good.

Julia was waiting for me anxiously in her room, sitting on her bed to avoid any unneeded pressure on her ankle. A surprised look crossed her face as I stormed in and grabbed my jacket. "What happened?"

I huffed, "I need to take a walk. I hate this place," and stomped back towards the door.

She called after me desperately, "Ivan! Wait. I can't walk on my ankle very well."

I stopped with my hand on the handle and rested my forehead against the door, feeling its coolness flow into my burning skull. "Right, sorry."

She patted the bed next to her. "Please talk to me, my love."

My rage faded a bit, and I took a breath. "Fine." I stumbled over to the bed and flopped onto it, facing away from her.

She laughed as I groaned. "Mother couldn't have been *that* bad."

"Try me."

She touched my back, running her finger down my spine. "What did you two talk about?"

You're not mad at Julia, remember that. I sighed and rolled over to face her. "Guess."

The gears turned in her head as she pursed her lips and analyzed my face. "She wanted you to do a mission for her?"

"Cold."

She scrunched her face in playful agitation. "It was related to us."

I looked into her eyes. "Warmer."

"She tried to break us up."

"Yup. She told me that our relationship will continue to 'erode' people's confidence in your family and that I'm a danger."

Her eyes were alight. "And what did you tell her?"

"I told her this is not a fling, and that there was a reason I sacrificed everything I did for your family."

She made an *ooh* face. "That's bold of you to say to her. I'm impressed."

I shrugged. "Yeah, but then she went on about how I'm tearing your family apart and know nothing about royalty.

She chuckled. "That's ironic, coming from her."

I clenched my fist just thinking about Vera's attacks. "It is, and I let her know it, telling her that she is the one tearing your family apart, so I don't have to. Then, I explained exactly why she can't get rid of me. Without me, she can't destroy the Fracture, she loses you, and then she'll lose Alex. After that, I bowed and stormed out."

"So much for diplomacy."

I groaned. "I tried that, but the only way I could prevent her from ending us is to beat her at her own game." I sighed. "To these people, that's all that power is, a game. They don't care that peoples' lives are at stake. Your mom, Bilgram, all of them will do everything they can to protect that power and move up the ladder. There are some lines we cannot cross, but if we're going to make you queen, we need to play the game, and we need to win. This kind of maneuvering is not that different from what had to be done in the Militia to prevent hostile takeovers. You want to stay out of the mud, but I can do it."

She ran her thumb along the back of my hand and reached for the Hughes family pin on my chest. "If we play their dirty games, we become no better than them. What you said to my mother was blackmail, and I don't like it." She sighed. "I understand that it had to be done in this case, but I don't want to be queen through shady deals and stabbing people in the back. I know it will make this so much harder, and there are *some* games we must play to win. I'm not naïve enough to not defend myself or attack when necessary, but we want to show the world a different way, though, a purer way. Let them dirty themselves in the mud. In the end, I will wear the White Crown. I know that I need to do this, and together, we can do this."

I sighed. While I didn't agree with the approach, she did have a point. I'd learned the hard way that I wasn't going to win in discussions like this, so I just nodded. "Ok then, it's your campaign. No mud."

She smiled softly and kissed me. "Thank you, Ivan."

I returned the smile. "Long live the queen."

Chapter 14

The set up for the nomination ceremony ball was my first return to the ballroom since my release. Just stepping foot into the room made me want to vomit. Everywhere I turned, I could see the death and destruction from the night of the coup. I stared at the spot where Isaac held a gun to the head of the woman I loved. *I almost lost her.*

"Ivan! Ivan!"

I shook myself out of my daze and looked towards the voice. Jonah was trotting down the ballroom staircase and towards me. "What's up?"

As he approached, he noticed where I was staring. "That asshole got what he deserved."

"I shoot him every night in my dreams. It's always the same, and I never regret it."

He nodded solemnly. "And every night I watch a bullet fly through my king's head as I stand there, helpless to stop it."

I placed my hand on his shoulder. "If it wasn't for your rallying of the servants, the entire family would have died. I would have died."

He adjusted his pin, keeping his head low. "Bravery is not hiding while your comrades are gunned down."

I sighed and kicked at the stupidly perfect floors. "Bravery is doing what is needed, no matter the risk. You did that."

He bit his cheek and dodged the topic. "Fix your tie, it's crooked."

I made a face but did as he said. "They failed to teach me tie etiquette when I became a servant. Phillip and Michael were too concerned with me saying 'sir.'"

Jonah laughed. "And they obviously failed at that. You should be headed to your post. The guests will be arriving shortly." He started walking away before spinning around. "Oh, and a certain princess looks wonderful this evening, but she told me she wants you to be surprised."

I raised my eyebrows as he grinned before heading back up the stairs to finalize the security measures. The spot still haunted me as I took one last look, sighed, and strode towards my post. *This is going to be a long night.*

Over the next eternity, guests arrived one-by-one. A caller announced each of their names and meaningless titles as they entered to the sound of the orchestral music. *I'm living in a demented fairytale.* Each of them was dressed to the max, and I wondered how big of an event this was for some of them. It was their one chance to make an impression before the coronation, so they planned to apparently over-do it as much as possible.

From my station along the left wall, I scanned the mingling Whites, attempting to identify who was friend and who was foe. It was impossible to tell. There were around a thousand royals of varying importance eligible to vote for the monarch, and it felt as if all of them had crowded into the palace for the nomination ceremony. Some cared about the competition, others jostled for power, and many more were simply hoping for a good show. Regardless of their intentions, they all eagerly awaited the campaign. Everyone knew this would be the first contested election in Northern Mississippi history. This was not an event they wanted to miss.

By that time, the minor royals had almost completely filed in. Franz Meier took his time with the stairs but looked absolutely excited to be there. His smile was the first genuine one I had seen so far that night, and his wife had to stop him from flying down the stairs and breaking a hip. That was a rare joy. *I see why Julia picked him.*

Alanna Lorenz was the odd-one-out. She had dressed formally, but her simple black dress made it obvious that she had avoided the excessiveness in an act of defiance to her peers. Ironically, her lack of effort to stand out made her the most unique of all, and her five children had followed suit.

The last royal to descend the staircase before the expected candidates was Alexander Hamilton V himself. The great-great-grandson of the second king of America strode down the steps as if he was, in fact, the king. His hand was stuffed into the chest of his navy and gold jacket, imitating Napoleon Bonaparte as some of the snobbiest royals often did. He held his chin high as minor royals greeted him at the bottom of the staircase. *Is he just that cocky, or does he have a plan?*

When Hamilton's walk was complete, the room quieted as the Bilgram children entered ahead of Duke Richard Bilgram and his wife, Ilana. The couple's obsidian and gold rings shone in the chandelier light. From my position, I could tell they enjoyed every second of the spotlight, taking each step slowly as they smiled to the crowd. The royals gave a mixed response, with many clapping and gawking at them while others sipped their wine and turned away in disgust. The slave trader was a controversial figure, but I had no doubt that he would be a force to be reckoned with.

Once the Duke reached the floor, he began his circle through the crowd, greeting each one as the vulture looked for his next prey. I wanted to take him down so bad, but we had too many problems to deal with already. For now, ensuring he didn't become king would have to do.

Next came the royal family. They were to enter from youngest to oldest, but in Helena's place, the caller asked for a moment of silence to remember her by. The warm atmosphere of the room chilled as they remembered her loss. Like the other guardsmen and servants, I wore a black armband in mourning for both her and her father. During the silence, I pictured the scene from the street: Julia emerging from the wreckage, Vera clutching her daughter's burned body, smoke hanging over the scene, and limousine parts scattered throughout the street. The Fracture would pay for what they'd done. *Even tonight is a step towards making things right.*

Once the silence had passed, the caller cleared his throat. "Princess Julia Elizabeth Hughes, Duchess of St. Paul." The doors slid open, and I gawked as Julia strode down the stairs in an ice-blue ball gown that hugged her frame before flowing into a wide circle. She shone even in the soft light, and there were audible gasps from the crowd. *Damn, I'm lucky. Maybe this fairytale isn't so demented after all.* She beamed at the crowd with genuine excitement. With everything that had happened the last few weeks, she must have been relieved to have a formal royal engagement to keep her mind occupied.

I couldn't help but smile at her from my post. She glanced towards me before she reached the bottom of the staircase, and our eyes met for a moment. That moment was enough to calm my worries. In the midst of the struggles and the chaos, we were a team and finally making progress. The fight was no longer about Coyote and the Militia against the world. It was on her shoulders now. The rest of us were just doing what we could to put her in the right position. We had found another way because of her, and I was happy for her to have a deserved moment in the spotlight before the real games began.

A few of the royals followed her glance, and I was met with a wide array of faces. Some of them that I recognized from the night of the coup looked at me with respect. Others, both familiar and unfamiliar, scowled in disdain at my presence. *Are they angered that I'm here or that I would dare consider myself worthy of Julia?*

She reached the bottom of the staircase and met each minor royal waiting to greet her. This was her natural habitat; her confident yet eloquent demeanor made navigating a crowd like this as simple as could be. For once, though, I was glad to be away from her side. While she ruled the spotlight, I preferred the shadows.

Wearing a simple black jumpsuit, Alexandria made much less of a scene than her younger sister, and I doubted that she wanted it any other way. Everyone in the crowd was too busy fawning over Julia, conspiring with the Duke, or anxiously awaiting Natasha and Vera's arrivals. She didn't bother smiling or putting on a show, and I lost track of her as she quickly moved on to probably something involving alcohol and a rebellious royal boy that didn't want to be there either.

Next came Natasha and then Vera, both drawing their share of attention, surprisingly, though, they were outshined by Julia and Bilgram. Natasha seemed uncomfortable in the spotlight and waited for her mother at the bottom of the staircase before moving through the crowd. Part of me felt for her. Her parents had deemed her the chosen one before she had a say in her future, and no matter how much they tried to prepare her, she still lacked the charisma of Julia. Vera, on the other hand, still carried the weight of her husband and daughter's losses, so she dressed more modestly in remembrance. Vera's strength was not as the center of attention but as the puppet master, and soon she would make her people dance.

With the painful introduction process completed, the fun and games began as royals talked, drank, and danced to the live music. The night was only just beginning, and I felt a serious need for more than one drink myself.

As security for an event like that, there was nothing to do but listen to the boring relays of "nothing to report" from the guards outside and observe the festivities. Security was much tighter after the Preus' stunt at the last gala, so inside the ballroom there was little to worry about unless two royals got too drunk and started to fight. On a crucial night like that, though, even those drunkards weren't that stupid.

Julia mingled through the crowd, meeting with key minor royals in what could appear to others as idle pleasantries. To anyone watching closely, though, it was obvious that she was speaking specifically with those who resided outside of major cities. Like our meetings in Wisconsin, showing the more remote royals that she not only knew who they were but also cared about what they thought was crucial. It wasn't a hard act for her to play, either, since it wasn't an act. While ignoring the power players could cause issues, the royals that Julia cared about the most were these forgotten ones: the rural lords and ladies who just needed to feel important.

I could have watched her meander through the crowd all night, her gown flowing along with her. I never knew how she did it, but with each conversation she had, her counterparts stared in awe as she told her stories about the palace or her love of the Black Tag children. She held so many of them in the palm of her hand, but unlike so many others, she didn't tighten her grip.

My heart twanged with jealousy as men, both young and old, pounced at the chance to dance with the beautiful princess. The elderly ones simply wanted to feel the thrill of dancing with a young woman again, while the younger ones blindly hoped to sweep her off her feet and away from me. *Good luck with that, assholes.* In those moments, my desire for the shadows failed, and I wanted nothing more than to be with her, to be the one making her smile as she spun around the dance floor. I remembered, though, that the royals had money, titles, prestige, and land, but I had what mattered: her. That was enough to make me smile as she endured their flirtatious advances, not that I forgot the suitors' stupid faces.

As the ball danced on, the royals began wobbling on their feet and scuttling off to remote corners of the palace to do what drunk people do in remote corners of a palace. I watched the organized chaos from my post and laughed to myself. This was why the royals were simply a means to an end when it came to changing things. Their failure to rule effectively was the reason the UPF had the chance to take over in the first place, but if Julia could become queen and push for change, maybe it didn't have to be the incompetent monarchists against the tyrannical socialists. Maybe there was another way.

At one point, Alex made her way over to me and looked towards Julia, turning the shaved side of her head towards me. Her burn was still obvious, but I had a feeling she enjoyed showing off her battle scar. While she was not one for the spotlight, she definitely did not enjoy blending in either. I followed her gaze as she mumbled, "She really does know how to work a crowd."

I smiled. "She has what it takes."

Alex raised her glass. "Thank God it's her and not me. I would rather not spend my time sucking up to these douchebags."

"How's your outreach going?"

She took a sip of her wine. "He's a good kisser… Oh, that's not what you meant." I laughed, and a few royals glared towards us with narrow eyes. Alex shot them a faux smile before turning back towards me. "She's got a lot of the younger ones. They hate how much their parents love my mom, so Jules is the obvious pick. We're in good shape, but you need to relax, Red. Tomorrow is for politics, tonight is for fun."

"Speak for yourself." I looked longingly towards Julia, who was thanking the musicians during one of their breaks.

A devious smile grew across her face. *Oh no.* "You know what would really screw with these cocky assholes? Go over there and dance with her."

I can't be a king... Every ounce of me wanted to dance with her, but it would require me to step into the spotlight of Julia's world, and as I watched the royals that night, I knew I didn't want to be one of them. Walking out there would make a statement to everyone that I was really with Julia, and she would be a candidate for queen tomorrow. "That would be finally admitting our relationship to them, beyond what Isaac said. It could risk everything for tomorrow. Plus, I'm supposed to be standing guard."

She took another swig of her drink. *Isn't wine supposed to be sipped?* "We need to make her stand completely apart from the others, to prove she really is different. You know, the people are tired of the old monarchy, and the royals our age are sick of the boring old drama. Give them something to be excited about."

"That's the most positive thing I've ever heard you say."

She sighed. "I'm spending too much time with my sister. Go, I need some entertainment."

I huffed and found Julia again, gracefully awaiting the next song. *Am I actually doing this?* When you think about the dancing with a girl, you're usually afraid of what she is thinking, not what the thousand royals in the room staring at you are thinking. I sighed, straightened my jacket, and started walking towards her as the next song began. *I need a drink.*

When I approached and placed a hand softly on her back, she turned, shocked, towards me. I held out my hand and bowed my head. "Would you like to dance, m'lady?"

Her ice-blue eyes were a clash of rebellious thrill and surprise. She understood what we were risking in that moment as well, but she didn't have much of a choice: royal courtesy demanded that she accept the dance. We were surrounded by a sea of eager eyes. *What are they thinking?*

Quickly, Julia broke out of thought, shot a thin smile my way, and placed her hand into mine. "Of course, Ivan."

As I led her onto the empty dance floor, my chest felt like someone had dropped a brick on it. I had been hoping that others would join us on the floor, but instead, a circle emerged as they watched us. *They're eager to see me fail.* Luckily, Julia had tried to teach me the basic moves of the waltz in the weeks before the coup in exchange for my teaching her self-defense. Those lessons had not been a fantastic success, though, and I could only hope that I would be better with everyone watching.

With my left hand raised and my right on her back, our eyes met. She was tense, but we both smiled in a moment of peace before I stepped forward, and the dance began. I drew a quick breath. It was always hard for me to pick out the flow of the music. I just didn't have the ear for it, but with a bit of help from her, we kept pace and moved throughout the open floor. Each step was taken one after another as I moved with no real plan or idea of what I was doing, but the royals did not seem to be laughing or booing. That was enough for me. Eventually, I threw in a spin, allowing her to twirl her dress for the crowd and sparking a few young royals to grab a girl themselves and join us on the floor. They may have been just trying to compete, but I appreciated the company.

It was hard to talk with the music, but she whispered in my ear, "Did Alex put you up to this?"

"Are you saying I'm not stupid enough to pull this stunt without some encouragement?"

She glared at me for long enough that I knew she wasn't happy. "You know everyone will be talking now, right?"

I smiled. "Exactly, about you. Not Bilgram, not Natasha, you. Besides, can't I share a dance with the hottest woman in the room without the whole country losing their minds?"

"The night before the nomination ceremony you decided that it was okay to announce our relationship to the world. This could ruin everything, Ivan."

"It could also show that you're genuine and transparent to the people you will rule. Look around, they love you, though, not as much as I do."

She bit her lip and gazed around at the gawking royals. "Stop acting cute so I can be mad at you for doing this."

Dancing with her for that song became one of my favorite memories. There was nowhere else in the world I would have rather been. It surprised me how easy it became to handle the spotlight around her, and I understood why so many of the royals were drawn to her. She held herself as an elegant princess yet didn't make those around her feel inferior. If anything, she did the opposite. My heart had raced before the dance, but once we began, it felt natural. We were connected. *Maybe I can do this.*

When the song came to an end, I smiled at Julia, bowed again, and kissed her hand, receiving audible *awws* from some of the women in the audience before I returned to my post. On my way, I spotted Bilgram, standing with his coalition. They looked pissed. *If this shocks them, they're in for some big surprises.*

Alex was talking with a royal boy and shooed him away as I returned. She looked smitten. "Impressive. I didn't expect you to actually do it."

I looked back towards Julia, who was blushing as she managed the swarm of women that had descended to gossip with her. "Neither did she."

Alex followed my gaze to her sister, who hadn't stopped smiling since the dance ended. "So, when are you changing your relationship status on social media, King Ivan?"

"I don't know if I could ever be king. I love her more than anything, but this isn't my world. What if I'm getting in her way?" Julia and my eyes met, and we shared a smile for a moment.

Alex shook her head. "It's not my world either, Ivan, but you just told her you're willing to do this with her. Ever since you two got together, she's been happier than I've ever seen her in my life. Don't take this lightly, because Jules sure as hell doesn't."

"I don't know how, but I'm willing to do it for her. She's already sacrificed so much for me." I sighed. "How was my dancing?"

"You're a sloppy lead. Still, you two have the cute factor, so congratulations, you won her the girls' votes."

"And probably lost the votes of the guys who are fawning over her."

She scoffed. "No, they'll stupidly follow her until there's no longer hope. They know the rules about a monarch's marriage, and besides, that's all they do anyway: stare at us and hope we fall in love with their riches. Pathetic." She scanned the crowd. "Now, I must find further entertainment for this evening. See you later, Red."

I laughed as she slid away. *At least someone in her family likes me.*

Over the next hour, the ballroom slowly emptied as royals headed off to their hotels or mansions for the night. Julia eventually glided over to me, her face showing her exhaustion. "How is my valiant bodyguard?"

I bowed to her and mimicked a royal voice. "Splendid m'lady. I quite enjoy watching drunk royals converse as I lose feeling in my feet."

"Try doing it in heels." She surveyed the now royal-less ballroom. "I still cannot believe you did that."

"I think it went well for my third time waltzing." I put my arm around her waist

Looking down at the ground, she hesitated before looking at me again. "You should have consulted with me first, but they say that fortune favors the bold."

"They also say that you should avoid Reds like the plague, so *they* don't seem to give great advice."

She rolled her eyes. "Walk me up to my room? I am exhausted, and we should probably both take time to rest ahead of the nomination ceremony."

I kissed her hand and bowed. "As you wish, m'lady." She shook her head with a smile, and we started walking back towards the staircase. "You really did steal the show. Everyone was watching you."

She ran her hands through her dress. "Do you like the dress?"

I smiled. "Jonah said that you wanted it to be a surprise. I love it, and you look beautiful. It wasn't just the dress, though; they just gravitate around you."

She dropped her head. "Some of them."

I pulled her closer next to me as we walked. "You're never going to make all of them love you. You're challenging their same old system. Some of them like it the way it is."

"Still, I don't enjoy the look of disdain some of them give me."

I sighed. "Imagine everyone looking at you like that."

She gave me a soft smile. "You are growing on some of them, though."

"Not enough. Sometimes, I feel like I'm holding you back."

She turned in front of me and held onto my jacket. "I could not do this without you. If I lose because they don't like you, then I lose. I never wanted to be queen. I still don't really *want* to be queen, but I know that what we are doing together can actually change things. They are not going to make me give you up, Ivan."

I hugged her in silence. She was sacrificing a lot for our relationship, in a way, we both were. We were doing everything we could to make it work, but even though we could laugh about annoying some royals, it was hard for both of us. It felt at times like it was the two of us and a few friends against the world. If we were going to change it, though, we would need each other, every step of the way.

134

Chapter 15

Nomination day had finally arrived, and the throne room was packed with the royals from last evening. The mood was very different, though. Instead of drinking and celebrating, the Whites were focused and negotiating.

I could see from my position the various factions of the royalty by where they chose to seat themselves. Vera's puppets sat in the front, and Bilgram's coalition was spread throughout the left. Julia's supporters were dispersed as we were still disorganized, partially on purpose. We didn't want to give Vera any reason to suspect Julia's nomination before it happened. Plus, it was beneficial to appear to have support from a variety of groups, something both Bilgram and Natasha currently lacked.

Julia sat with Alexandria on the right side of the room, near the front. She was dressed for business in an ice-blue blazer and slacks, and as she studied the crowd, her eyes were alight in anticipation. Alex, on the other hand, casually browsed her phone and yawned. She cared about her sister's nomination, but she didn't want to show it.

The Royal Council took their positions to the left and right of the throne itself, and the room quieted down as the head of the Royal Council, George Foster, cleared his throat and spoke, "Thank you all for joining us for our fourth royal nomination ceremony. I hope you all enjoyed last night's festivities, but now it is time to begin the process of choosing those who will vie for the White Crown. It is my honor to declare the nomination process open." He raised his arms out as if declaring the end to a firebrand sermon.

There was silence for a few moments. We all knew that Natasha would, as per tradition, be nominated first, but nobody knew who the nominator would be. Eventually, Alexander Hamilton V rose, and murmurs began among the audience. *The old guard protects the old guard.* He spoke proudly, "I, Count Alexander Hamilton V of Madison, do hereby nominate Princess Natasha Vera Hughes, Duchess of West Minneapolis."

His declaration was met with royals from the front shouting out, "Hear, hear!" Julia had explained to me ahead of time that it was an old tradition from Britain. I expected nothing less from the royals, but it was a nice tool to see the initial amount of support for a candidate. Natasha's support was significant, though it was nowhere close to a majority.

Count Alexander continued, "The princess has demonstrated her poise under pressure during these harsh times for our country. She has followed in her father's noble footsteps and would ensure that the monarchy remains a stable institution in Northern Mississippi. In times of crisis and trial, it is time to reaffirm what we believe, not radically change our beloved monarchy for the worse. Let us coalesce in unity around our common values, and let us coalesce in unity around Princess Natasha as our next queen."

The same crowd clapped as Natasha stood and straightened her skirt. She smiled proudly. "I accept the nomination." They whooped again in celebration, but most of the crowd remained deathly silent. Hamilton V had called for unity, but, as we suspected, there was little to be found.

Foster nodded. "Thank you. Do we have any more nominations?"

Franklin McGill stood and proclaimed, "I, Lord Franklin McGill of Osakis, do hereby nominate Richard Abraham Bilgram, Duke of Milwaukee, as our next king."

That must have been a nice slave-whiskey trade. Ever since I'd overheard his conversation with Bilgram about trading illegal whiskey for legal slaves, it was obvious he was a part of some plan. It was surprising, though, that such a minor royal was nominating Bilgram. It was also not surprising that Vera had not blackmailed him, yet. The idea of turning the nominator against his nominee after the ceremony was a tantalizing prospect, and I doubt she would hesitate to use it.

The surrounding royals, all elderly, chanted their own, "Here, here," in response. It was comparable, if not louder than Natasha's supporters. I stole a glance at Vera, wondering how she would respond, and watched her swallow what must have been a bit of her pride before lifting her head as if to shake it off.

McGill continued, "It is past time that we address the rot that has set into this great institution. We must re-legitimize our influence in this country and ensure that we are using every bit of royal influence to its maximum potential. Duke Richard is the only one who can ensure that. Let us make our monarchy into the force that it once was."

The Duke's large body rose as his supporters clapped. "It is with great honor that I accept this nomination."

His coalition stomped their feet in applause before Foster raised his arms to quiet them down and called for any additional nominations. He looked around, not expecting another, and began to speak again before Franz Meier stood slowly. Foster paused, a shocked look on his face, and then nodded.

Franz Meier supported himself on his cane as he spoke, "I, Lord Franz Meier of Rheinlander, do hereby nominate Princess Julia Elizabeth Hughes, Duchess of St. Paul, as the first elected queen of our great country."

A gasp came from much of the audience before a moment of silence and an array of murmuring. I had to hold in a laugh as shock and anger crossed Vera's face, and pride swelled in my chest as she glared at her daughter. With the surprise royals didn't know how to react, and they all looked around, seeing how others would respond. I took the initiative upon myself and yelled, "Here, here!" from my post in the back corner. The royals hesitated before Alanna Lorenz echoed the response, and an avalanche of replies followed. *Just needed a push.*

The room had gone from dead silent to a roar of support within a few seconds, and I couldn't help but grin. Many royals had needed a moment to consider her as a possibility before calling out in support. Countess Alanna looked back at me, and we nodded to each other. Together, we had allowed others the opportunity to show their support, and we heard it from people we never expected. It was not a majority, but it was at least as large as Bilgram's coalition and much more excited.

Foster raised his hands to silence the crowd before gesturing to Lord Meier to continue. Franz scanned the crowd with a gentle smile. "Princess Julia has proven that she is willing to put the peoples' interests ahead of personal power or prestige. To me, the ultimate symbol of humility is the desire to improve our world without the desire for power, and the princess is the noblest person I have ever met. She has demonstrated to me and many others, within the royalty and beyond, that she is the leader that this country needs. It is time for Northern Mississippi to heal the festering wounds that have existed for a century. It is time for Princess Julia to be the first elected queen."

A chorus of claps came from around the room, and I couldn't help but join in. *Screw formality.* Julia stood with her face aglow, trying to maintain her poise through her excitement. "I am humbled to accept Lord Meier's kind and generous nomination."

When she finished, I saw her eyes flick to her mom, who was still glaring at her with the ferocity of a thousand suns. Her supporters in the crowd hollered as she sat, but tension filled the room. Everyone knew what this meant, but no one knew what to expect. *Let the games begin.*

Foster shouted for quiet with his arms raised as Julia's rowdy young supporters continued. He almost looked reluctant to ask the question again. "Are there any further nominations?" After not more than a few seconds of hesitation, he broke the silence. "Then I hereby call this nomination ceremony to a close. Thank you to all of our nominators and nominees. As a reminder, the election will be held in three months' time. Per royal law, the votes will be counted by round, with the lowest vote-receiving candidate being eliminated if no candidate receives a majority on the first ballot. I look forward to seeing all of you here once again for that joyous occasion, where we shall choose our next monarch. For now, though, the Royal Council and Hughes family would like to wish you safe travels back to your residences."

I wished I had popcorn for what was to come. Vera was fuming. Natasha's supporters were trying to congratulate her, but all her mom could do was glare at Julia, who was surrounded by enthusiastic supporters of her own. Our surprise had worked, and there would be consequences.

As the royals passed me on their way out, the occasional one nodded at me in respect, while others, mostly from Bilgram's group, spat at me. Once most of the royals had cleared out, Vera swooped in and grabbed Julia's arm, yanking towards the small parlor. I followed along with Alex in hot pursuit, both for Julia's protection and pure curiosity.

When we entered the parlor, Vera threw Julia onto one of the couches and began her verbal assault as her face raged bright red. Julia's eyes peeled back in shock at her mom's violent reaction and shielded herself with her arms on the couch. I tried to put myself between Vera and her daughter, but she shoved me aside.

Natasha entered behind us, her head drooping as Vera ranted at Julia, "How dare you go behind my back! That was absolutely insulting to me, your sister, and this family. We have agreed for years that Natasha would follow in your father's footsteps, but instead you selfishly decided you want the crown for yourself."

Julia glared back at her. "You know that isn't true! I never wanted this, but it is what I need to do. Our country is falling apart, mother, and all we've done is sit back behind our walls and do nothing about it. That needs to change." She looked away, towards the fire, and spoke softer, "Besides, it is what father wanted."

Wait, what? Everyone was as stunned as I was, but Vera looked like her daughter had just ripped her heart out. "How can I believe anything you say anymore? How *dare* you use your father's death for your personal gain."

Ironic.

Alex sprung at Vera. "How dare *you* use dad for your gain. All you have ever done is try to control us and him. You just want Natasha on the throne so you can have another servant with a crown."

Natasha let out a cry, "I am not her puppet! All you've ever talked about is how mother wants me on the throne, but have you ever wondered why I am doing any of this? Any of you?"

There was silence. She was right, we hadn't. She had never openly expressed many thoughts, so we had all made assumptions. Even her sisters had failed to see her as much more than their mom's favorite.

Lost with how to respond, we all just stared at Natasha, dumbfounded. She groaned. "Of course you haven't! Our country is falling apart, and if the Duke wins, he is only going to deepen the divides. Now is not the time to follow his route to return the monarchy to power, and I'm sorry Julia, but we cannot afford to start another conflict with the Front to end the Prism Test. Our only option is to adapt to the world we live in today, to cooperate with the Front, and to negotiate so that we can work together to fix things."

Julia shook her head apologetically and tears began to stream down her face. "Natasha, this is not a personal attack against you. Please, believe me. Before father died, when Isaac was punished for attacking Ivan, he told me that he feared he would die. He didn't know why, but he knew something would happen. He said that he wanted me to be the queen, but I told him that I didn't want it and that you had been groomed for the position, not me. He wanted me to promise I would run, but I couldn't do it..."

I felt out of place in this family duel. Obviously, I wanted to be by Julia's side, but all of this was as surprising to me as anybody else. For once in my life, I didn't know what to say. *Why didn't she tell me?*

Natasha shook as she listened to Julia. She was not as forceful as her sisters, but it was a big change to see her fight for herself. Her response got even sharper, "I understand why father would do that; I'm not the pretty and perfect one like you are. I just want to protect all of us. We're in danger constantly and fighting the People's Front is only going to lead to more deaths. Don't you see how you're risking all of our lives? A queen's job is to keep her people safe, not to flirt with Red boys and almost die sneaking into the work cities!"

Julia rose and walked slowly towards her sister, quieting her voice. "A queen's job is to keep *all* of her people safe, not just the royals or the favored ones, all of them. That includes the Reds in those camps, the Oranges struggling in the ghettos, and the Yellows whose standards of living are constantly slipping lower and lower. You haven't stepped into the real world and seen how much damage we allow to happen while we isolate ourselves from our own people. Cooperating with the Front will not fix our country, Natasha. We have to change things, or we're complicit."

Natasha swung her arm down sharply. "I'm sorry sister, but I cannot risk all of our lives to fight a battle that we have already lost. We must protect what we have left."

Vera stepped forward, the blaze of the fire creating an aura around her. "Natasha is correct, and that is why she *must* be queen. Julia, I expect you to rescind your name from the election immediately."

Julia looked to Alex and me for support, and we both shook our heads. She crossed her arms and looked directly at her mom. "I'm sorry, mother, but I have made my decision, and I have father's blessing. If you wish to punish me, you can take it up with him." She took a sharp breath. "Now, I must go. The orphanage is nearly complete, and I would like to assist in the process. Please, do not worry about my safety, mother. We have extra security there as always. Any of you are of course welcome to join me." She stormed out of the room with Alex and I in tow.

Chapter 16

The orphanage was in downtown St. Paul, just north of the Mississippi River and only a couple of blocks away from where Julia and I first met. I looked down the street towards that abandoned warehouse, remembering the thugs grabbing at her, my blade in the Yellow attacker's neck, and his knife in my abdomen. Everything had changed that night, for both of us. Coyote died months later, but that night, I left a part of me behind at that street corner, sacrificing it to save her. Everything that had happened since felt like a new life.

It was weird to think about what could have been different if I hadn't taken that route or had stayed a few minutes longer with Aaron. Would Julia have survived? Would Wilhelm be on the throne? Would I be leading the remnants of the Militia instead of Delaware? It was impossible to know.

The last five months had been the longest of my life. Julia had once said that she didn't know if fate or luck had put me on that corner. I wasn't religious, but it was hard for me to believe that all of this had been because of luck.

That feeling was reaffirmed as I looked up at the almost complete orphanage. If it hadn't been for my encounter with Lt. General Gilvan's crying daughter during my vengeance mission for Alex, it never would have been built. Julia had wanted a charity, and my grief was the spark for her. It would be the first orphanage that didn't force children to work, unpaid, as slaves. Instead, they could be cared for and given a real chance. It would be a rare safe space in St. Paul.

For my entire life, St. Paul had always been the poorer of the Twin Cities, but with the Fracture's takeover of the west-side, it was split further among control by the Militia, the Fracture, the UPF, and various minor gangs of Oranges and Reds, making the situation even worse.

As I stood there, I could hear the echoes of shots being fired from not far away. It was impossible to know who was shooting and who was the target. All I knew was that St. Paul was a powder keg waiting to blow at any moment. I only hoped we could dismantle the Fracture before they started an unwinnable and bloody war.

We were safe with the extra security around the building, but we still hastily shuffled Julia and Alex inside the double wooden doors, just in case. Once inside, we could relax, and I scanned the entryway with awe. It was built like an upscale house, not an orphanage for the lost and abandoned. A curved staircase hugged the walls on each side, meeting at a balcony that oversaw the foyer. The place was empty for now, but I could picture the little Black Tags running around, feeling at home for maybe the first time in their lives. This place could give them the chance that I never had. They'd still endure the Prism, but at least they wouldn't go through hell beforehand.

A stocky Green was walking Julia through the details while I meandered behind, ignoring the technical parts. It was amazing how much work had gone into the old house since I'd last seen it, and Julia smiled as she looked at the improvements. I was proud of her. In a few months she had taken a broken old home and turned it into something grand and important. It would do wonders for her political reputation as well. I knew she didn't think about it like that, but one of us had to.

The nomination ceremony had only been an hour ago and still hung in my mind. It had gone as well as could have been expected, but Vera had been harsh. This was not going to be easy, politically or emotionally, for Julia. She would need to take advantage of the little things that she could.

I watched her glide throughout the house and impatiently waited to speak with her about what had happened. In addition to all the drama among the women in the family, I was still shaken from her revealing her dad's wish for her to be queen. It must have been why she was so quiet about her discussion with her dad after Isaac's punishment. *But why couldn't she trust me with that?* She had talked with Alex privately before we came here, and I couldn't help but wonder why I was excluded again.

My thoughts were interrupted by static blasting over my radio. Delaware's voice crackled through. "Ivan, we need to talk, now. I'm out front of the orphanage."

What's so urgent? Delaware had never demanded I break away from bodyguard duty, so something had to be up. Julia looked back at me, having heard the message, and nodded her head, telling me it was okay to go. I nodded and grabbed the radio. "Heading out."

Delaware was waiting in front of one of the royal guardsmen, who was holding her back. I gestured for him to let her pass, and she pushed past him. Her round cheeks lacked their usual pep as she approached, and mumbled, "I need to show you something."

I narrowed my eyes, confused by the secrecy, but nodded and followed her down the street, taking a look back at the orphanage along the way. We walked bristly down the broken sidewalk in silence, heading over the highway and into the neighborhood on the other side. I eventually broke the silence. "What's with the urgency, Del? We've been doing what we can about the supplies, but with the nomination ceremony, Jonah and I have had our time really split."

She took a sharp breath and kicked at a stray stone. "I'm sorry you've had a *busy* week. Must be hard trying to get your princess to be queen."

I was stunned. "Del, we're working the same thing here. Without her leading the monarchy, we don't have the power to change things. We've lost so many..."

She stopped and glared up at me, her eyes like daggers. "What happened to my best friend? What happened to the guy who would do anything for the Militia, to save the Reds? You get sick of us up there with the royals?"

I raised my hands defensively. "What are you talking about? I'm trying to help!"

Her brow furrowed. "Everything the last few months has been about Julia with you. Even with Operation Blackout, everything was put on me to deal with the details. And ever since that night, ever since you got out, you've been so distant. It's been almost a month, Ivan, and you haven't visited the survivors even once. You haven't visited *me* once. What happened to my best friend? You told me you'd never lie to me again, so answer this: what matters to you more, her or us? Would you sacrifice all of us to make her queen?"

How can I choose between the girl I love and the people I swore to fight for?

I clenched my fist. "I gave up Coyote to keep her alive, but I would never sacrifice you for her to be queen. This isn't about power for her, for either of us. My goal is the same thing it has always been, Del, but it isn't as simple as we thought it was. We don't have the power to change things from outside the system without starting another war that we're doomed to lose. The Militia can't go on without the monarchy's help. Without Julia as queen, the Fracture recruits the Reds, not us, and they run around chopping peoples' heads off."

She crossed her arms and looked at her feet. "Then why have you ignored us? We're starving. I'm trying to hold people together and gather more recruits, but every day people look at the Fracture and start to think that they're the better option. I know you let Coyote go, but we need you, Ivan. The whole point of you working with the royals was to make us stronger."

I sighed and looked into the sky. She had a point. I'd been so focused on helping Julia and attacking the Fracture that I'd lost sight of the people in the Militia and our fight against the UPF. There were just so many hoops to jump through just to consider challenging the Prism. I bit my cheek and looked down at her. "I'm sorry. There's been so much going on. I almost died, we lost so many people, and with Julia losing her dad and sister, I just got caught up in the craziness. I'm living my life in two different worlds, and without Coyote, I feel like I'm getting split in half."

Her eyes softened. "I get it. Just know that I almost died too. Remember?" She hesitated. "I want Julia to be queen, they all will once the news gets out that she's a nominee. I know that you're trying to help, but don't forget about us. Okay? I need my best friend back. You're a hero to a lot of these guys, and it would really help if you made an appearance."

I smiled. "Okay, we have a deal. I'll try to get out to your safehouse more often and will see about those supplies. Julia refused to run them through the orphanage, which makes sense, but we need an alternative, and I think I have one. We still have those shitty old vans from the Enclave, right?"

She shrugged. "Yeah. Why?"

I pointed towards the abandoned warehouse back near the orphanage. "If we get the supplies to a warehouse, do you think you guys can handle the transport from there? That way, we aren't bringing them directly to you and exposing your location. Plus, with the UPF's cameras out, we should be in the clear."

She thought for a second and scrunched her nose. "It's not perfect, but it'll have to do. When did you start coming up with the good ideas?"

"Long before you met me. Now, what is it you wanted to show me besides this nice twenty-year-old pothole." I pointed to the cracked street.

"It's hard to explain. Just trust me on this one." She started walking briskly once again.

I saluted. "Aye aye Captain Delaware."

She laughed. "Why do you get your real name back but not me?"

I shrugged. "What? The codename I give you isn't cool enough for you?"

"It's weird calling you Ivan. I don't know, the whole codenames thing doesn't work when you're kind of apart from the Militia."

I raised my arms in surrender. "Okay then, *Naomi.*" *That felt weird to say.*

She squirmed. "It feels like it's been forever since someone has said my name."

"That's part of the sacrifice of joining the Militia. Nothing in this world comes without losing a part of yourself. We've both learned that the hard way."

She looked towards the setting sun and squinted. "We need to hurry before the gangs come out. The Fracture has turned this place to hell. We're trying to keep people safe and fed in Payne-Phalen, but with the failures of the collective farms and the damn UPF's restrictions on trade, people are desperate. Even the Yellows are willing to kill you for some rations."

We ran up a few more blocks before turning down a side street full of abandoned houses. Delaware was unusually quiet as we stopped in front of one. Its siding had all but fallen off, and the windows were covered in old wooden boards. She just stood, staring at it for a minute, her eyes lost in another world. Eventually, she took a step forward. "Ashland Avenue, I missed you."

I stood there, silent, as she approached what must have been her old home before her dad died. My heart twitched at the thought. *I took this from her.* We walked up the rickety front steps and onto the rotting porch. She reached for the door handle before there was a loud *crack*, and her leg broke through the wood.

I jumped forward, grabbing her quickly and pulling her out before there could be any serious damage to her leg. "You alright?"

She was in a daze for a moment before she struggled to her feet and brushed herself off. Mindlessly, she muttered, "Yeah," and walked through the door.

The floor crunched beneath our feet as we walked along the broken window glass. The house looked ransacked. It was hard to know if it was because of the UPF after her dad's death or from the gangs looting everything they could. Delaware shuffled towards a wooden dresser along the wall and shakily grabbed a picture from the floor in front of it. Her whole body shook as she stared at the picture, but I was too far away to see what it was.

I looked up the collapsed staircase as she remained there, motionless beyond her shakes. *How many homes were destroyed like this one? How many families ruined?* There was almost nothing left in the kitchen either. A few broken pots and pans were scattered across the counter, but anything of value was long gone.

Eventually, Delaware spoke weakly, "I never thought I'd see their faces again."

I walked over to her and looked down at the photograph. It was her dad holding a younger, even cheekier, Delaware on his shoulders as what must have been her mom laughed. A tear streaked down her face and onto the glass covering the photo. She sniffled and wiped it off with her dirty coat sleeve.

I bit my cheek before hesitantly speaking, "You looked like a happy family."

She shut her eyes tightly before popping them back open again. "We were, but when mom died, dad was working at the factory so much to get rations…" She sighed. "He shouldn't have been there when that bomb went off."

I hung my head. "I'm so sorry, Del…. He deserved better. You deserved better."

She looked up at me before back at the photo. "Did I ever tell you how mom died?" I shook my head. "She went down to the store to try and get some extra bread. It was a long walk, but we were having people over, and she wanted to be a good host." She took a deep breath. "Mom never came back. We never found out why, but the UPF grabbed her somewhere between here and the store. When we submitted the paperwork to contact her, they claimed she never existed. Dad was destroyed, and he worked to keep his mind off it. I never forgave them."

I put my hand on her shoulder. "That's terrible."

She took a deep breath and smashed the glass on the dresser before pulling out the picture, folding it up, and placing it in her pocket. I looked down at the fractured glass scattered across the dresser and floor before I noticed her looking up at me. "You never know what you've got until it's gone. The UPF took my mom, and the extra work took my dad. They did this, all of it, and they'll pay." She sighed. "Let's get out of here. I don't want to see this shithole ever again."

Chapter 17

It was late when I got back to the palace. A soft snowfall had begun, and I swiped at the flakes on my coat as I entered Julia's room. Her and Alex's matching eyes watched me hang up my peacoat, but they said nothing. *Something's up.*

I smiled at Julia softly. "Am I interrupting something?"

She pursed her thin lips and looked to her sister before responding, "No, you're fine. How is Delaware?"

I sighed and sat on the couch opposite of Alex. Julia paced as I spoke, "Weird. She was upset I hadn't visited the Militia since the pardon, which is fair. We worked out a smuggling system I think, but I'll have to run it by Jonah."

Julia thought for a moment, her eyes wandering. "You were gone for a long time."

Is she mad about something? "Yeah. She wanted to show me her old house, the one that they lived in before... you know."

Julia nodded solemnly. "Right." Alex looked lost but didn't say anything.

I took a deep breath. "I don't think she wanted to go in alone. We didn't talk much, but she showed me an old family photo and talked about how her mom died in UPF custody."

Alex looked down. "Damn."

"Yeah. It was awful, and to know that I'm partially responsible for her losing her dad... So many people have died."

Julia whispered, "Too many."

An eerie silence filled the room. The only sound was Julia's soft steps as she paced in thought. I'd learned that she would talk when she was ready, but if something was affecting her that much, it was serious. Alex scanned her phone aimlessly, obviously waiting for her sister to speak. My chest was tight as I waited. It felt like the whole room had dropped a couple degrees, and I still had no idea what was wrong.

Julia eventually turned to speak, but she didn't have the chance. My radio buzzed, cutting her off before she could start as Jonah's voice pushed through the static. "Ivan, I need you in security, stat. Grab your gear."

I stood as Julia looked at me like a wounded animal. If Jonah was calling me like this, it was urgent. I looked at her hopelessly. "I'm sorry. I'll be back soon, hopefully."

She shook her head. "It's fine, go."

My heart sunk, and I closed my eyes for a moment before hurrying out the door. The last thing I wanted was to leave before she could speak, but I had a job to do. I ran down to my tiny room on the other side of the palace, grabbed my new black protective gear, knives, and royal guard issued pistol, and met Jonah in the security room.

The monitors in the room buzzed with the constant flow of electricity. Guards were seated in front of each of them, watching entrances into the palace and the royal territory in general. As a natural rebel, the place gave me the creeps. It was hard to remember that these guys were on my side, mostly.

Jonah was on the opposite side of the room, looking over the shoulder of one of his sergeants. The sergeant was analyzing something on his four different monitors and typing furiously. He didn't look up when I leaned on the back of his chair. "What's up?"

Jonah turned towards me slowly. His eyes were wide in fear. He nodded towards one of the screens and whispered, "Watch."

I looked at the screen as the sergeant clicked play on a video. What I saw made me want to vomit. The Mountain, flanked by Cockroach and Max, was holding a knife to Delaware's neck. *They must have grabbed her when we separated on the west-side. Shit!*

Cockroach spoke first, "Hello, Ivan. Rumor has it, your little princess has decided she wants to be a queen, and we think it's time for us to make a deal." He looked down at Delaware. "We don't want hurt her, so you have a choice."

Max continued where he left off. "It's time for you to prove your loyalty to your people. In order to root out the great corruption in our system, we must destroy the puppet masters, the first of which is the supreme manipulator, Vera Hughes. Bring her to us, and Delaware can go free. Fail to do so, and we will know where your true loyalties lie."

A smile had crept over Max's face. "You know the web she has spun. You know the levels of her deceit. In your heart, you despise her as much as we do, so why sacrifice the girl you saved for the crooked queen? You have until midnight. You know where to find us. If you bring any royal guards, we'll know, and your friend will die."

With that, the screen descended into a blast of static. I clenched my fist. *I'm going to kill them.*

Jonah looked up at me. "I'm sorry Iva…"

I didn't hear him finish, because I was already out the door and on my way to the garage. I knew where they'd be. There was no choice. As much as I didn't like Vera, I couldn't throw her to the slaughter.

Jonah called after me from the hall as I flew into the garage and grabbed the cheaper sedan. I didn't have time to ask for permission. The engine roared to life as I turned the key in the ignition. My mind was racing, but I couldn't think.

As I drove through the Minneapolis night, speeding towards St. Paul, my phone rang. Julia was calling, obviously concerned for my safety, but I had neither the will nor the mental capacity to talk with her. She would try to talk me out of it. There was no turning back. I'd all but abandoned Delaware the past month, and now she was in the Fracture's hands because of me. It was my problem to fix.

The wind howled as I parked the car and approached the warehouse where I'd chased down Cockroach. There was no doubt in my mind that I was walking into a trap, but any back-up would mean her death. This was the risk that I had to take.

I shuffled through the snow, pistol in hand. Breathing out in a puff of fog, I flung open the door, entering the dark warehouse. The cold chilled me to the bone as I slid along a line of shelves. *Where are you?* There were no noises beyond the soft shuffling of my shoes along the cement floor.

Suddenly, a few of the overhead lights flickered on, illuminating Delaware, tied to a chair, and the Mountain standing behind her. I raised my gun but had to hesitate from hastily pulling the trigger as a gun cocked behind me.

Cockroach emerged from the shadows, his weapon pointed at the back of my head. "Tsk, tsk. You disappoint me again, Ivan. What fun is it if you can't play the game right?"

I shuddered with rage. "This isn't a damn game, Roach. You had to know there was no way I could bring Vera, even if I wanted to."

He sighed, disappointed. "Drop the gun. Max may not want you dead, but I recommend not giving me a reason to squeeze this trigger."

I bent down and placed my gun on the ground before kicking it back towards him. As he reached down to pick it up, his gun wavered from my head. I spun swiftly, pulling a knife from my sleeve and cutting his arm. His gun dropped from his hand as shock crossed his face. Before he could react, I was behind him with a knife of my own to his throat. He just laughed as the rest of the lights sparked to life. The Fracture thugs who inevitably were hiding nearby encircled us. *Déjà vu.* I had no idea what I was doing, but acted resilient and shouted, "Drop the guns or he dies!"

Max stepped out of the shadows and stood next to Delaware. "'I only regret that I have but one life to lose for my country.' That was a quote from a soldier in the Continental Army. He understood the crucial importance of a person's love of their country, of its people. Kill him, and he will have died as a soldier in the fight to save Northern Mississippi."

I scowled at her. "Save? You're creating chaos. Things were bad before, but you've turned St. Paul into a war zone."

She paced around Delaware, examining a small knife. She stopped and held the knife between her two pointer fingers, the sharp tip digging into the first few layers of her skin. "Crimson must rain for the sun to shine. Crimson must reign for the light to rise."

I scoffed. "You're a lunatic."

She narrowed her eyes and spun the knife around her finger. "I am a visionary. I see the world not as it is but as it could be. I see that the route to such a world is not an easy one, but it is the one we must walk." She sighed. "You came without the Queen."

My lip twitched. "She was busy."

Max shook her head. "A shame. You could have been a part of the bloodletting instead of resisting it. You cannot stop the change, Ivan. This world shall..."

A shot rang through the warehouse, interrupting her mid-sentence. The thugs looked around in shock as the Mountain dropped his knife. Blood squirted from his shoulder as a series of shots followed, and a shootout began between the unknown attackers and the thugs. The sound of bullets smacking cement and metal surrounded me.

Cockroach took the distraction as a chance to escape. He tried to elbow me in the gut, but I spun, knocking him off balance, and tightened the knife around his throat, drawing a small trickle of blood.

Max watched the skirmish unfold, her eyes wide in fear. *Not so tough now.* The Mountain scrambled towards her, trying to shield his leader from the bullets. Together, they stumbled towards the central door that must have led to another section of the warehouse and abandoned both Cockroach and her thugs. *What a leader.* Cockroach groaned, trying to call for Max but was held back by the knife at his throat.

With their leaders gone or captured, the thugs quickly fell around me. They never had a chance with the inability to see their attackers. I held Roach tightly and looked around the warehouse, trying to figure out who the hidden saviors were.

When the last thug fell, Delaware struggled against her gag and rocked the chair back and forth. I shuffled towards her, pulling Cockroach with me. "You alright?"

She nodded as a figure appeared behind her, and my heart stopped. Then the figure stepped into the light, and I took a breath. Snapback reached around her neck, catching her by surprise, and pulled the gag from her mouth. She turned to see her boyfriend and yelled, "Not funny Snap!"

He laughed and untied her from the chair. "I don't know, I got a kick out of it. How about you, Ivan?" He smirked at me.

I smiled. "Leave me out of your relationship drama." Snap laughed and raised an eyebrow at Roach. I looked at my captive. "Thanks for the help, but I had the situation under control."

Snapback flipped his iconic hat backwards before giving his girlfriend a hug. "Sure looked like you did. Surrounded by armed thugs is always a good position to be in."

Delaware clenched her fist as seven other Militia members emerged from behind the shelves. "Enough joking around. I'm glad you guys saved me, but this is serious. I almost died, and the Fracture is only getting stronger."

I nodded. "You okay?"

She huffed and rubbed her exposed arms for warmth. "I'm fine. Where'd they put my damn jacket?"

Snapback took the cue and flipped off his ragged leather jacket, placing it over her shoulders instead. I smirked. "Adorable."

Delaware scrunched her nose at me as Snap escorted her outside to the rusted van they came in. The other Militia members helped me load Cockroach in the back as he yelled and struggled against us.

Besides Snap and Del, I'd never seen any of these Militia members before. They introduced themselves to me one by one, and I smiled with pride at some of the codenames Delaware had come up with. Unlike the Fracture, she had managed to keep recruiting both Reds and non-Reds into the Militia, and the group had an Orange and even a Yellow. *Julia may be able to unite the people in the light, but Del can unite those in the shadows.*

As they shook my hand, their eyes were full of adoration; it made me uncomfortable. The only people I'd ever really wanted the attention of as Coyote was the UPF, but being possibly the best-known rebel meant I had somewhat accidentally gained a following.

The rest of the team climbed into the van as Snapback and Delaware stood outside with me for a moment. I shivered and looked up into the sky. "Sorry this happened so quick, Del. I didn't realize..."

She raised a hand. "It's not your fault. I knew what I was getting myself into when I became captain." Her eyes flicked to her boyfriend. "We're both lucky Snap knew where to find us, though."

Snapback laughed. "Actually, I didn't. Jonah radioed me from the palace and told me what happened." *That must have been why Julia was calling...* "He thought this was the location, so I rounded up a group quick as I could. Couldn't let my girl lose her pretty...

160

head?”

I chuckled. “Smooth as always. Seriously, though, thanks Snap. I didn't know what I was going to do, to be honest.”

He beamed. “Glad to see nothing has changed with you.” He pointed his thumb back at the van. “You comin’?”

I held up my hands. “I promised Del —I mean *Naomi*— I'd visit soon, but it's been a long day, and I ran out of what I think was about to be an important conversation with Julia to get here.”

He nodded his head. “Keep the princess happy, we're counting on her. I'm going to get my little captain to sleep.” He rubbed the top of Delaware's head, agitating her. “We'll let you know if we manage to get anything out of Cockroach.”

I gave a salute. “Later, and good to see you again. I missed that stupid hat.”

He just winked, climbed into the cab, and started the van.

When I returned to the palace, Jonah was waiting for me in the Great Hall, his face smug but tired. “You're welcome.”

I raised my arms in surrender. “Thanks for bailing me out.”

He rolled his eyes. “If you had waited a few more seconds, I would have told you my plan.”

“Why have a plan when you have the element of surprise?”

He crossed his arms. “Next time, talk to me first before you run off and almost get you and one of our allies killed.”

I nodded and faked a military salute. “Yes, Chief Jonah, sir!”

He rolled his eyes. “I'll never know how you've lasted so long in this place.”

“The secret is flirting with your boss, and speaking of my boss,

I believe she needs to talk to me."

He raised an eyebrow. "*To* or *with*?"

I made a not-so-confident face. "I have a bad feeling it's *to*."

With a wave of his arm he gestured me on. "I believe she and Princess Alexandria are in the parlor."

I nodded and walked quickly through the Great Hall to the north-wing of the palace. My palms began to sweat as I opened the door to the parlor. *Why does this feel just as dangerous as trying to save Delaware?*

Julia and Alex were seated next to each other on one of the velvet couches. The fire was dying slowly, and the slight smell of ash filled the room as I sat across from them. "Sorry about that. Just had to prevent my best friend from being killed. Normal Saturday stuff."

Alex bit her cheek, trying not to laugh as Julia crossed her legs, her face serious as she spoke, "Are you alright?"

I leaned forward. "Yeah, thanks to Jonah calling Snapback and the Militia for back-up. They would have seen royal guardsmen coming, but he caught them off guard. Del's safe, and we caught Cockroach, but Max got away."

Her eyes widened. "Wait, you caught him? Maybe mother won't hate you."

I nodded with a half-smile. "Yup. The Militia is going to question him, but I wouldn't count on being on Vera's good side."

She took a deep breath. "I'm glad you're okay. When Jonah told me what happened, I was so worried."

I smiled softly at her. "I'm sorry. I probably should have figured out a plan with him first, but I needed to save her."

She thought for a moment. "I understand, Ivan, and I'm just happy you are both okay and alive." She shifted uncomfortably before continuing, "But, I have something I need to tell you."

I interjected, "I know. I'm sorry for running off at the orphanage, not answering the call, and staying involved with the Militia. I told you I would be done with it."

She shook her head. "No, it's not that. You've already sacrificed so much for me." She paused, as if searching for the right words. *What is wrong with her?* "You have been honest with me, completely. I'm so sorry that I haven't done the same for you." I tried to calm her, but a look from Alex stopped me. Julia continued, her voice rough. "Father didn't just tell me he wanted me to be queen during our conversation." She stopped, her body shaking as Alex rubbed her back.

I scooted to the edge of the couch. "Whatever it is, Julia, you can tell me. I'm not mad about that, and whatever this is, we can work through it."

She pursed her lips and looked down. A tear smacked into the carpet before her eyes met mine. "I know who your parents were."

I just sat, looking at her, too stunned to respond. *My parents?* I hadn't thought about my parents in a long time. It always seemed like an unimportant fact that they'd died when I was little, like so many other Reds, and that led to me being sent to the River Falls orphanage. Was that not true? If it wasn't, did I really want to know? Part of me said no, but now that Julia had said those words, there was no going back. I had to know.

Julia's eyes were full of desperation. "Ivan?"

I was lost in a daze for a moment and had to force myself back to the real world. I tried to respond but could only mutter, "Who?"

She took a deep breath. "Henryk and Janica Matelski."

I narrowed my eyes. "I don't know who they are."

Julia hesitated before responding, "They were elite Purples within the People's Front. Your father was the Secretary of the Prism, and your mother was one of his analysts."

Chapter 18

I wanted to crawl into a hole in the ground. *My dad ran the Prism Test?* I slumped back in the couch and stared up at the ceiling. Rage boiled inside me, and I didn't know whether I was mad at Julia for not telling me or at my parents for being my parents. I was fine being who I was and never really cared about who my parents were. My life had always been mine, not defined by a family. Now, this could upend everything I knew. *When will this day frickin' end?*

Julia spoke softly, "Talk to me, Ivan."

I closed my eyes. "Why'd you wait?"

She took a breath. "Because my father is the reason your parents were executed."

My chest tightened. It was hard to breathe as I lifted my eyes back to her. "He did what?"

She swallowed. "Father said that Henryk had been working to take the General Secretary position for himself. Apparently, Henryk believed the General Secretary at the time was too much of an idealist, and he reached out to my father for help in the coup. The two of them were old friends, despite their political differences, but that was not enough to convince Father to violate the Treaty of Minneapolis." Her voice faltered as she shook. "Father knew that our family's lives would be in danger if he went along with Henryk's coup, so he exposed the plan to the Front."

I shook my head. "This is insane. My father wanted to lead the UPF?"

Julia's face drooped. "He did, and when my father exposed him, your parents were arrested. Henryk was killed after two weeks in custody, Janica... she died months later." *Months of torture, I'm sure.*

I took a deep breath. My mind was spinning. "How did they cover this up? I mean, even if there are different factions within the Front, my dad was in charge of the Prism. They couldn't just kill him without people noticing."

"Both my parents and the Front agreed to keep the whole affair quiet. They claimed Henryk had resigned for medical reasons and died from complications in the hospital."

"Of course they did." I groaned and rubbed my temple. "Where do I fit into this?"

Alex jumped in, impatient. "You were a baby when they were captured. Dad ensured they didn't kill you, and instead, you were sent to that orphanage." Julia gave her sister a harsh glare. "What? You were extending an already awkward conversation."

"Why would he allow me to live but be fine the UPF killing my parents?"

Julia sighed. "Father was not cruel. He saw no reason for you to suffer because of them."

I scoffed. "Bull. He sent me to a work orphanage, telling himself that I'd be fine and that he'd never have to see the skeletons in his closet again. He knew what they did there, didn't he? Didn't he?!"

"I will not make excuses for my father's actions. I'm so sorry,

Ivan." Her words felt like frost as another tear streaked down her cheek.

Raged burned inside of me as I scowled. *I hate royals. What am I doing here?* "Anything else you've been hiding from me?"

She looked at me, wounded. I took a deep breath and tried, reluctantly, to redirect my anger. I peeled apart my clenched fists and attempted soften my tone. "I'm sorry. This isn't your fault, but this is insane. You're telling me not only were my parents elites within the government, but they were also betrayed by your dad and probably your mom. I don't want this. I'm happy with who I am."

She sighed. "Ivan…"

I rose without thinking. "I need to go. I need to think."

Julia followed me as I stormed towards the door. "I can come."

I shot my arm up, "No," and flew into the hall.

Julia tried calling after me, but I was already running towards the Great Hall. I threw open the back doors of the palace and entered the stormy night.

The world was nothing but a haze of white swirling around me, threatening to pull me off my feet. Part of me wanted it to. Maybe it would drag me to somewhere where I wouldn't have to deal with all this crap: the UPF, the corrupt royals, the bloodthirsty Fracture, my starving friends in the Militia, and now my family's past. I didn't want it; I didn't want any of it. Everything I'd worked my whole life for seemed to take me in circles while the puppet masters laughed at me flailing uselessly. My parents may have been pursuing political power, but even they were killed in the unending tide of violence. *Why would I be different?*

My ears numbed as I ran through the garden, losing myself in the maze. I ran past the spot where Isaac had smashed my head with a rock. The path had obviously been scrubbed, but a slight crimson tint remained on the pavement, and my mind flashed back to the horrific scene in front of the prison. *One thing never changes: no matter who rules, crimson reigns.*

I stopped in front of the statue of King Timothy III, the man who threw my parents to the slaughter. His statue glared at me from atop its horse. For the first time, I didn't feel guilty about failing to save him. I didn't know if what my parents had done was right, but Timothy sacrificed them both and lied to my face. He insulted me for being a Red when he was the one who made me an orphan in the first place.

I knew what it was like to hold in the truth. What happened with Delaware's dad was an accident, though. This was a conscious decision. I didn't know if I could have forgiven him if he'd been honest enough to tell me, but I knew that he'd left Julia to pass on the information after his death, and that was unforgivable. *Coward.*

I bent down and grabbed a stone from the side of the pathway. Rolling it in my hands, I felt its smooth sides against my freezing fingers. With a look up at the statue, I hurled the stone, striking the King dead on the nose and visibly chipping the marble. It was the punch in the face I couldn't give him in life. Besides, the nose was wrong anyway.

The snow collected around my feet as I stared and thought. I was born to Purples by birth, but nothing changed. I was still a Red inside and by law. I'd gained a whole new set of burdens and a family history that held nothing but conflict and questions.

I picked up a second, more jagged, stone but stopped as the snow crunched behind me. Breathing out a puff of fog, I spoke, "How am I supposed to move forward? The Prism made me a Red. Your father made me a Red. Everything made me a Red, except my parents."

There was only silence in response. I let out another breath before turning around to meet Julia's eyes of ice. The wind smacked at her hood as she fought against its force. She looked more exhausted now than when her father or her sister died. She had said it felt like someone tore out her heart and put it back in backwards. Now, it looked like her heart had not been put back. She looked at me with a deep sadness as she kept her distance. *Is she afraid of me even now?*

We stood, just staring against each other through the wicked snowfall, the world nothing but the few feet separating us. I felt betrayed, even by her. From the beginning, I did everything I could to reveal my skeletons, to show her the dark side of my life. She couldn't do the same for me, even when it wasn't her own failures that needed exposing. Because she didn't tell me, I almost died trying to save the man who pushed my parents to their deaths. We had promised to be open and honest. Instead, she preferred to protect her white-washed family ahead of our relationship and the trust I had in her. I sacrificed everything I knew for her, and she couldn't even tell me a simple truth.

With each passing second, she looked ready to speak, only to recoil at the last second, unsure what to say. I looked at the snow-covered ground, now splattered with drops of blood. My hand was bleeding from how tight I gripped the stone, and as I watched the drops hit the snow, I thought about what Julia said after my pardon. *If we're all born White, then why does our blood stain the world crimson?*

When I looked back up at her, her eyes watched in horror as the blood trickled from my hand. I sighed and dropped the stone. "You have nothing to say?"

Her cheeks were covered in tears. "I have too much to say."

"What are we without honesty?"

She took a step towards me, pleading. "Ivan..."

I scowled. "Nothing! I thought that you really were different, but no, you're just like all the other damned Whites. You'll lie and hide the truth to exploit people for your gain. Telling me sooner would have threatened your precious family reputation. Instead, you've ruined our trust."

She stepped forward further, shouting over the storm, "You're right, Ivan! You're right. I lied, and I deserve for you to be mad at me, but please let me explain."

I clenched my fists. "Explain what?"

She was only a few feet away from me now, and I felt my heart be pulled in so many different directions. Anger, sadness, love, and confusion all threatened to tear apart my sanity. Julia shook from both the cold and fear. "The Front doesn't know who you are. Father covered up your identity to protect you, and I... I was worried that telling you would change how you saw me, saw us."

"Then why now?"

She sighed. "I'm a nominee for queen now, and you deserve to know the truth about both of our parents if we are going to go on together. I know that I should have told you before. I'm sorry."

I shivered as the cold wind pierced through my thin jacket. "You don't get it. You didn't tell me about not just this, but also your dad wanting you to be queen. Both of those things affect me, and you pulling them out as a surprise now just makes everything more difficult. You broke my trust. I told you every painful thing I've ever done, but you couldn't do the same for me. 'Sorry' doesn't fix that."

She stepped closer. "What can I do that will?"

I looked to the sky, flexing my hands in frustration. "Prove that I can trust you, or I'm not sure what we're doing together."

The tears continued down her cheeks as she tried to grab my hands. *She has nothing to say to that?*

I stepped away from her and looked across the garden. "Maybe Vera was right. Maybe we shouldn't do this."

She pled, "Ivan, please," but I trudged past her through the snow, heading back towards the palace. She called after me, "Ivan!"

I didn't look back.

Chapter 19

Angry or not, my job was still to be Julia's bodyguard, and the next morning, I waited outside her door. Rage was the only thing that stopped my heart going completely numb as I stared at the wall, mentally and physically exhausted. Between the nomination ceremony, Delaware's capture, and Julia's reveal about my parents, my mind had been far too busy for sleep last night. I lay in my tiny room and stared at the ceiling for hours, trying to decide what to do. In that time, I had decided on absolutely nothing. My world felt shaken, and I didn't know whether to take charge of my future or escape it entirely.

When Julia finally emerged with Rachel and Anne in tow, she offered a timid smile. I was too exhausted to bother reciprocating. It was hard to know where we stood after last night. While it was probably up to me to figure that out, I had no clue. I loved her, but could I trust her?

I trudged behind them as we headed towards the SUV waiting out front. Alex met up with us on the way. Overall, the girls were silent, beyond Julia's normal formalities with the servants. *Do the handmaidens know what happened, or can they just feel the tension?*

After closing the door to the back for them, I climbed into the passenger seat and nodded to the chauffeur. He looked at my bandaged right hand. *You should see my arm.* I shot him a glare in response. "I cut myself on a piece of glass. Go."

He muttered something under his breath and drove out of the loop in front of the palace, heading towards St. Paul. Today was the opening of Julia's orphanage. It should have been an exciting moment for the both of us, but with the current state of our relationship, I wasn't feeling anything but anger at the world.

As we drove, we passed by line after line of Yellows and Oranges in Minneapolis hoping for food at the rationing stations. Rations had not been officially cut for as long as I could remember, but the UPF's claims didn't disguise the ever-shrinking amount of food the lowest colors received on each trip. People had begun waiting outside, hoping to receive any possible stale leftovers that had not been collected.

A few years ago, it was only the Reds and some Oranges who were struggling. After a few bad winters, mismanagement on the government run farms, and the restrictions on trade, though, the Yellows had fallen into the pit of starvation too. *How can we fix this?* We were on the good side of town. If it was getting this bad over here, it made sense why St. Paul was in such bad shape.

When we arrived at the orphanage, I opened the girls' door and followed them as they entered. Many of the "honored guests" had already arrived, and the Blues and Greens greeted Julia with enthusiasm, having heard about her nomination. Those that didn't support her didn't bother attending. At this point, even showing their face at her charity event could be seen as a political error, especially for a Purple, and among the elites, those errors could be fatal. *My parents found that out the hard way.*

Even when Julia was in a rough mood, she could still play the part. She moved through the crowd, shaking hands and smiling with the guests. She made her way towards the stairs up to the balcony, where a small horde of Black Tags was waiting for her, their little faces nervous as they looked at the crowd in front of them. When she reached the balcony, she hugged each of them and listened to their ramblings. As I watched her, I couldn't help but be reminded why I fell in love with her in the first place. *Why couldn't you just be honest with me?*

Eventually, she finished her hugs with the children, and it became time for her to give a short speech. She hesitated as she scanned the crowd, and her eyes stopped at me for a moment, saddening before she regained her poise. She took a deep breath and forced a smile to her face. "Thank you so much for joining me here today…"

A buzzing came through my earpiece. "Ivan, we have an issue out here."

I touched my finger to my ear. "What's up?"

The guard from outside continued, "There's a crowd of Yellows, Oranges, and Reds out here. They want to see the speech."

I looked up at Julia. She was speaking passionately, and with the crowd, there was no way to interrupt. I couldn't ask her, but I knew what she would do. "Check them for weapons, but let them in. I'll open the door."

"You sure?"

No. "Yes." I walked over to the front door and opened it as the first of the lower colors arrived, excited to see Julia speak. The Blues and Greens looked back in shock as a crowd of lower colors flooded into the room. Despite their surprise, the higher colors didn't leave, though the Blues shuffled into their own area. We were making progress, but for some of these people, the colors were still their life.

As they entered, many of the Oranges and Reds stopped to shake my hand or give me a hug. I always forgot that, without Coyote, everyone knew who I was now, and that was a weird feeling. *I don't like being a celebrity.*

Julia had paused her speech with the commotion. I looked up to her and was met by one of the biggest smiles I'd ever seen on her. I couldn't help but smile back. This was probably the first time that a crowd this diverse had existed since the creation of the Prism, and it was because of what we'd done, together. In that moment, it was hard to remember that I was mad at her.

When the crowd had entered and the doors had been shut, Julia smiled to them, took a breath, and spoke again, "You have no idea how amazing it is to stand before all of you today. To see people from every color, Blue through Red, along with royals in one room... That is truly special. This orphanage, it's not about me. It's about this."

She swept her arm across the crowd in front of her and back towards the kids. "It's about this community that we have been missing for so long in this city, in this country. When we put aside our differences, we can accomplish beautiful and amazing things together. It is my hope that this orphanage can be both a home for those without one and a symbol of unity in this community. The children here will receive the education that has been denied to so many children, and it is my hope that as queen, I can extend this opportunity to every child left behind by the People's Front.

I will ensure, then, that the opportunities they have when they are grown are determined by the brightness of their minds and hearts, the strength of their souls, and their determination to succeed, not the color of an earring. By educating even the poorest of children and allowing entrepreneurs and individuals to create businesses and choose where they work, we will take a giant leap towards fixing our broken country."

She paused for a moment as an applause interrupted her. "Please, take the time before you leave today to get to know someone you never would have the chance to talk with anywhere else." She looked at me and smiled. "It might change your life."

There was a pause as the crowd wondered if she was finished. We were both caught looking at each other, wondering what the other was thinking. *Stop making me proud.* After a few seconds, I flicked my eyes to the crowd and then back to her, reminding her to finish. Her eyes filled with realization quickly, and she looked back towards the crowd as her cheeks flushed. "Thank you, all of you, and I hope that, together, we can unite this city."

When her speech ended, the crowd erupted in applause. I smiled in pride for her, but my chest still felt like a weight had been dropped on it. I'd reminded myself why I loved her, but that made her betrayal hurt even more. There was so much we needed to talk about. I didn't know where I would even begin when the event was over.

As we drove back to the palace, Alex practically bounced in her seat. "I normally hate stupid events like this, but that was awesome. Well done breaking protocol, Red."

I shrugged. "We did check them for weapons at least."

Rachel smiled. "I was genuinely surprised at the calm of it. You would normally expect more conflict with Reds and Blues in the same room."

Julia ran her hands through her hair. She'd been quiet up until that point, and I could tell she was busy thinking. "That was one of the most stunning sights I have ever seen. I'm touched they came." A rattled sigh passed through her lips. She was still holding back.

I smiled back at her, fighting my feelings for now. "They came for you."

She bit her lip. "Maybe we can do this. If only they could vote."

Alex wrapped her arm around her sister. "Queen Julia Elizabeth Hughes, Duchess of St. Paul, Lover of Reds, and Uniter of the Colors."

Everyone had to laugh at that. Even with our tension, Julia's eyes met mine, and we shared a smile. *Why is it so hard to be mad at her?*

Chapter 20

As we pulled in front of the palace, I fiddled restlessly with the bandage wrapped around my hand, and, once we parked, opened the back door of the SUV for the girls. We entered the Great Hall and began towards Julia's room, but along the way, Vera interrupted us. She didn't even look at Julia. "Ivan. You and I have something we must discuss."

Julia bit her cheek before nodding sharply to me and proceeding towards her room. *Why does everything get in the way of us talking like a normal couple?*

There were a hundred different things Vera could have wanted. All I could think about in the moment, though, was how she had a part to play in the death of my parents. I bowed to her. "Of course, your highness."

I followed her to the parlor. She sat on one of the couches while I stood along the wall, as far away as physically possible. Her eyes judged me. "Jonah has informed me that your *friends* apprehended the man responsible for my daughter's death."

So that's what this is about. I crossed my arms. "Yes, we did. The Militia is holding him along with Otto Preus."

Her eyes challenged me. "Where would that be?"

"Why do you ask?"

178

"You cannot possibly understand how much I want him in our custody."

I paced towards the fireplace, rubbing my fingers together on my non-bandaged hand as I thought. It was a reasonable request, but he was an asset. We weren't just going to hand him over. Plus, I was not in the mood for listening to royal demands. "We have our own history with Cockroach."

She clicked her tongue. "You are playing a dangerous game, *young man.*"

"I've been playing a dangerous game my entire life, *your highness,*" I turned towards her again, "and I play to win." She scowled as I continued, "We're not just going to hand him over. Besides, we have information that we need to get out of him."

Vera straightened the skirt of her dress, stood, and walked towards me. "This is not a negotiation, Ivan."

With a laugh, I waited a moment before replying, "I have someone you want, and you don't know where they are. Good luck getting him without me. Veiled threats are not going to change anything."

"I ensured you were pardoned, but I can send you back. You have caused more problems than you are worth." Vera stepped forward, coming within a foot of me.

I raised an eyebrow. "Worried that your chosen one is going to lose the election?"

She waved her hand dismissively and circled around the other end of the room, "I am worried that you are jeopardizing my family's safety and everything we have worked for. Prove me wrong, or I'll hand you back over to the Front. My daughter will get over her silly fling with you when you are gone."

"Nothing has changed. You still need me to get Cockroach. Handing me over to the UPF would ruin you, but I guess it's just in your nature. You'll just try to get rid of me, just like how you and your husband threw my parents to the dogs."

Shock filled her eyes. "How do you..."

I stepped forward, unrelenting. "The King told Julia before he died. I know everything, *your cowardess*. I know how you betrayed my parents' trust and tried to keep it quiet. I know how you sent me to a work orphanage, probably hoping I'd die. You're no better than the UPF. You're part of the corruption that plagues this country. So, if you want Cockroach, you better have something good to offer, because I've got plenty on you."

Her usual cold front was shattered as she stumbled over a response. "I... What do you want?"

I stepped forward again. "I want the truth. Why'd you do it?"

She scoffed. "Henryk was a fool. He came to us, claiming he could fix the relationship between the monarchy and the Front if we helped him become General Secretary. He may have been Timothy's friend, but we could see the desire for power in his eyes. Your father was no better than the man he hoped to replace. We had no choice but to report him. Not doing so would have risked the safety of my family, my daughters. I couldn't do that."

I crossed my arms. "So, you sacrificed them when they wanted to overthrow the worst faction of the UPF? Maybe, he could have changed things, but instead, you'd rather sit here in a shell while people starve and suffer beyond your walls?"

180

She was stern. "Do not claim to know anything about your father's intentions, or mine. You would not understand unless you had children of your own."

There was nothing but silence for a moment as I thought. "You sacrificed me, too. I've spent my life as a slave because of you, and you both were too afraid to tell me when I showed up."

She looked into the fire. "I wanted to send you away when you saved Julia. Timothy is the one who decided to keep you here. He felt guilty for what happened to you. When we turned over your parents, we considered allowing the Front to take you as I feared that they would punish us for protecting you. Against my recommendation, Timothy ensured you were smuggled away from their eyes." She sighed. "Now, I regret our decision to let you live at all. Timothy and Helena might be alive if it wasn't for you."

I ignored her jab. "Next, you will not interfere with Julia and my relationship."

She responded sternly, "No."

I shrugged. "Then I can't wait to let everyone know how the great Vera Hughes threw her friends and their baby to their deaths to avoid political drama. I'm sure that would go over well."

"That does not mean you can make any demand you wish."

I laughed. "You were happy to marry her off to Isaac, yet your only reason for me being too dangerous was because I'm a Red. You're blaming me for your cruelty."

Vera looked to the ceiling as she paced. "I will not interfere if she decides that she is foolish enough to stay with you, but I will not accept it." She sighed. "Is that all?"

"No, you will use your connections to ensure the supplies that we are smuggling to the Militia actually make it to them. I know your web extends throughout the cities."

She narrowed her eyes. "I was made aware of this recently. While I do not necessarily approve of you both acting behind my back or smuggling supplies, if that is what is needed to finish this, then I will ensure that your operation is unhindered."

I nodded. "Fine, then. We will hand him over in a few days." I pushed my way past her and to the door. "Anything else, *your highness*?" She shook her head, so I rushed back through the doorway, back into the hallway, and up the stairs. *One confrontation down…*

The handmaidens rushed out of Julia's room as I entered. Anne diverted her eyes, and Rachel looked concerned. Julia was waiting on the couch, her hands playing with her family ring. As I watched her there for a moment, I took a breath as my heart raced. Facing Vera had deflected my anger towards the woman who really was to blame for what happened. That didn't mean I was happy about Julia not telling me, though.

She gave a closed-mouthed smile as I slowly walked towards her. I ran my hands along my pants, trying to calm my nerves as I sat across from her. She pursed her lips before she spoke, "How are you?"

I don't know.

Her concerned eyes scanned me, ending at the bandage on my hand. She said, "You have the right to be angry. I should have been honest with you from the start."

"I'm not mad at you." I followed her gaze to my injured hand. "I don't know what I am with you."

She bit her lip. "Are you doubting our relationship?"

"I did for a moment. It's hard to trust you right now. You hid probably the most important piece of information that exists between us. Still… I need you, and I love you." I paused and sighed. "I don't understand. Why didn't you tell me sooner? Did you think I'd kill your parents or something?"

She shook her head. "I don't… I don't know."

"You couldn't be honest with me then. Be honest with me now."

"Yes." Her head dropped.

I nodded to myself and took a deep breath. "So, after everything…"

She cut me off as tears began running down her face, "I was wrong, Ivan. I should have trusted you. I am so sorry. It's just… No, no more excuses. There's nothing else I can say. What can I do?"

Seeing her cry poked at my heart, and I moved to her couch. "You can start by never lying to me like that again." I held her hand. "You get that I wouldn't have killed them, right?"

She nodded quickly. "Yes. I was just scared. With Isaac, your concussion, father saying he wants me to be queen, and then this… I messed up."

I nodded. "I can't say I'm over it yet, because I'm not, but thank you. I appreciate the apology. Besides, I got to take out my rage on your dad's statue and your mom."

She ran her thumb along my fingers. "I noticed the statue's damaged nose. Maybe they will get it right this time." We both laughed through the tension. "What happened with mother?" I smirked, and she winced. "Oh no."

"She wanted the Militia to hand over Cockroach."

Curiosity replaced her look of surprise. "What did you say?"

I shrugged. "I told her no. She threatened me, saying you'd get over our 'fling' if she sent me back to the UPF. I told her that I knew what she did to my parents."

Her surprise returned. "Ivan!"

I shrugged. "It worked, though! She told me more about how your dad wanted to protect me and how she wanted me dead."

She took a sharp breath and examined her family ring. "The more I find out about my parents, the less I'm honored by this ring. What else did you get from her?"

Looking down at the floor, then back at her, I continued, "She also agreed to help protect supply runs to the Militia with her network."

"Do you think she will actually follow through?"

I shrugged. "I don't know. She's your mom. Is the potential of that getting out enough to scare her?"

"If I know anything about my mother, it's that she always has hidden plans. She might help for now, but she'll be looking for a way to get revenge." I nodded, and she continued. "Was that all?"

"She also reluctantly promised to continue tolerating our relationship, for now." I smiled.

She bit her lip. "So, we are okay? I mean, you can't be *that* mad at me if you asked her that."

I raised an eyebrow. "Try me. You don't realize how important honesty is to me, Julia. Like I said, I'm not over it, but I still love you."

She gripped my hand as if she were worried I'd let go. "I love you too.”

I shut my eyes and leaned my head back against the couch for a minute. “Everything has been insane. My parents were part of the fricking UPF, and my dad ran the Prism. How do I go on with that? On top of all this crap with the Fracture and the election, now I have to figure out who I am.”

She placed a hand on my cheek and I reluctantly let it rest. “You’re Ivan, the man who saved my life, twice. You’re a Red with the blood of a Purple. You’re the one who opened my and so many others’ eyes to the suffering of the Reds. Nothing about who your parents were changes who you are.”

“What do you know about my family, the Matelskis?”

“I don’t know much. The Front scrubbed their information from any historical records, and my parents obviously were not open in discussing them. All I know is what Father told me. I’m sorry, Ivan.”

I huffed. “So I still know nothing about my family, except that they were part of the group I’ve been fighting my whole life.”

She held my hands. “They were fighting for what they thought was right, just like you.”

Chapter 21

"Hit him again." A bruised and bloodied Cockroach sat tied to a chair in the old apartment building in Payne-Phalen that the Militia now occupied. Delaware ordered one of her newest recruits, a bulky Orange they called Paul Bunyon, to keep punching Roach in an attempt to get some information out of him. Each hit caused the cracking sound of bones smacking into bones to echo through the small room. Snapback stood in the corner and watched the mess.

The Militia's new HQ was where nobody would bother looking. The building was falling apart and looked completely abandoned from the outside. A few days after Julia and my step towards reconciliation, I was part of the first supply run to the Militia. It was a good excuse to get away from the political and personal tension that hung around the palace. Plus, I needed to follow-up on my promise to Delaware. Her new recruits wanted to meet me, and I wanted the chance to see what remained of the Militia within the Twin Cities.

We had brought the supplies through the back of the building and into a few apartments that had been set aside for storage. The place was in shambles, but it was someplace to hunker down; for so many, that was enough. Families of Reds and Oranges had greeted me ecstatically as I made my way up towards where Cockroach was being held. The looks on their faces told me the pain they'd experienced since the safehouse raids and the beginnings of the UPF's relocation of the Reds. I was glad the Militia could still provide a somewhat safe place for these people, but we had so much to do to keep them safe and give them a chance.

When I reached the interrogation room, I saw the torture that Delaware had Paul unleashing on Cockroach. It was horrifying. Cockroach sat slumped forward in the chair, conscious yet dazed.

I rushed forward and pulled Paul back before glaring at my mentee. "What the hell are you doing?"

She swung her arm towards me. "We're trying to get him to talk!"

I pointed to his destroyed face. "By beating him into submission? Del, this isn't what we do." I shot my glare towards Snapback. "And you just stood there and watched?"

He stopped leaning against the wall, took off his cap, and scratched his head before returning his lucky hat it to its usual place. "I tried, man. She insisted."

Delaware stepped forward. "He hasn't given us anything. We needed to give him a reason to talk, and I wanted to give him a taste of his own medicine."

She had a point, but I wasn't going to resort to torture for the sake of information. "This is the kind of thing that makes us no better than them. You can't just beat his face in."

Delaware crossed her arms and shook her head, not responding. Snapback sighed. "Well, he ain't talking. Not sure what you want to do with him before we give him to Vera."

I groaned. "You didn't get anything from him?"

Delaware paced. "Besides an overplayed story about how Max

appeared out of the ashes of the safe house raids to lead the Fracture forward, no."

I ran my hands through my hair in frustration. "Where the hell did she come from, and how did they get all these heavy weapons?"

"No idea."

I crossed my arms and looked at Cockroach. "Max showed up promising weapons, food, freedom, whatever to these desperate Reds. She started eliminating the people who claimed to be were better than them. Of course they worship her."

Delaware played with the buttons on her jacket nervously. "Then what do we do?"

I crouched in front of Cockroach, staring at his bloodied face. "We need to eliminate her. She's got everyone in a trance, and if we don't, they're going to start a civil war," I muttered.

Delaware cracked knuckles neck. "I call dibs. It's only fair I get to put a knife to *her* throat after what she did to me."

I shook my head. "Killing her makes her a martyr. We should try to expose her for what she is: a mass murdering psychopath who can't support the Reds. Break the trance and her power goes away."

Cockroach struggled to open his eyes and gave a weak laugh. "We've started a movement. You can't stop it. We will burn those who've looked down on us."

I cocked my head to the side and glared at him. "I have a feeling you won't be doing anything once Vera is done with you."

Snapback sighed. "How do we do that: break the trance?"

I stood. "Show a more peaceful alternative, build the Militia into a coalition large enough to make a difference, keep recruiting the Yellows and Oranges along with the Reds, and show them that we're together. We have plenty of time to organize before, hopefully, Julia becomes queen. Then, we raid the camps and free the Reds with the help of the royal military. When Max refuses to work with us, she'll look like a fraud."

She shook her head. "You want us to just sit on our asses and wait until then? That psycho just kidnapped me!"

"No, I want you to organize and prepare. If we act now, we'll lose. We need to build up, ensure our allies are in position and only then act. It's no use fighting a war we can't win. Nothing has changed there."

Snap smirked at Delaware. "You know he's right, Naomi."

She stuck her tongue in her cheek. "Fine. We'll organize, but I don't know how you expect us to convince so many Yellows."

I shrugged. "We'll find a way. We always find a way. Now, I need to take Roach to Vera. She's upholding her end of the bargain, and I don't want to make her even angrier at me. There's enough damn drama in that family with Julia running for queen."

Delaware laughed through her stiffness. "Ooh. The rebel and the queen."

I shook my head and laughed. "Shut up!"

Chapter 22

The droning of the plane's engines filled the cabin as we flew. This was my first flight, and I was not enjoying it. The pressure change was hurting my ears, and I sat, watching the world fly by, in extreme discomfort. *How long is this damn flight?*

We were on our way to Chicago in the Hughes family's private plane. Julia had explained that the American countries of the socialist Fifth International had called a surprise conference, and the royal family had been invited for diplomatic reasons.

The only reason I wasn't fearing for my life on the plane was the words that had greeted us as entered: *Made in the Appalachian Confederacy.* Just like the cars, everything we made in Northern Mississippi was useless: The designs, the production, the supply chain, everything was constantly wrong. During my time at the steel mill, I saw so much borderline useless steel being sent off for use in various products. If it hadn't been for trade, we would have failed a long time ago, and now even that was nearly impossible with the UPF's embargoes on the few remaining non-socialist countries.

I looked across the aisle at Julia, her nose buried in a book. I admired her love of reading. She would always say it gave her hope to read of worlds different than our own. Both the time to read and access to books had become a luxury, though. Anything considered remotely opposed to the UPF's rule had been banned, taken, and burned. The royals only managed to keep their own books through their exemption from UPF laws.

She looked up at me occasionally, flashing a smile when I caught her eyes. I would force a smile back, but I was unnerved. The truth about my parents still weighed heavily on me. *Why couldn't she tell me sooner?* I was starting to understand why she chose to wait, though. Nothing was simple in the royal political game, and she had plenty of turmoil in her own life to deal with.

A copy of the *St. Paul Free Press* was spread across the seat next to me. It was the only paper left in Northern Mississippi that wrote anything resembling the truth, and it amazed me that Aaron still managed to keep it running with the conflict in St. Paul. Two stories battled for control of the paper's cover: "The Socialists Dance in Chicago" and "The Fracture's Crimson Reign."

I picked up the paper and glanced over at Julia. "What is this conference about anyway? The *Free Press* seems to think it's about border disputes involving the People's Republic of Huron."

Julia set her book down and placed a bookmark in it before looking up at me. "Huron has been *problematic* for sure. They want to bring Chicago back into Illinois, and their new Premier, Nathaniel Taggart, has an eye on us too. This conference is about more than that, though. Huron isn't the only country seeking to expand: Canada, California, and The Commonwealth are all looking beyond their own borders. The Fifth International has avoided internal wars for a long time, but socialism isn't enough to unite them anymore."

"They aren't more concerned about the non-socialist countries?"

She shrugged. "The Appalachian Confederacy, Kingdom of New England, Dakota Republic, and Republic of Texas together are a threat to the socialists. With the Anglo-Nordic Coalition in Europe successfully overthrowing the socialists in Denmark and the Netherlands, they definitely fear the same thing could happen here. A few ambitious leaders, though, care more about their country's power than the stability of the Fifth International."

"You've been doing your research."

Glancing out the window, she hesitated before responding, "If I am to be queen, I need to understand what is happening in the world. I don't plan to treat the crown as purely a ceremonial role in diplomacy, unlike my father."

I smiled. "He would be proud of you."

"I hope so." She sighed looked down at her family ring. "It feels wrong for me to leave the Twin Cities while the Fracture is killing so many people."

"You are the Duchess of St. Paul, I am St. Paul's most famous rebel, and Delaware is the Captain of the Militia. Together, we'll show the Reds there's another way, one without mass murder."

A small smile crossed her face. "We will."

The pain returned to my ears, and I winced. Julia chuckled when she saw me scrunching my face. "You need to release the pressure from your ears." She demonstrated how: pinching her nose and then blowing through it.

As I tried to follow her instructions, she watched, entertained. Eventually, after many failed attempts, the pressure released from my ears in one of the weirdest feelings I've ever had in my life. She laughed as I squirmed, said, "That was worse than jail," and gave a small smile. "Thanks."

She gave a bow of her head. "Anytime, my love. I forgot that you have never flown before."

"Never left the country before, either." I looked out the window.

She followed my gaze out the window, her eyes full of excitement. "The world is a beautiful place. Hopefully, I will get to show you some of it. Though, even I have not seen as much of it as I would have liked."

I moved across the aisle to sit next to her and held her hand as she continued admiring the view. "We'll explore it someday, together."

She kissed my cheek. "I would love to explore the world with my future king."

That thought still unnerved me, but I forced the feeling away and smiled, laying my head back against the headrest and closing my eyes. "He sounds like a lucky guy to have an amazing woman like you."

"Promise you'll be there no matter where I go?"

"I'll never leave your side. I promise."

I felt her nuzzle her head into my neck and take a slow, deep breath. "Good, because there's no one I'd rather have there more than you."

We awoke as the plane landed in Chicago. Julia held my hand to reassure me as the plane screeched to a halt. When we finished taxiing, she smiled softly. "Ready?"

I cracked my back and straightened my tie. "Ready as I'll ever be for a fancy evening with a bunch of socialists. At least we don't have to deal with Isaac this time."

She groaned. "Let's not talk about him. He makes me remember my father, and right now I would rather not get emotional."

I squeezed her hand. "Of course, I'm sorry."

She half-smiled. "Don't worry." She paused as the pilot came over the intercom, announcing that we could now exit the plane. "Time to go. Got the bags?"

I stood, offering my hand to help her up. "Of course, m'lady."

Alex popped her head around the corner, yawning from her nap in the sleeping area. "Come on! I love Chicago!"

We both laughed as I grabbed the luggage and followed the princesses out. Vera, Natasha, and Benjamin were already in their car, and the chauffeur helped Julia and Alex into the second car while I loaded the luggage and shuffled in behind them.

Julia laughed as I took a deep breath. "Happy to be back on the ground?"

I looked out the window as we drove. The Chicago skyline was just becoming visible in the early afternoon sunlight, and it was breathtaking. "Maybe a little, maybe a lot."

Chicago's weather was no better than the Twin Cities'. Snow carpeted everything in sight, and with the black cars, grey buildings, and overcast sky, you could have been forgiven for forgetting that color existed at all. I tended to like the snow and winter, but it was late February; I was ready for it to be over sooner rather than later.

Julia and Alex idly chatted about their royal friends and other gossip that I had little interest in. The royals were always jostling for influence or prestige, even in the little things, but to me, the squabbles were petty distractions. It was nice, though, to see the sisters enjoying a small moment together. Alex was one of the few people Julia seemed comfortable around anymore, and I did not want Julia to lose her.

We eventually arrived at the location of the conference: a ritzy hotel along the Chicago River. I had flashbacks to the St. Cloud conference months before as I opened the door for the princesses. Unlike that one, though, there would not be leaders from outside the Americas, and I also didn't need to worry about Isaac's advances on Julia. A bad taste filled my mouth just thinking about that bastard. The coup felt like an eternity ago, but the horrors of that night would be stuck in my mind forever.

Paparazzi were everywhere as the royal family walked down the carpet to the hotel. I followed to the side with the other bodyguards as journalists started asking them questions. Julia beamed at the photographers and quickly responded to their questions about the election and being a princess. Then the questions came that we had both hoped to avoid: "How is your Red Tag boyfriend? Will he be the king if you win your election? Why would a princess date a murderer?"

While she suffered the interviews, I noticed more than one camera pointed in my direction. The paparazzi and tabloids were obviously very excited to get a picture of Princess Julia's forbidden lover. I did not appreciate the attention, and with each *click* of another camera, I squinted and flinched.

With Northern Mississippi's tight controls on newspapers, this was an entirely new experience, and I only hoped Julia was handling it better than I was. All I could do was try and maintain my composure and silence as the cameras flashed and similar questions were asked to me. *Leave me alone.*

After a few minutes of that torture, I tried to force open a path for Julia, shoving paparazzi out of the way so that she could make her way into the hotel. They pushed back against me, trying to get a closer shot of her, but I was not in the mood to tolerate them. I wielded a glare, and with help from the other royal guards, we cleared a route to the doors.

Once we were inside, the family was greeted by the Director of the Chicago Union, Jamal Brooks. From what Jonah had told me ahead of the trip, the workers' union had replaced the government in Chicago after the Third Civil War, making Brooks effectively the country's head of state. It was an intriguing concept, but I wouldn't have time to learn more. I had a job to do.

Julia swept her way into the ballroom, her black dress flowing behind her as she went. While I hated those events, I enjoyed being able to stand to the side and watch the beautiful girl that I loved work the crowd. Still, I preferred my spot on the sidelines. Unfortunately, though, if she wanted me to be king, I wouldn't be there for long.

The night seemed uneventful at first with the usual speeches by various leaders, including Bachton, and as the night dragged on, the guests drank way too much as they forgot about the important meetings tomorrow. *My parents would have been here. Did they hate these things too?*

My thoughts were interrupted when a security guard tapped me on the shoulder. "We require your assistance."

I looked at the bulky, bald man and shook my head. "I'm sorry, sir, but my job is to protect the princess."

He placed his hand on my shoulder. "Listen, we need a representative from your security team for a quick briefing. It'll be quick, I promise."

I took one last look towards Julia. My heart felt full watching her in her element. We were slowly working past her lie, but it would take time. For now, though, she was safe, and if I was needed for a stupid briefing, I was needed for a stupid briefing. I sighed. "Fine. Lead the way."

The security guard escorted me down a side hallway, his massive build blocking my view of what was ahead. The hall seemed to stretch on forever as the soft *thuds* of our feet against the black stone floor echoed with every step. Along the way, we passed more than one drunk couple that had hoped for a bit of privacy away from the party, but one look from the massive guard had them stumbling their way back towards the ballroom.

Eventually, we turned down what seemed like a maintenance hall. The cracked cement on the ground and strong *buzz* of the overhead lights contrasted sharply from the elegant halls we'd just left. *Where the hell are we going?*

Still, I continued to follow the guard. We had to be close, and considering his size, I didn't want to upset him with more questions. I liked my chances in most fights but not when the opponent was twice my size.

My bored mind wandered, wondering if I could kick him in the head, and what he would do if I tried. This lack of attentiveness became apparent to him when he stopped at a door, and I smacked into his back. He glared down at me and nodded towards the door. I raised an eyebrow but opened it. Not a moment later, pain filled the back of my head, and the last thing I saw was the floor flying towards my face.

I woke up in a dark room, illuminated by nothing more than one hanging lightbulb. They had me cuffed to a chair, and my nose felt like it was broken. I muttered to myself, "Damn it."

After what could have been minutes or hours, a mustached balding man in a pinstripe suit entered, flanked by two large guards. He smirked at me. "Ivan 181375, the slave who wooed a princess."

I rolled my eyes. "What the hell do you want?"

Crack! One of the guards punched me in the face. I cried out as the pain seared through my cheek. When I recovered, I opened my mouth to cuss them out, but a second blow shut me up before I could speak.

He raised a finger and wagged it back and forth. "You are in Chicago now. Things work differently here."

I spat at him the blood that had seeped into my mouth.

The man clicked his tongue for a moment. "You're a cheeky one, aren't you?"

I glared. "Where is Julia?"

He sighed and shook his head. If I hadn't been handcuffed, I would have jumped out of the chair and beaten that condescending look off his face. It was the only look I'd been given for so many years of my life, and I was sick of it. "The princess and her family are safe and enjoying their evening."

I groaned. "Then what do you want with me?"

The other guard cracked his knuckles and nailed me again. My head spun as I struggled to retain consciousness, and I groaned as a smirk crossed his face. "You'd do best to stop talking. It'll make this quicker."

I raised an eyebrow. "If you're going to kill me, I'll go down talking, thank you very much."

He laughed and pulled out a revolver, holding it up for me to see. "I'm not messing around, kid."

Well, shit. "You going to tell me who paid you to do this? Because the royal family is going to be pissed at whoever the bastard is."

The man checked the bullets in the revolver and spun it back into place. "Ironic. Your queen is the one who wants you dead. I don't know what you did, but she paid good money."

I sighed and shook my head. *So, this is how she bites back.* "Just get it over with."

He chuckled, raised the gun, and cocked it in a fluid motion. I flinched at the *click*, more afraid than I was willing to admit. I didn't want to die. Even with the struggles and the conflicts, I'd finally found something and someone to live for. Now, in one quick turn of events, it was all going to be over. I'd challenged the black widow, but I was trapped in her web the whole time.

My heart sunk as I thought about Julia. She had lost her dad, her sister, and now her boyfriend. I had disappeared, and she would only hear of my death when my body washed up on shore somewhere, if it was ever discovered at all. Things were still tough between us after she revealed what she knew about my parents, but I loved her more than anything. Even with her mistakes, she was a pure white dove trapped in a violent, dark world that didn't deserve her. I wanted to protect her from it all: from my violent past, from the UPF, from the Fracture, from her mom. I couldn't do it. I played a dangerous game, and I'd lost.

With my eyes shut, I took one long, shaky breath. I thought it would be my last as I pictured his finger tightening around the trigger. When the *bang* came, the sound echoed throughout the cement room. *I'm sorry, Julia.*

Chapter 23

Two more shots followed the first in quick succession. I shook in my chair, too afraid to open my eyes. *Why am I not dead?*

A rough voice came from the other end of the room. "You can open your eyes now."

Reluctantly, I forced my eyes open and reentered the world of the living. In front of me were the bodies of the man and the two guards, a bullet hole in each of their heads. A middle-aged man stood over them, the dangling lightbulb illuminating his bald head.

My face must have been full of shock, since the man just chuckled to himself. "You're alive, kid, for now."

I nodded towards my hands. "I don't know who you are, but you wanna un-cuff me? Or are you here to kill me too?"

He gave a smile and bent down to grab the keys off one guard's belt. He unlocked the cuffs, and I rubbed my wrists as he spoke, "Name's Chuck."

I stood. "I assume you already know who I am."

"We've been watching you for a long time, Ivan."

I frowned as I grabbed my knives and guns from the corner. "We?"

"You're not alone. There are more of us that want to see things change. We are the Minutemen."

The Minutemen? "Like from the American Revolution?"

Chuck cracked open the door, looking out into the hall. "Yes, but we don't have time to talk now. They're going to notice the guards are missing, and when they do, they're going to come for you."

I groaned. "Who are *they*?"

He mumbled something to himself and slid into the hall, motioning for me to follow. "The Chicago Union's political police. Your Queen Vera has a lot of friends. They're not going to let you get away easily."

He flung something at me, and I bobbled it before finally gaining a hold. It was a key fob. "A car?"

With a quick turn, he began down the hall, forcing me to follow at a jog. "There's a black sedan waiting for you in the garage. Look for the flag of the Thirteen Colonies window sticker. There is a number on the phone in the glovebox. Drive back to Northern Mississippi and call it. I'll tell you everything. Don't worry about the princess, she'll be fine. Ready?"

My mouth gaped as my ringing head tried to unpack what he just told me. "Wha... I guess."

He nodded and ducked into a side closet in one of the halls, leaving me a sitting duck in the middle of the hall. I waited a few seconds before peeping in behind him. He emerged, smacking into my face but ignoring the contact. A police uniform was in his hands. "Put this on. Hopefully it'll hold your cover until you can get out of the country."

"How did..."

He shoved me into the closet and threw the uniform after me.

"No questions. Hurry up."

What is happening? I didn't have much of a choice if Chuck was right about the cops, so I followed his directions and changed into the disguise. The outfit included a winter police hat, allowing me to stick my tag out of sight, at least if someone didn't look too closely. My hands still shook in fear from my narrow escape. *Not free yet, focus.*

When I emerged, Chuck just gave a quick nod, pointed, said, "The garage is that way. Call me when you're out of the country," and ran off the opposite direction.

I watched him go, confused. *Thanks for saving my life, I guess?* I wanted to know more, but I needed to escape first. They'd caught me once. I didn't want to have a gun to my head a second time that day.

The garage was on the opposite end of the building, meaning I had to pass by a lot of security and police on my way out. I lowered the cap on my head and looked at the floor as I walked, trying to avoid any eye contact. The last thing I wanted to do was leave Julia behind, but Chuck assured me she was safe in the ballroom. There was no way I could get to her with all the security around the room; I'd text her when I was free.

Nobody I passed seemed to care about me, but when I was closing in on the door to the parking garage, one security guard studied me closely as I passed. With less than ten feet to go, he yelled from behind me, "You! Stop!"

I didn't stop. Instead, I flung open the door to the parking garage and sprinted along the line of cars, searching desperately for the old flag of the Thirteen Colonies. I winced as a bullet whizzed by my head, followed by more shouting. *Apparently, they shoot first, ask questions later.*

I ducked behind a car to my right and aimlessly returned fire, hoping to slow them down. There was no way to know where the black sedan was as I zig-zagged through the cars. At least half the cars were black too, making life even more difficult. *Why couldn't he have picked yellow?*

Bullets flew over my head constantly as more guards and cops entered the garage. I turned, placing my forearms on the top of one of the cars, and fired back, hitting as many of them in non-lethal areas as possible. After a couple shots, my ammo ran out, and I ducked back down before spotting the sedan on the next aisle over. I just had to make a clear sprint.

Two steps into my run, though, a cop knocked into me, and we both fell to the ground. In the resulting struggle, I hit him with an elbow, only knocking him out for half a second, but it gave me time to grab his gun and sprint towards the car. Another wave of bullets flew around me as I pointed the gun wildly and fired back, shattering glass, denting cars, and causing one cop to cry out. *Almost there.*

I dove into the car and started it as the police closed in, shouting and shooting at my tires. The car was quick, though. With the noise of the V6 echoing through the garage, I stormed out of shooting range and onto the street. Moments later, sirens wailed behind me as I put my foot down, completely unaware of where I was going. According to the badge on the steering wheel, the car was from the Appalachian Confederacy, like the plane, and I just hoped the police had nothing better than the crappy ones from the state-owned factories.

It felt freeing to fly through Chicago with a horde of police trailing behind me. I tested the car's limits on the tight city streets, but it responded to everything I asked of it. There was no way for the police to keep up as I stormed through the night.

Chicago felt like Minneapolis on steroids. Even with the speed I was driving, I could see both the skyscrapers and the food lines. They didn't have a Prism of their own, but even here, people were struggling. I wished I could have spent time talking with its people, seeing what life was like here compared to Northern Mississippi. Surviving was more important, though, and I needed to get back home.

I was free and clear when I reached the highway, just another black car under the night sky. I drove through the wintery night with no sound but the vents blasting welcome hot air onto my face. The drive gave me time to clear my head and try to comprehend what had happened. *Vera is willing to kill me, and she's going to try again.* I didn't know what I was going to do about that fact. All I knew was that the last thing I needed was another threat within the royalty.

I tried calling Julia, but she must have still been too busy at the ball. A text would have to do. At least then she would know why I was gone and that I was alive. I'd deal with Vera when the time was right. Someone had to destroy the black widow's web.

The difficult part of the journey would be the border. While Northern Mississippi and Chicago had a warm relationship, there were many efforts made to prevent the free flow of people into and out of each country. On top of that, wanted messages would have been sent to the border patrol by the time I made it. It was obvious that I would try to get back home, and there was only one highway that ran between Chicago and Wisconsin.

After almost an hour of driving, I needed time to think of a plan, grab some gas, and take a break, so I pulled into a gas station near the border. For a minute, I just sat there. It had been a long day, and the events in Chicago had more than shaken me. On top of everything else I was already dealing with, my girlfriend's mom now had a kill order out on me. I was stupid to face her without truly understanding who I was dealing with. To make things worse, the Fracture's threat only grew as we fought within the Hughes family. Tensions would boil over soon between the UPF and the Fracture, and I didn't know who would snap first: Max or Bachton. All I knew was that I didn't plan on finding out. It was hard to prevent a civil war, though, when I was running for my life.

Eventually, I took a breath and climbed out of the car. As I filled my gas tank, I pulled my police cap down over my head. *Don't act suspicious.* Nobody seemed to give me a second look as I fed the bills into the machine. *Please accept Northern Mississippi Dollars...* The machine stuttered for what felt like an eternity as my heart was raced. *Stay calm.* Eventually, the whirring of the machine stopped, and it spit the money back out before shouting, "Please see an attendant for assistance!"

I jumped back at the noise, and another person pumping gas raised an eyebrow at me but quickly looked away when I shot him a glare. I ripped the money from the dispenser and walked quickly into the mini-store.

A man who looked like he hadn't slept in months was at the counter. His head was craned forward like a turtle, and he showed no emotion at the sight of a police officer. "Pump four?"

I was caught a little off guard and stuttered in response, "What was that?"

His eyes showed even more disdain for the world. Something which I hadn't thought possible moments before. "Your car is at pump four, officer?"

I nodded too rapidly. "Yes, it is. Do you accept Northern Mississippi Dollars?"

He gave me a confused look, probably wondering why a Chicago police officer wanted to pay in a foreign currency. Apparently, asking wasn't worth the effort, though, and he just sighed before punching the amount into the cash register and holding out a hand. I placed the money into it, and he haphazardly dropped the bills into their slots. I nodded and turned, starting to walk away before there was a cough behind me. My heart stopped.

"Officer, your change."

I let out a breath in relief. "Of course, thank you." I shook my head to myself as I walked away with the change. *I'm an idiot.* As I exited the store, I half-jogged to the car, pondering what other routes could be possible. Chuck hadn't given me any hints, so I was on my own.

Lost in my thoughts, I forgot to check my surroundings and nearly fell when I heard a shout from behind me. When I turned to see who it was, I froze. The cop had his window down and was looking right at me. *He must have pulled in when I wasn't looking.*

I turned only half my face towards him as he spoke, "You hear the reports from downtown?" I shook my head. "Some maniac shot up the Fifth International conference. Rumor has it, it's that nut *Coyote* from up north. Keep your eyes out. They say he might even be dressed as one of us."

I nodded. "Appreciated. I'm off my shift for the night, but I'll keep an eye out." I opened my door.

He raised an eyebrow. "Say, what precinct are you from?"

Don't make me kill you. I really don't want to. "Uh, six. Must have just left before the call went out."

He narrowed his eyes for a moment before slapping the side of his car. "You better check your personal radio then before someone hears its broken." I nodded, and he rolled up the window as he pulled into a parking spot. *Too close.*

I avoided going back on the highway. I needed to find a way north that wasn't going to be guarded. The small town by the gas station seemed safe enough, so I looked for a road heading north and took the worst built one, hoping it wouldn't be patrolled. I was so close to the border, so close to home.

My hopes faded after when I saw the lights. Both in front and behind me, police were closing in. The cop at the rest stop must have recognized me, and now, I was surrounded. I grabbed Chuck's phone, slammed on the gas, and drifted into a side street, hoping to buy myself a bit of time. The phone rang as I called its one stored contact. The time between each ring could have been hours as I sped through the unsuspecting neighborhood, the sirens closing in around me.

Finally, there was a *click*. "Hello, Ivan?"

In my panic, I shouted into the phone, "The cops are in hot pursuit, and I need a way across the border. I'm skidding through side streets two exits from it."

Chuck's voice was stern. "Stay calm and listen to me. There's a set of railroad tracks just east of you. Take those north and across the border. Call me back when you're clear."

I skidded through a red light exiting the subdivision, heading back onto a main road as I yelled for him not to hang up. He did anyway, and I winced as a loud *crash* came from behind me. The rearview mirror showed the carnage I caused by running the red light. An SUV had rear-ended a pickup at the intersection, blocking the cops' path. I wanted to scream in frustration and cheer about my luck at the same time, but I instead focused my energy on putting my foot down and pushing the car to its limit.

With the cops delayed, I needed to get to the railroad while I was still out of sight, but I had no idea how far it would be. Traffic swerved and honked out of my way as I sped by, the V6 roaring through the innocent town now caught in the middle of a battle of international espionage. The sirens roared in the distance as I reached the train tracks. If it hadn't been for the lights on the tracks, I would have missed them. The problem was: the lights signaled for the train that was speeding through the intersection. I was trapped.

I faced a massive dilemma. The cops were closing in and would catch me if I waited, but the train blocked my only way across the border. I thought fast and turned the wheel sharply, sending the car off the road and blazing into the grass alongside the tracks, each bump jolting me rapidly along the way.

The car was not built for off-roading. It took every bit of my strength to keep it in a straight line as the rear wheels spun, ripping up every plant in their path. The train steamed ahead next to me as I skidded along, cutting through the darkness. I had no idea how far the border was, and I was too focused on handling the beast to care at the time. One mistake and I would slide under the train and to my death.

After a few minutes of battling with the steering wheel, the train passed by, leaving me skidding in its wake. It's flashing red lights taunted me as I drove up the slope and onto the tracks, finally gaining a decent amount of traction. With time to check my rearview mirror, I could just see the flashing lights flying by on the street I'd left behind. Luckily, they hadn't seen me turn. I was finally free, unless they had yet another trick up their sleeves.

Soon, the lights of the first road in Northern Mississippi came into sight. The road was empty as I turned onto it, but I did not want to spare a second of time getting as far from the border as possible. I was done with risks for the day.

A few towns down the road, I stopped at a small shop and changed clothing. Even after taking off the hat, face-wrap, and badge, the Yellow cashier gave me a weird look. He didn't say anything, though, as I flashed my Hughes family pin, and his eyes widened with recognition after a moment. He swallowed as he read out the price.

I only smiled and handed him the debit card Julia had given me in case of an emergency. I figured being on the run as an international fugitive was an enough of an emergency to buy some crappy jeans. His hand shook as he slid it through the machine. If

I hadn't been so on edge, I would have laughed it off and told him not to worry. Instead, I rapidly tapped my foot and stared out the window.

I changed quickly before heading back to the car. When I got there, I found myself unable to drive. I could only grip the steering wheel and take deep breaths in an attempt to calm myself down. *I'm in Northern Mississippi. I'm alive. Chuck said Julia would be okay.* It didn't work. All I could think about was how I fled without her. If something had happened to me... *Don't think about it.* In the moments before I thought I'd die, the resentment I had felt towards her was gone. Now, all I wanted was to hear her voice. I tried calling her again. Her phone rang and rang before, "Hello, you have reached the phone of..."

Rage flooded into me and I threw my phone into the passenger seat. "Damn it!" I smacked the steering wheel as tears ran down my face. Everything was insane, and now I was alone, somewhere in Wisconsin, while she was stuck with her murdering mom.

I pulled out Chuck's phone again and dialed the number. When he picked up again, I didn't give him the chance to speak. "Who the hell are you?" He just laughed, and I scoffed. "How is this funny?"

There was more laughter on the other end and then, "Calm down, kid. Everything's fine."

I yelled in frustration, "Fine? Things are not fine! Vera bribed Chicago's cops to kill me, the Fracture is killing people left and right in St. Paul, my friends in the Militia are starving, we've done nothing to end the Prism, and Julia is caught with the woman who wants me dead."

"Yet, you're alive. The fight continues."

I rested my head on the steering wheel. "The damn fight never ends."

"Tyrants never rest, so neither do we."

The lights above the parking lot flickered. "Who are you, 'the Minutemen'?"

He sighed. "We are an international group fighting quietly for what America was supposed to be. We were founded by James Madison and Benjamin Franklin shortly after the end of the First Civil War and have tried to intervene throughout America to push things in the right direction behind the scenes. We were the reason Lincoln became king and, after the Third Civil War, eventually succeeded in establishing the Appalachian Confederacy and Dakota Republic. In most other countries, though, we've struggled."

"Why have I never heard of you?"

He waited a moment before replying. When he did, he seemed to be picking his words carefully. "When you run a network of agents that infiltrate governments, it is beneficial to not be known."

I shook my head. "How do you know so much about me? How did you know they would try to kill me?"

"Long story kid, but we've been looking for potential members in Northern Mississippi. You fit the bill, and when our network discovered Vera's plan among the Chicago PD, we felt it was time to bring you into the fold. Unfortunate that it was under such chaotic circumstances."

I laughed. "I'm used to chaotic."

He chuckled. "So I've heard. Now, you've got yourself quite a solid little group there. We believe you can actually change things. That's actually why we tried to not get involved for so long. We didn't want to interfere in the progress you all have made."

"What progress? Nothing has changed."

"Kid, you'll realize when you're my age that things move slow as hell in this world. The fact you managed to take out the Front's cameras, prevented a coup, got your girl into a legitimate position to become queen, and started a movement against the Prism in less than a year is impressive. I've been in this for most of my life, and I haven't felt real hope in this fight until you and your princess joined up. It ain't gonna happen tomorrow. Just keep doing what you're doing, and hopefully our network can help."

I shivered as the cold crept into the car, and I finally mustered up the effort to turn the key. The blast of warm air was a relief, mentally and physically. "Thanks for the praise, but you're telling me there's nothing you and your super-secret spy organization can do to help?"

His voice sounded like that of a disgruntled dad. "Listen, kid, we just saved your life. The only thing we can offer with our limited resources right now is the continued influence we have among some of the royalty. Many of them are still on the fence. We'll make sure they come down on Julia's side."

My eyes tired as I pulled back onto the road, continuing my journey home. All my body wanted was the quiet of my closet-sized bedroom in the servants' wing. It had been a long drive already, but part of me was happy to not be flying again. "Thanks for that, I guess. We have a good feeling about the election, but everything helps."

He responded in the most serious tone I'd heard from him yet, "Everything revolves around her becoming queen, Ivan. Everything."

Chapter 24

The drive back to Minneapolis would be more than four hours, even with me speeding the whole way. To kill the time, I could only crank up the heat and flick on the radio. It was a boring trip. With the rapid pace of the day, though, I was still wide awake.

Between old rock songs, the radio commentator read the censored news for the day. At first, there were the usual announcements about the number of people who passed through the Prism, the bullshit "amazing" growth of our economy, and accusations against both the Militia and the Fracture, who they claimed were conspiring together against the people. I had to laugh at the irony of that. Either they were idiots and actually believed we were on the same side, or they didn't care about the differences.

What really piqued my interest were the updates from around the world. Apparently, the situation in the Netherlands and Denmark had begun to deteriorate. The republican rebels supported by the Anglo-Nordic Coalition had managed to seize both countries' capitals in recent weeks, and an emergency meeting of the European branch of the socialist Fifth International had been called to address the conflicts.

The USSR especially would be concerned. If the republican forces could gain a foothold in Central Europe, then they could soon be knocking on Moscow's door. It seemed the Fifth International was less powerful than they let on, yet I wondered why they hadn't intervened in the conflict sooner. After the pseudo-meeting the night that I met Isaac, they had applied embargos against the Coalition, hoping to choke them out, but apparently, it had done nothing to push them back. Weakness in the Fifth International was a good sign for us, but if war came to Europe, then America would not be far behind.

Half-an-hour from Minneapolis, Julia called me. It was two in-the-morning, so my heart jumped a bit when my phone rang, half from surprise at the new noise during the long ride and half from excitement. Her voice was frantic. "Oh my gosh, Ivan are you alright?"

I laughed. "I was kidnapped by your mom's hired goons, was saved by a secret international republican group, shot my way out the hotel, and terrorized the streets of Chicago. I'm alive, somehow. I'll take it."

"I heard that your escape was… eventful…" She sounded worried. Her voice hung on the last word, avoiding talking about the people I'd shot.

I sighed. "That's one way to put it. How was the conference? I felt really bad leaving so fast."

She interjected, "*You* feel bad? I put us in this mess. You were right about my mother."

"None of that matters right now. It doesn't matter who was right or wrong. We're in this together. We're alive." I put as much intensity into my voice as possible without being too forceful.

There were a few moments of silence before she spoke again,

"We are a team. Even when we mess up."

I nodded, despite the fact she couldn't see me. "Exactly."

She sighed. "So, what happened?"

I explained how I was taken to the back and knocked out, how they almost killed me, and how Chuck swooped in to save my life.

She listened silently the whole time until I finished. "Ivan, I'm so sorry, but I'm happy you're okay. I... I don't know how to deal with my mother. This is insane."

I hit a bump in the road and groaned in pain. The beating I'd taken had left its mark. "In some twisted way, she probably thinks she's protecting you."

She scoffed. "From the guy who has saved my life more than once."

I laughed. "There's multiple ways to look at it I guess." My smile faded when I thought about our next steps. "She wants me dead, Julia. I don't know if I have much of a choice of what to do."

"*We* need to beat her at her own game."

I looked at the St. Paul skyline in the night. "What if we already lost?"

She pushed harder. "Ivan, you're alive, you broke out of a deathtrap that she set for you, and we're in a spot to win this election. We know her schemes now. If anything, we're the ones winning."

I sighed. "Sure doesn't feel like it sometimes."

"Don't worry, my love. We will find a way, we always do. For now, though, I must go speak to my mother about this. I don't care if it is two a.m. She just tried to kill my boyfriend."

"At least she won't kill you."

She sighed. "I hope not. Love you. Drive safe."

When I returned to the palace, I found a spare spot in the garage for the car. Part of me felt a bit of pride about that car. It was mine now, and with what I had to go through to get it home, I felt like I'd earned it. Taking one last look at it before turning off the light, I smiled to myself, and stumbled towards the showers.

The mirror reflected my bruised and battered face. A black bruise graced one of my eyes. *Hot.* I spat into the sink. The bleeding had stopped, but the iron taste lingered in my mouth. I was a mess: The mutant that stole the heart of a princess. Taking one last look in the mirror before I left for my room, I silently hoped it would look better tomorrow so Julia wouldn't have to see me like that.

The old door to my room creaked as I entered. As usual, it took three tries to actually get the dang thing shut once I'd entered. It was a daily battle, one that I'd learned to just laugh at. Tonight, though, I wasn't in the mood. It had been a long day. I didn't want a stupid door to stand between me and sleep. When it finally clicked shut, I groaned and threw my clothes onto the floor. The cold air stung my skin. They never heated the servants' wing enough.

Exhaustion ruled my mind and body, so I just stood and felt the cold. When I opened my eyes, I looked down at my scarred and burned body. Each mark carried its own story, each one another time someone tried to kill me and failed. That night had been the closest I'd ever come to death. A second later and my brains would have been blown out by that mysterious man. Instead, he lay dead on the floor while I continued my fight. Many had tried. All had failed. I just wondered in that moment: *When will my luck run out?*

Chapter 25

eat them at their own game. I hid my scowl as Michael stopped by my room the next day with a message from Vera: I was to join the Hughes family for their dinner that evening. It took everything I had to not tell Michael that Vera could go to hell. She was trying to keep her eye on me, to manipulate me further, but I'd learned my lesson the hard way.

Every time I thought I'd won my confrontations with her, the opposite had been true. Her attack in Chicago proved she had no intentions to uphold her side of our deal, and now she had Cockroach. I could still blackmail her with the information about my parents, but that had its own risks, and I didn't want to expose my true bloodline until the moment was right. I had no idea how deep her web ran, and I was fighting desperately to escape now.

Julia and I had not spoken much after the phone call. She was busy, and we were both too shell-shocked. It was all overwhelming, but we had to take everything one problem at a time. Somehow, we had to balance handling her mom with preventing a civil war and getting Julia elected, and unfortunately, those three things were very different tasks. We were no closer to defeating the Fracture, freeing the Reds, or creating a coalition for Julia beyond the minimal help the Minutemen could provide. All I'd manage to do was waste another day, fall into Vera's trap, and barely survive. She would have never killed her daughter, but I was fair game.

Julia's day had been full of meetings with various royals at the palace. The results were mixed, but earning a couple votes and moving a family in the right direction was at least somewhat of a success. She knew what to offer to who and how to speak with them. Even with the less friendly Whites, she was making progress.

One of the royals had specifically asked whether I would be the king if she won, and Julia just looked towards me and then back at him. "You might want to ask him about that one. That is one tradition I do not plan on breaking. Though, I hear the standard for a queen's ring is much higher than that of just a princess."

The royal was charmed like they almost always were, and the bullet was dodged. I wondered how much of her statement was a joke and how much was real, but I doubted she would reveal that information herself. For now, though, there were higher priorities than our way-too-rapidly moving relationship. Whether Julia thought the same was a mystery.

In preparation for the meetings, we had Alex conjuring up as much gossip about each family as possible, ensuring that Julia had at least some insights into what they wanted. I was becoming more familiar with the names and faces, but I still got lost every now and then. Luckily, I was just standing in the corner, not the one doing the talking. Part of me wished I was the one negotiating the political scene, but Chuck was right. Our fight was so much bigger than me now. This was Julia's time to shine.

Ahead of the dinner, Julia gave me a warning as we walked the halls. "Don't let mother or any of them get to you."

I bit my cheek. "She tried to kill me."

She stopped and sighed. "I know, but we have enough problems without you trying to do the same to her. I questioned her about the attack last night, but she acted offended that I would accuse her. We will ensure she pays for this, but for now, we need to play her game. I'm sorry we haven't had a chance to talk about everything today. With everything that has happened, I feel like we haven't had any time together."

I gave her a closed-mouth smile. "Don't worry. Campaigning is more important, and listening to cranky royals rant about their petty problems is better than me talking about my emotions anyway."

She intertwined her fingers into mine as we walked. "Well, I like it when you're open with me." She kissed my cheek. "We shouldn't leave them waiting."

I held her other hand. "I love you."

Her smile grew. "I love you too."

The table was quite literally set. An ice-blue tablecloth stretched the length of the intricate wooden dining table. A line of platinum candelabras split the table, their flames blowing wisps of smoke into the air, only slightly obscuring the glare on the Queen's face. The delicious smell of cooked meat filled the room, and each of our steps sounded like an army marching to war.

The servants were waiting for us all to be seated, but the stare-off between Vera and I had frozen time. Julia nudged me along, trying to get me to my seat. Her words rang in my head, but a stronger thought replaced them. *She dies, or I die. Crimson reigns.*

Crimson falls. That woman had killed my parents, tried to kill me as a baby, and tried again a day ago. If I let her live, she would try again. There was no denying it, and I wasn't going to find out if the third time was the charm.

Julia yanked me to my seat. Her glare was colder than her mom's, and a chill went down my spine. *Why aren't you glaring at the woman who tried to kill your boyfriend?*

Vera gave a smirk as I sat. "Thank you for joining us this evening, Ivan."

I raised an eyebrow but said nothing. I was too angry to come up with a witty response, and by the time I could collect my thoughts, the food was being served.

It felt wrong to be at the table, being served by Blues and Greens who had scowled at me when I first arrived at the palace. Even after everything that had happened, their eyes still judged me as they placed the plates. Doubts about the Prism had taken over the lower colors, but most of the higher ones still looked upon us as inferior, no matter what we did. A Red dining with the royal family was damaging to their pride. A few months before, I would have been happy knocking them down a notch, but now, I pitied how petty they were. There were so many problems we needed to solve, yet they were too focused on an earring to see them.

As I criticized them in my head, I realized that I had not been so different until recently. Even though I rejected the idea of the Prism, it had for so long been the center-point of so much of my life. My fight had always been against the Prism, and in the long-run it still was, but I still noticed people's color and judged them on it. I had been stuck in the dark, blind to the intertwined and complex problems that we now confronted. I was starting to see more as the light crept into the cracks within the country, but there was no way for these servants to know all of it. We were all caught in our bubbles. *Is it fair to judge them for focusing on their own problems?*

I was ripped from my internal dialogue when Julia spoke, "I had a fascinating discussion with the President of the Great Plains Collective about a new type of corn that they believe could survive the winter. Just imagine how important that could be for us."

I smiled to myself. She was genuinely excited about things like that, and she knew it would distract people from the obvious tension in the room. *This is her family, remember that.*

Natasha nodded. "It would be quite impressive if they were to succeed in these temperatures."

Vera took a sip of her white wine. "Unfortunate that we could not research such things ourselves."

Julia smiled. "Yes, it is, though, if we allowed more people to openly practice the sciences, perhaps we could. Still, it is an amazing feat, and I hope that soon we may use it to address the food shortages. Don't you think that it's important, Alex?"

Alex was caught off guard with a glass of red wine at her lips. She quickly swallowed, her eyes wide in surprise. "Yeah, corn."

We all laughed. It was rare to have such a warm moment when the whole Hughes family got together, but it was a welcomed one. With all the tension lately, it was easy to forget how much loss this family had suffered in the last couple months. They deserved some happiness. *Maybe this dinner won't be as bad as I expected.*

The dinner carried on in a lighter atmosphere. Jokes were made, gossip was whispered, and old family stories were shared. *Is this what a real family is supposed to be like?* I hadn't seen the Hughes family as a normal one until that moment. Even if Vera wanted me dead, it was new to see her as just a mom with her kids. It didn't change my anger towards her, but it was important for me to see.

Near the end of the dinner, Vera scanned the candelabras before focusing on Julia, her tone serious. "There is something we must discuss."

Julia shifted uncomfortably and held my hand under the table. *Here we go.*

Vera leaned forward. "I believe that in one way or another, we are all aware of the events that occurred yesterday evening." I gripped Julia's hand a little too hard, prompting a quick glare from her as her mother continued. "There seems to be a misunderstanding within the family."

Alex scoffed. "I think we understand things perfectly."

Julia responded, softer than her sister, "It would be difficult, mother, for me to misunderstand an attempt to kill Ivan. I would be interested in hearing what possible excuse you could have for that."

Vera's eyes narrowed. "Why would I attempt to murder Ivan? Was it not me who had him pardoned? That was entirely Chicago's doing, not mine."

"Bullshit!" The word flew out of my mouth before I could think, and everyone except Alex gaped at me. Alex just laughed.

Vera stood and gripped the edge of the table. "Watch your mouth when you're around your betters! You have caused nothing but trouble ever since my husband invited you into our household. Now, when I invite you to our table, this is how you act?"

Benjamin interjected, "Can we not enjoy the meal instead of quarreling?"

I stood sharply. "Says the one who wasn't almost murdered yesterday!" A look of fear crossed everyone's faces. I looked at my hand, extended towards Benjamin, a steak knife in its grasp. *Now I screwed it up.*

Vera looked at me condescendingly, her lips curling in the corners. *I fell into her trap.* I knew she'd won, but I was too enraged to back down. My fuse with her had grown very short, and the only thing running through my head was everything she'd done wrong to me, to Julia, to everyone. I drove the knife into the table, rattling the glassware and prompting another audible gasp from the family and servants.

Taking a breath, I looked around, my hand still gripping the knife. *Damn it.* I didn't know what to do or what to say, so I ran out of the dining room and through the halls, leaving the chaos in my wake. The tension in my heart had been building and finally reached its peak. Only one of us could live, and I was going to make sure that it was me.

Chapter 26

A cold western wind whipped across the old High Bridge, smacking constantly into my face. From my seat along the edge, I looked beyond my dangling feet to the half-frozen water fifty meters below, watching the Mississippi River send thin sheets of ice crashing into the supports.

After the fight with Vera, I needed to get away from the palace. I had grabbed the Minutemen car and drove without a destination in mind. Somehow, I ended up there, my favorite place.

Just a few months before, Julia and I had sat at that exact spot, looking at the view of Minneapolis's halo in the night. As much as the rest of that night had been filled with chaos, it had been one of my favorite memories. For the first time, I had been able to show her part of my life, the good and the bad. Then, I thought my world was dark, but now, I saw hers was just as dangerous, with threats veiled in secrecy.

I had calmed a bit, but the thought remained in my mind. *Vera dies, or I die.* There was no way to escape that fact. It was a distraction, though. We were trying to stop the Fracture, to end the Prism, and to make Julia queen, but my personal issues with Vera were constantly getting in the way. I wanted to push them to the side, but beyond the rage I felt towards her, the situation was truly about life and death.

A puff of fog appeared in front of my face as I blew out a long breath. I had hoped the bridge could be an escape from the thoughts that haunted my mind, but instead, the quiet created a void for them to fill. My hands shook as I ran them through my messed-up hair. I thought I could handle the pressure, handle the immense challenges that stood in front of me, in front of all of us, but I couldn't. Everything was a distraction from another goal. It felt like everything and everyone was working against me. I was sick of it.

The *crunch* of footsteps on the snowy broken cement approached. I sighed and looked down at the river. "How'd you find me?"

Julia joined me along the ledge, much more confident than the last time she sat there. She looked at me with concern and a half-hearted smile. "Where do we go when we need to be alone and to think? Our favorite quiet place. I go to my room or the forest, and you go to your bridge."

"You remembered."

She placed her hand on my leg. "Of course I did. This bridge is important to you, so it's important to me. Besides, you opened up to me that night, and it meant the world to me." She sighed and looked out over the water. "It feels like yesterday and an eternity ago at the same time."

I followed her gaze, watching the leafless trees shudder in the wind. "Ever since I was a kid, after Poseidon rescued me from the orphanage, I had wanted to test if I could walk all the way across the river on the ice. I never had the guts to do it, but a few years ago, Snapback dared me to. Delaware had only joined a few weeks before and was still a little shy, so I made her do it with me. It was hard to convince her, even though she was more of a daredevil than me once she got comfortable. I got her to do it, though, and when we tried to cross, the ice was not very thick. My first steps had already started to crack the ice, but we were still young and stupid, so we kept going."

Julia's eyes filled with curiosity. "What happened?"

Chuckling, I replied, "The ice started cracking, so I decided to sprint across instead, throwing caution to the wind."

"Did you make it?"

I shrugged. "I did. She didn't. When my sprinting broke the ice, Snap had to dive into the river to save her. Pretty sure he was fine getting to save the new girl he had a crush on."

"Like how you saved me from the thugs downtown and then in the Enclave?"

I felt my cheeks flush in response. Somehow, she knew how to break down my guard. "I was a little more worried about keeping you alive, but saving a cute girl was a plus. It was even better when I got to know that girl."

A smile crossed her face, and she laid her head on my shoulder. A calm feeling flowed over my body, and I shut my eyes. The silence was suddenly peaceful with her there, unlike the chaos that had ruled my mind alone. *I need her.* I didn't want that moment to end. It felt like the eye of a hurricane, a brief respite from the storm before the waves struck again. We could forget all the craziness of the world for a few moments and remember that we loved each other.

I wrapped my hand into hers and ran my thumb along hers. After a few minutes, she sat up again and breathed out, releasing her stress. "I love you, Ivan, and I'm so sorry, about everything."

I gave her a soft smile, said, "We're in this together. That's all that matters to me," and kissed her for the first time in what felt an eternity after the stress of the last week. With my eyes shut, enjoying that moment, I could have forgotten we were high above a deadly river on a freezing night. All I felt was her warmth.

Her eyes glimmered in the moonlight as she gazed into mine. "I was worried that, after everything, you had begun to doubt us. The way you looked at me when I told you about your parents… You looked at me as if I had killed them, and you have seemed so distant since then. I understand why. Just, please don't shut me out. I know it sounds selfish, but I need you, especially now."

She paused and looked down at our hands before back at me. "I have lost everyone in my family, except for Alex. So much has happened so quickly, and my family has fallen apart because of it. You two are all I have left."

I pulled her into a hug, and my heart twanged. I had been too busy worrying about my own problems and fighting against the Fracture to think about the impact things had had on her.

I said, "I'm sorry I've been distant. I'm not mad at you. Things have just been going so fast that I haven't had time to think or talk with you alone." We released each other, and I looked at her concerned face. "I don't feel like I'm in control of my mind or my life anymore. No matter what we do, nothing changes. There's too many enemies and not enough allies. We haven't stopped the Fracture, we haven't freed the Reds from the camps, we haven't ended the Prism, we haven't beaten the UPF, we haven't…"

Julia grabbed my hands. "Shhh. Ivan, it's not your fault that everyone is this broken country is fighting against us. We have accomplished so much, and we have only just begun. Nobody else could have done what you have."

I laughed sarcastically. "Or maybe nobody else is stupid enough to try."

She shook her head. "A lesser man would have killed Razor, Wilhelm, and my mother. A lesser man would not be able to look his enemies in the face and beat them at their own game. You have done that consistently."

I sighed and looked over the river. "Vera has beaten me every step of the way. I keep falling into her traps. You said a lesser man would have killed her, but that's all I can think of at this point. I can't see how we can both live on like this. She's already tried to kill me once, and she'll do it again. I know she's your mom and this is hard to hear, but I don't know what else to do."

She released my hands, stood, and paced across the bridge, her lips pursed in thought. "You are not one to take the easy way out."

I forced myself to my feet, groaning in pain from the beating I took in Chicago. I spoke intently, my voice wild with emotion, "You really think this is easy for me? I don't want to kill your mom. I told you, I hate having to kill, but what choice do I have, Julia? We both have seen what evil she has unleashed, and we don't even know the tip of the iceberg when it comes to her. I can't win at her game, and I'm losing my mind trying to find another way. Maybe we're all born White, but all I can see is crimson everywhere I turn."

Julia bit her lip and looked into the sky. As I watched her ponder, all I could think about was how I wished we could be a normal couple, spending a night grabbing ice cream or something, not considering killing her evil mother. Then I remembered that there weren't really "normal" couples. Everyone from Yellow down was struggling, and my romanticized view wasn't a reality for anyone but maybe the Blues and Purples. The rest of us were caught in the middle of a war for power, just hoping to survive.

Her face was full of sorrow as she turned towards me. "We *are* born White, but this world paints us crimson. There's blood on all of our hands, Ivan, directly or indirectly, even mine. My mother, she has more on hers than most, but you can't just kill her. We have her cornered in the area that matters most: the election. We are making so much progress, and when I become queen, I will have her arrested for her crimes. She will be punished, but resorting to murder does not make things right."

I took a deep breath and examined the St. Paul skyline. The old capitol building stuck out into the night sky, the lights illuminating its marble face and flag. I scowled. "I don't like it, but it is an option. Unfortunately, there's over a month until the election and longer until the coronation. How are we going to prevent her from ruining everything until then?"

She moved towards me and pulled me closer by the chest pocket of my peacoat. Her eyes stared into mine with care and passion. "Together. In everything, we do it together. Jonah, Alex, and I will all watch your back. My supporters and their families have resources as well. With everyone watching her, she wouldn't dare touch you. Mother's reputation means too much to her to sacrifice."

I wrapped my arms around her. I still was not convinced about her plan, but I loved her, and deep in my heart, I knew she was right. As I gazed back into her eyes, I accepted that if this is what it took to make things work, it was what I would have to do, even if it meant fighting the constant nagging in the back of my head every step of the way. "We'll make it work, together."

She gave me a quick kiss. "I love you."

I smiled. "I love you too." The Cathedral of St. Paul's bell clanged for nine o'clock. Both of us looked towards it for a moment before returning to each other. "We should probably head back."

She gave a soft smile, her arms still wrapped around me, "Maybe a few more minutes," and she kissed me for more than a few minutes.

Chapter 27

When General Secretary Bachton's face appeared on the TV, we were all caught off guard. It was rare for the General Secretary to give a speech in front of the People's Assembly. It was even rarer for him to do so with no announcement ahead of time.

Julia, Alex, and I had been preparing for the day's campaign meetings with various royals in Julia's room when the TV screen popped on, as always happened when the general secretary spoke. During my time at the St. Paul steel mill, I'd heard my share of stories and jokes about what people were doing in private when the "great leader" appeared on their TV, phone, and computer screens.

In her surprise, Julia dropped her notebook and knocked over a glass of water all over the letter I was writing for the Free Press. I scrambled to salvage my writing as Bachton began his speech. Between me drying the paper and Julia apologizing, we missed the start of it, but our eyes were drawn to the screen when Alex shakily pointed at it and whispered, "Guys, listen..."

Julia and my eyes met, and we thought the same thing. *If Alex is wound up, it can't be good.*

Unlike when we spoke after my release from Prison, Bachton wore a military uniform with far more medals than was believable, especially since it was well known he never served. *It's all about the show.* Behind hind his bald head was a massive bronze Prism symbol that surrounded him like a halo from a medieval painting. The members of the People's Assembly were applauding what he'd just said, and he raised his hand in recognition.

When he spoke again, his deep, powerful voice echoed through the assembly hall, "Today, we face many threats to our great collective, both internal and external. To ensure that our people can feel safe in their homes, we will be taking measures to defend against these threats." He paused and raised his round chin. "This morning, as an effort to shield ourselves, I signed an executive order declaring an official state of emergency until these threats are extinguished. The Prism and our great collective will resist the attacks of traitors who do not value the common values of this great nation and will purge the terrorists within the so called 'Fracture' from our society."

The assemblymen jumped to their feet in applause, forcing Bachton to pause.

I was the first to react, "They're taking advantage of the Fracture's attacks."

Julia nodded and placed a finger in front of her lips before nodding towards the TV. I winked at her and was met with an eye roll.

Bachton had regained control of the crowd. "Furthermore, to achieve our security goals, we will be instituting military patrols within all major cities. Color-based travel zones will be enforced by physical barriers and the military presence, allowing us to confine the terrorist threat before it is exterminated. Until the terrorists and our enemies are eliminated, we must make the necessary sacrifices for the good of the collective."

I gripped Julia's hand so forcefully that she yelped. I quickly apologized, but it was the only thing I could do to prevent myself from throwing something at the TV in rage. They were confining the colors to certain zones. The Reds that had yet to be sent to camps and many Oranges would be trapped in the slums with no escape. It would be an effective containment of the damage that the Fracture could cause, but it would also enrage even more low-colors to take up the fight. On the bright side, though, this would be a perfect recruitment tool for the Militia if Delaware and Snapback could take advantage.

Julia's eyes met mine as I shared my idea, "Our current smuggling system isn't going to work. We're going to need more supplies: food, water, whatever. We can recruit from this, but this isn't about just the Militia anymore. We need to keep people alive."

Julia nodded. "We will make sure of it. I can try to secure the supplies and find a guard that will let you through. I do not have many friends within the Front, but I will see what I can do. You should coordinate with Jonah and Delaware to find a way to handle the distribution." She paused and pursed her lips. "The Fracture is not going to tolerate this."

I shook my head. "No, they're not, but apparently the UPF isn't going to tolerate them either. While they're busy trying to start the next civil war, we'll keep people alive and win some friends along the way."

Alex stood quickly and turned off the TV as the General Secretary rambled on with closing remarks. "Ivan, let me talk to some of my friends. Depending on where they set up those barricades, we might be able to find secret routes around them."

Julia laughed and beamed at her sister. "Of course you know the secret passages around the cities. I would expect nothing less."

I ran my thumb nervously across the back of Julia's hand, trying to comfort myself more than her. "This really does change everything."

Julia squeezed my hand and whispered, almost to herself, "In the midst of chaos, there is also opportunity."

I sighed. "Sun Tzu."

She raised an eyebrow. "When did you read *The Art of War*?"

I smiled wryly. "I stole your copy a while ago." I laughed as she furrowed her brow. "Don't worry, it's back where it belongs."

She shook her head. "You do realize you can just ask to borrow any of our library's books, right?"

Alex walked towards the door, shaking her head. "You could steal anything, and you took a book? I expected better from you, Red."

I smiled, stood, and copied her sarcastic tone. "I am sorry, m'lady. I shall do better next time."

She laughed as I bowed. "Glad to hear it, Red. Let me know what you guys learn. I have *business* to attend to. Later Jules."

Julia smiled. "Talk later, Alex."

Alex shuffled out the door, leaving us alone. I sat back down and looked at our interlocked hands. "What the hell have we gotten ourselves into?"

Without a response, she squeezed my hands tighter. The anxiety in my chest eased a bit, and I rested my head against hers. In that moment, the world felt like little more than the two of us and her room. While I still felt some residual tension from last night's fight with her mom, she knew how to calm me down.

With little noise but her soft breaths to distract me, I felt the exhaustion of the past few weeks hit me all at once. We had a couple of hours until her first campaign meeting, so I just shut my eyes and took a deep breath, fading to sleep. *Enjoy this moment of peace. Chaos is coming.*

Chapter 28

St. Paul was a warzone. What little food could be scavenged had been forcefully collected by the Fracture and various other gangs days ago, leaving many Oranges and Reds with nothing left to eat.

In the days after Bachton's announcement, we started hearing the screams. The second that the walls went up and the patrols started, the Fracture had seized near complete control over the neighborhoods around West 7th Street, just north of the Mississippi. It had always been their home base, and now the walls kept their competition out. Unfortunately, the walls also kept many defenseless Oranges and Yellows in, and they were being enslaved and slaughtered. Technically only Reds were legally restricted to stay in West 7th, but with the Fracture's rapid takeover, the military had placed the neighborhood on complete lockdown.

Underground social media sites were full of horrific pictures and videos of what was happening in the neighborhood. Decapitations and torture were rampant in the Fracture's territory against those unwilling to submit to them, but the military did nothing. They sat outside the walls, content to confine them and allow them to commit mass murder against the lower colors. No one could go in to stop them, and no one could flee from them. If the Fracture somehow managed to break through the Front's containment, the city would burn, and none of the city's Oranges, Yellows, or Greens would be safe. I remembered Max's crazy call: *Crimson must rain for the sun to shine. Crimson must reign for the light to rise.*

There was nothing we could do for West 7th while the military had it locked down, but we could try to save the other slums. In a massive coordinated effort, Julia had secured food and clean water, Alex had prepared a way through the checkpoints, and I was helping transport the supplies to all the other Orange and Red restricted zones.

We knew this chaos would happen. Max had already built a reputation of decapitating non-Reds, and as I drove along the border of the restricted zone, heading towards the Militia's territory on the east-side, I tried not to picture what was being done to the innocent people on the other side of the cement wall. Even with the windows up, each cry pierced into my soul. All I could do was grip the wheel harder and drive on. As much as it hurt, we couldn't save everybody. Not from the UPF or the Fracture.

Beyond the screams, I was rattled enough already. I'd seen military patrols searching, beating, and shooting people in the streets as I drove through St. Paul. The UPF had gotten desperate. They didn't care if someone seemed like a harmless Yellow. With people growing ever angrier without food and the emerging threat of the Fracture, they were prepared to ensure order with whatever force they deemed necessary. I saw far too much crimson running down the pavement that day, but I drove on with a pit in my stomach. *We're saving everyone we can, but it's not enough.*

240

Infantrymen shot me looks as I drove, but so far, the plan was working. Using a transport van and some scrubs Alex managed to "borrow" from the Royal Hospital, I was well disguised. The military wasn't friendly with the royals, but even they wouldn't try to stop a medical van. At least we hoped they wouldn't.

As I pulled up to the gate to Payne-Phalen, a soldier looked me up and down before examining the forged papers we had Aaron print at the *St. Paul Free Press*. I tugged down on the ear flaps of my winter hat, ensuring my tag was covered. It only took a minute for him to read the papers, but it felt like hours as the glares from the other soldiers burn into my head.

The soldier grunted. "What business does the Royal Hospital have here? This is a long way from royal territory."

I sighed in fake annoyance. "Did they not tell you that Princess Alexandria has a friend that needs transporting?"

The soldier glanced back to what must have been his captain and scratched the back of his head. "They did, but I don't..."

I opened the door just enough that he could hear it *pop*. "It would be a shame if I had to call the princess all the way down here to explain the situation to a soldier who doesn't understand his place."

He shook his head, reluctant. "Fine, just go."

I gave him a smug look and slammed the door shut. He held out the papers, and I snatched them as the van lurched through the gate and into Payne-Phalen. *Too close.* They were frightened for now, but I would have to be careful on my way back out.

The neighborhood was in bad shape. It had always been a poorer part of town, but the gang conflicts over the last few months had taken a severe toll on what was left. Many Yellows, Oranges, and Reds had fled to the area from the Fracture-controlled west-side after Max took over. Now, Delaware and Snapback had brought them into the Militia's fold, making the group into somewhat of a force once again. With how bad conditions had become, they had turned the Militia's focus to defending the vulnerable lower colors and ensuring as many people as possible were cared for. The fight against the UPF was still important, but for now, we just needed to keep people alive.

I quickly ran into the Militia patrols and started handing out supplies to whoever needed them. The food and water were for the people trapped in the zone. The weapons and ammo were for the Militia to hold off the military for now. We didn't want a war, but we needed to be prepared for one. The Militia couldn't afford to be defenseless while the Fracture and UPF went at it.

When I reached the HQ, I found Snapback bent over a table, looking at El Capitan's old pool table map on the first level of the apartment building. Relief crossed his face as he saw me. I'd never seen him so stressed before. "Ivan! Maybe we won't starve to death." He ran towards me and threw himself into a hug, forcing me to catch him more than return the gesture.

All I could do was shake my head and laugh. He was one of the few people who I knew that could laugh along with me when things were at their worst. "Hopefully this stuff will hold you down for a while, but it's going to be hard to make too many more trips. They're skeptical already."

He shrugged. "We'll make due. Show me the good stuff."

I leaned against the wooden dining table he'd been using to

hold his plans and crossed my arms. Nodding towards the Reds carrying in the boxes, I responded, "Straight from the royal supply. Way better than the shit we got from Dakota." Snapback grabbed one of the rifles and held it up as if he was ready to shoot. I grabbed part of the scope and pulled it to the side. "Ever use a hybrid scope before?"

He grinned like a kid with a bucket of candy. "We can kill so many of those bastards with this. Up close or real far." He mimicked a shot, making a *pow* sound with his mouth. "Think we'll get the chance to use 'em?"

I looked up at the ceiling and then back at him as he played around with the rifle. "We've done everything to try and stop a civil war, but I think we failed. Things just keep getting worse, and until Julia becomes queen, we won't have the royal military to back us up."

He held the gun in one hand, pointing it upwards like a rebel posing for a photoshoot. "Hey, there's not much else…" In one quick swoop, Delaware popped into the room and grabbed the gun from his hands. His mouth gaped open. "Naomi!"

Del laughed. "Maybe if you'd stop playing with the guns we could actually get something done." She raised her eyebrow at me.

With my arms still crossed, I shrugged. "Not my job to babysit him. He's *your* boyfriend."

She weighed the rifle. "Don't taunt the girl with a gun in her hands."

I raised my eyebrow back. "Don't mess with the guy who has the ammo."

She laughed, put the gun down, and hugged me. "Missed you, big bro."

"Missed you too, Captain Delaware. How are things?"

Delaware hopped up onto the table and groaned. "The military has us trapped with no food, there's about to be a civil war, and we're just doing the best we can to maintain some order in the zone, so everything's peachy, thanks for asking."

Snap grabbed her hands. "But at least we've got a ton of new recruits, and with these guns, we can try to raid the camps."

I paced around the room, kicking dust with my feet. "It's a risk, but it might be the only way forward. With the military controlling the streets, there's no way we can do much in the city, and if we can free people from even just one of the camps, then we'll prove the Militia is a legitimate force again. The Fracture will look weak, unable to actually save the Reds."

Delaware puffed out her cheeks in thought. "Max will get desperate."

I nodded. "Good. She'll be more likely to slip up and either be killed by the UPF or her own fanatical followers."

Snapback sighed. "How are we going to raid the camps without the monarchy's back-up? We've got some awesome new guns, but you said so yourself, they're heavily guarded."

I resumed my pacing. "It'll be risky, but with so much of the military moved into the cities, they're leaving the camps much less defended."

Delaware cocked her head to the side. "What if you're wrong?"

I stopped. "Then we fail to save the Reds, and we'll all be dead."

Chapter 29

"I love it!" Julia's eyes lit up at the kitten in my arms. "She's adorable!"

I rocked the small kitten back and forth as it slept. "Want to hold her?"

She nodded, and I cautiously slipped it into her arms. The white ball of fur squirmed for a moment, its little blue eyes fluttering open before she sliding back into the embrace of sleep. Julia smiled at her before looking up at me. "Where did you find a cat?"

I shrugged. "She was wandering Payne-Phalen when I was on my way out. There's always stray animals running around the worst areas, but that one was just a baby. It looked desperate. Plus, it's someone's birthday next week." I winked at her.

She bit her lip and smiled cheekily before returning her eyes to the kitten. "You remembered."

Stepping forward, I stroked the top of the kitten's head with my finger. "Of course I remembered. The country is falling apart, but I can still try to be a good boyfriend. And don't worry, you'll get a less haphazard gift on your birthday if we don't all die before then."

She gave me a quick kiss. "I love you, and I appreciate the confidence."

I flopped down onto couch. "Now that I have you in a good

mood. We need to talk about the next steps."

She narrowed her eyes. "What is it?"

I avoided eye contact. "The Militia is going to raid at least one of the work camps and try to free the Reds."

Her eyes were wide with surprise. "You're going to lead them?"

I nodded. "Someone has to."

She looked at the kitten and joined me on the couch, bouncing her leg anxiously. "What about the Fracture? What if they interfere?"

I shrugged. "They're too busy with the military to do anything outside St. Paul, and the UPF is focused entirely on them. I think this is our shot to take down the camps while they're exposed."

She looked at me inquisitively. "You really have thought this through."

I smiled at the cat. It didn't smile back. "If I don't plan this right, if I mess up, a lot of people are going to die. Too many people."

Julia was shaking. "I saw those awful camps. If this is your chance, then you need to take it. You've fought hard to avoid more deaths, but I am telling you now that I understand that innocent people will die if we want to change things, and you can't blame yourself for the actions of the Front. Everyone they kill, every life they ruin, that is on them and only them."

I stroked her hand. "I never expected to hear you say that."

Her words were singed with anger. "I've seen the darkness of our world now. I was blind to it for so long, but I see the crimson staining everything, even my family. Maybe we're not all born White after all."

I tried to give her a reassuring smile. "You've been the one giving me hope all this time. You were right when you said that it's this stupid world that ruins people. I've seen so much darkness in my life, but because of that, I see the little glimmers of light more clearly. You're one of those little lights breaking through the crimson-stained darkness, Julia, and I won't let you give up like that. You're our only hope. If you give up, then there's none left for the rest of us."

She pursed her lips. "I never wanted this, any of this. I never wanted to be queen, to divide my family, to have everyone relying on me. I just wanted to be a good princess, to help people when I could. All of this, I don't know if I can do this, Ivan. Everyone is dying around us, and every second I worry if you are next. You say I'm everyone's only hope, well you're mine."

I couldn't help but laugh through the pain I felt in my chest. "We could have kept our heads down and just lived our lives, but I don't think that's either of us. You have to be queen *because* you don't want it. The path we've chosen is not the easy one, but if we don't do this, then no one will, and neither of us can live with that."

"Are you sure you haven't been stealing my philosophy books as well?"

"I took some when I became your bodyguard." She rolled her eyes and shook her head. "Hey, I had to figure out who that Ari-whatal or whatever guy was. You mentioned him in our first real conversation, so I felt like it was important to you."

She raised an eyebrow. "Aristotle. So, you were trying to find out more about what I was interested in, huh?"

I blushed and shrugged. "I plead guilty."

A wide smile crossed her face as she wiped the last of her tears away. "Well, whatever you did, it worked, but please refrain from stealing my things."

I bowed my head. "As you wish, m'lady."

The kitten, which was now tangling itself around the coffee table, let out a little yelp for attention. Julia scooped down to pick it up, and it was already purring before it was even in her arms. "We need to give her a name."

I held up my arms in surrender. "She's your cat. Not my call."

Julia narrowed her eyes as she looked to her right, thinking. After a few seconds, she looked the cat in its eyes and gave a soft smile. "Hope. We'll call her Hope."

Chapter 30

As we prepared for our assault on the camps, the situation in St. Paul continued to deteriorate. The Fracture began raids for food outside of West 7th, sparking another intense round of skirmishes between them and the military. We had no idea how they managed to hold their own in the fighting, but we knew that the more they kept the UPF occupied for now, the less attention would be paid to us.

With the fighting, though, people were afraid to even go outside. Everyone had seen the chaos in the streets, and they just wanted it to end. They hated both sides, but there was nowhere else to turn. We hoped to offer them another option, but it would take time.

Aaron had agreed to open the *St. Paul Free Press* for our planning meetings. It was a good middle point since Delaware and Snapback would never make it into the palace undercover, and it was already hard enough to get into Payne-Phalen without two princesses and the chief of palace security. Besides, Aaron liked the company.

I was driving Julia, Alex, and Jonah to the meeting in an old delivery van that we hoped would allow us to fly under the radar. Even with the Free Press being outside the restricted neighborhoods, we needed to be careful. The last thing we needed was an overambitious soldier trying to find out who was in the van.

We kept to the side roads and managed to avoid any patrols as we parked down the street. I nodded to Julia, and we both flipped up our hoods before stepping out into the night. The side door groaned as I slid it open and came face to face with Jonah. He looked uncharacteristically nervous. When I'd brought up the meeting, he'd been resistant because of the obvious risks involved, but we needed to meet in person for the plan to work. Both Julia and Alex had insisted on coming, so he had reluctantly agreed to as well out of concern for their safety.

He peaked out the doors. "Ready?"

I nodded. "Street is clear. Let's go."

He helped Alex out of the van and slid the door shut as I turned down the street. Julia took my hand as we walked. "I finally get to meet Delaware."

"I forgot you'd never met, but I'm glad you get the chance to. You'll like her, and she'll love you, everybody does."

She smiled. "It will be nice to meet part of your family." I raised an eyebrow. "You know what I mean. Your Militia family."

"Vera did a great job making sure neither of us would ever meet my real family."

She squeezed my hand. "I'm sorry, Ivan. I wish I could make it right."

I shook my head. "Nothing can, but, hopefully, we can prevent her from killing anyone else, including me, and figure out what my parents thought could destroy the UPF."

"We will confront my mother when the time comes, I promise."

I squeezed her hand back. "I trust you." We stopped walking as I looked up at the old brick building where Aaron lived. "We're here."

Letting go of Julia's hand, I used our coded knock on the door. There was a pause for a few seconds before some shuffling on the other side followed by the door popping open to reveal Aaron's smiling face. "Well if it isn't my old friend. Come on in. You guys are late."

I gave him a hug and led the rest of the group into the entryway that was little more than a hiding place for the entrance to Aaron's print shop. "How have things been at the old print shop?"

Aaron took a last look outside to ensure no one was watching before shutting and locking the door. "Considering my distribution network is ruined with these patrols and so many of my contributors are dead or missing, not well." He slid open the secret door to the print shop. "But seeing you all gives me a sense of hope."

"Glad we can give someone hope."

Aaron bowed to Julia and kissed her hand. "It is an honor to finally meet you m'lady."

Julia smiled. "And it is a pleasure to meet you. Ivan has told me much about you, and I have always been quite the fan of your work. Perhaps one day I could contribute a piece of my own if we ever succeed at eliminating the Front's control over the press."

Aaron held his hand to his heart and looked at her with awe. "You are too kind." He bowed to Alex and repeated the pleasantries. "Never in my life did I expect to have two princesses in my house."

Alex nodded. "It is impressive how you've managed to go undetected for so long."

"I've had my scares, but the Militia have always helped ensure anonymity." He smiled at me.

I faked a bow. "Always happy to help. Let's head down. Would hate to leave Delaware waiting."

We walked down the stairs and into the print room, where, as usual, the smell of ink and paper overwhelmed my nose. Waiting for us were Snapback and Delaware. I greeted Snap with an old Militia handshake before hugging Delaware. When I stepped back, I waved Julia over. "Princess Julia, meet the Captain of the Militia."

Julia smiled and met Delaware in a quick hug. "I am so excited to finally meet you. I have heard so many stories about you from Ivan. It is like I am meeting a legend."

Delaware laughed. "You feel like that? I'm meeting a princess." She looked around Julia to Alex. "Two princesses. Damn, I would have worn my nice clothes if I knew the whole royal family was coming."

Julia chuckled. "I am sure you and I will have plenty of stories to share."

I jumped up onto one of the printers, sitting on its edge. "I really don't like the sound of that."

They both laughed as Aaron said, "Ivan, why do you always have to sit on my printers?" His furrowed brow always made me smile. Those printers were his babies, and I had a knack for not respecting them because of how much I loved his reaction.

Julia gave me a side-eye that said to give in, so I made an exuberant sigh and jumped down from the printer. "Sad to see that you're still no fun, Aaron."

He chuckled. "Complimenting my paper, getting you off the printers, I like your princess already." He turned to Julia with a massive smile. "Do you know how many times I've told him not to sit on those things? If I knew all it would take to get him to follow my directions was a pretty girl backing me up, I would have changed my approach a long time ago."

Julia laughed, and I wrapped my arm around her waist. "Hey, this is my pretty girl. Get your own."

He patted the printer. "These babies are all I need in my life."

Delaware stepped forward, her voice stern. "As much as I enjoy hearing about Aaron's love life, we really need to focus."

Either she's really taking this captain position seriously or that kidnapping has gotten to her head. Maybe a bit of both.

Jonah looked around the shop, winding around the machines. "No matter what we do, there will be significant risks. We must accept that going into this, we really have no idea what we're walking into besides the little information Ivan and Julia were able to collect from the camp they saw in Wisconsin. I suggest we plan for the worst."

Silence hung in the air for a few moments before Julia spoke, "While I am usually not one for these types of missions, I have seen the horrors that occur in those camps. Many royals believe they must be freed. Even friends have asked me to convince the Royal Council to involve our troops, but the Council refused, as I expected."

Delaware spat. "Cowards."

Snapback put a hand on her shoulder. "I think what Delaware means is that it is unfortunate we will not have the support of the royal military."

Jonah quit his pacing next to Aaron. "It is unfortunate, but, and I think Julia would agree with me here, there's not much we can do until the election. Unless you want to hold off for a few more weeks, there will be no royal back-up."

Julia nodded. "While I believe that we will have enough support to win the election, I have no real power until then. The Council is controlled by my mother, and she is not interested in helping us. When I become queen, you will have the assistance of the royal military, but until then, you are on your own."

Delaware shook her head. "Then how the hell do we survive? Even with the weapons from the Whites, we can't fight tanks and an air force. This could just end up as a suicide mission, and then our people will be defenseless against the Fracture."

I made a downward motion with my hands, trying to calm her. "You might be right."

"Then why are we here?"

I looked up to the ceiling before back towards her, collecting my thoughts. "Because, Del, if we do nothing, then more of them are going to die, and we won't have enough people to fight if a real war comes. I know you're mad at Max, but there's no way for us to get to her right now. There's the whole UPF military and Fracture forces between us and her. The only way to draw her out is to convince the Reds we're their real allies."

She took a deep breath. "Fine, you might be right."

Jonah replied, "And, if I may, we do have a chance against the camp guards. It is unlikely that there will be any tanks or air force support at any of the camps. They are not built to maintain that kind of armored presence."

Snap nodded and moved on quickly. "Alright, so how many camps are we gonna hit? We don't exactly have an army."

I made eye contact with Jonah, and he nodded. "I suggest that, with your... our... limited resources, we strike hard and fast at one location, New Ulm. It will allow us to send our message and free as many Reds as possible without risking a complete failure."

I nodded. "Then one it is."

Delaware held up a hand. "Don't you think I should have a say in this as captain?"

I stepped back. "Of course. What do you think, Del?"

She looked at the ground before scanning the faces in the circle. "I wish we could save all of them, or even a couple of the camps, but if this is what it takes, if this is what we need to do, then I'm in. My only condition is that I get to name the mission this time."

We all laughed, and the ever-diplomatic Aaron stepped forward. "Make sure it's something that sounds good on a headline. Not like your solar energy rambling."

Delaware gave a smug look. "Operation Phoenix."

Her suggestion was met with a series of nods, and, with that agreement, Snapback reached into his bag and pulled out a rolled up sheet. He unbound the rubber band and let the sheet unfurl across the floor, revealing the El-Capitan's old map. "If we're going to do this, then we need a way out of the city first. We'll also need vans, and a butt load of them."

Julia smiled. "I may not be queen, yet, but I will ensure there is an adequate amount of transportation for both our troops and those we rescue. There are bound to be some spare royal vans lying around somewhere, and securing a few buses shouldn't be too difficult with some eye batting to the right people. The Front hasn't blocked access to the Enclave from the west, so we can send them through Minneapolis to meet you south of the river." Her eyes met mine, and I nodded.

Delaware sighed. "But how are we going to get to the vans? We know the passages to get beyond the walls by foot, but how do we get out of the city?" I smiled maniacally. "Ivan, I don't like that look."

I chuckled. "I hope your ice-walking has improved."

Chapter 31

We didn't leave each other's side for a couple of days before the raid. It took a lot for Julia to accept what we needed to do to free the Reds from the New Ulm camp. We had become more than just a team or a couple in the recent months. We'd survived so much trauma together that even when so many forces wanted to drive us apart, we needed each other more than anything. The constant campaign meetings kept her mind busy, but I could tell the anxiety stuck with her. She clung to me like each moment could be our last, her wintergreen perfume hanging in the air wherever we went.

Operation Blackout had been one of the hardest things I'd ever done, but Operation Phoenix tore at my heart in a different way. This mission was more than just putting my life on the line to save the trapped Reds, it was risking everything for her as well, and that hurt. I knew how alone she'd feel while I was being shot at, and I wished there was something I could do to make it better. There wasn't. There was only the time we had together in the present. The touch of her skin against mine and the warm feeling of her in my arms was what reminded me why I needed to live no matter what. I loved that amazing girl, and no bastard with a gun was going to ruin the happiness I felt just thinking about her.

The morning of mission day, we just lay in bed feeling the air fill and flee from each other's lungs. Neither of us wanted to leave.

I could have stayed there forever and forgotten the Prism, forgotten the Fracture, and forgotten all the responsibilities I had. Julia had been quiet for what felt like hours. I knew she hadn't slept well as the thoughts of the mission haunted her. Eventually, though, she broke the silence. "When you first became my bodyguard, you said you believed in a peaceful resolution to all of this. Do you still believe in that?"

I kissed the back of her neck. "I think there is a way to fix things without another war. I thought it would be easier than this, but there is still hope."

She breathed deeply. "What if a war comes anyway?"

"Then we will fight for survival, for those we love, and for a better future. That's all we can do, fight until the end."

She took a shaky breath. "That reminds me of an old poem. I don't remember much of it, but I know the ending:

And you, my father, there on the sad height,

Curse, bless me now with your fierce tears, I pray.

Do not go gentle into that good night.

Rage, rage against the dying of the light."

My mind felt drained. "I can't tell if that's sad or beautiful."

She rolled over to face me, her caring eyes studying my face. "I think it's both." I smiled at her and moved her hair over her ear as she spoke again, "Promise me you'll come back."

I kissed her. "My heart will never leave you." She didn't accept that answer and scrunched her nose. "I promise that I will always come back. Just try not to get kidnapped by your insane ex this time."

She playfully scowled at me. "He wasn't my ex!"

I kissed her again. "Didn't mean I wasn't jealous of him for a while."

She bit her lip. "Oh, I know."

"That obvious?"

She chuckled. "Ivan, you can fool dictators and mass murdering zealots, but you cannot fool me."

"Well, then I'm glad, because that means you're not a dictator or a mass murdering zealot. In this country, that's about all it takes to be queen."

There was a knock at the door. She sighed, and I groaned. We both rolled out of bed, and I answered the door.

Jonah was looking way too well rested. "It's time to go." He peeked in at Julia and smiled to himself. "I hope you slept well."

I bit my cheek and chuckled. "I'll be ready in a minute. Meet you at the garage."

He nodded and waved to Julia, who returned the gesture, before turning back down the hallway.

I looked back towards Julia. "I'll be back soon."

She glided towards me. "Be careful. Coyote may be dead, but please save those people." She gripped my shirt and looked down at her shaking hands. "I wish I could do more."

I kissed her forehead. "You are doing more than anyone else in your position would. We're fighting so *you* can end all this, and besides, I would rather not worry about you being shot during the raids. You've had enough scares outside those camps. Do your thing here: inspire the kids, convince the Whites, and keep an eye on your mom."

She struggled to smile as I wrapped her in my arms. "I shall do my best."

Chapter 32

We waited for sunset before making our way towards the Mississippi. Moving almost a hundred armed Yellows, Oranges, and Reds through the St. Paul streets would be difficult, even in the dark. We would be sneaking through multiple zones that were patrolled by both the military and various minor gangs. Despite our numbers and guns, we wanted to avoid any conflicts or loud noises until we reached the New Ulm camp; anything that made the UPF suspicious could ruin the mission and kill us all.

Alex's connections had revealed a passageway through an abandoned building on the southern edge of the neighborhood that would allow us to escape. The back wall of an old house was so cracked that a person, with all their gear, could easily slide through.

The smell of mold and rotting wood filled the air as Delaware and I led the way into the house. Each of our steps creaked the floorboards. *Step carefully.* It was obvious that no one had lived in the place for at least a decade, probably longer.

The Payne-Phalen neighborhood had been a low priority for the UPF to rebuild after the war, so it wasn't a surprise to see another building in this shape. The neighborhood had always been inhabited by mostly Oranges and less well-off Yellows, but with the forced evacuation of the Enclave, the Red refugees almost outnumbered the other colors combined. It was a miracle that Delaware and Snapback had managed to unite most of the people behind the Militia in such terrible conditions.

Del was growing up quickly. I was proud and worried about her at the same time. She knew how to work hard and unite people, but she also had a strong desire for revenge. If she could use her rage against the Fracture to keep rebuilding the Militia, she would do great things. If she held onto that rage too tightly, though, it would burn her to ashes. I'd seen it happen too many times before. *She's better than that, I hope.*

Her flashlight scanned the floor, making sure there were no holes before we moved to the back of the house. She called back to the rest of the group, "Grab hold of someone's arm. If you fall through, they'll hopefully catch you."

There was a murmuring of agreement and repetition of the instructions to those further back before Delaware nodded and turned, shining the light onto the crack.

I touched her arm. "Keep it away from the hole. If someone outside sees it, we're screwed."

She nodded and swallowed, trying to hide her nerves. The flashlight turned off with a *click*, leaving us in the dark. Delaware looked through the crack and then back at me. "Can you go first and scout a good place for everyone to wait until the whole group is through? I want to stay back and make sure everything is fine back here."

I tried to give her a reaffirming smile, but my own nerves were on end. This was the riskiest thing we'd done yet, and we both knew it. "If anything goes wrong, pull everyone back, promise me."

She breathed out shakily, a puff of fog filling the gap between us. "I promise."

I pulled the rifle off my back and climbed through the crack, returning to the frigid March night. The snow still lingered on the streets, and each step I took created a *crunch* that left me hoping each time that there was no one nearby to hear it.

My breaths fogged up the air as I scanned the street. *Empty.* We were in the clear. I turned back towards the house and whispered, "Clear. Send 'em."

The first of the Militia members climbed through, and I made my way across the street, towards a park with some trees that would provide good cover while we waited. I never lowered my gun completely. There was no way to know where the patrols would be, or if there were any gangs looking for trouble. Fortunately, there were neither so far, and soon, everyone had gathered within the park.

Jonah had taken up the rear and nodded to me when he arrived. With one look at me, Delaware signaled once again for me to take lead, and I waved on our people. We'd made it out of Payne-Phalen, but we still had a more than two mile walk to the Mississippi. There was no time to lose.

We crossed over Phalen Boulevard and approached Dayton's Bluff, winding through various houses to avoid any patrols that might be on the street. Like West 7th, Dayton's Bluff was restricted to only Reds in an effort to control the conflicts in the area. While the Fracture had a larger presence in the western edge of town, they had a smaller force here as well, and the result was a battle for territory between them and the gangs that had held control of the neighborhood for years. The fighting was still scattered, though, with the Fracture focusing mainly on maintaining control of their home territory and terrorizing the neighboring area of Cathedral Hill.

The residents of Dayton's Bluff either didn't notice us or were too used to seeing armed men moving through their neighborhood to care. For so many at this point, they just didn't want to die. The Reds in much of the area had avoided being sent to the camps for now, and many wanted to keep quiet to avoid the terrible fate that would await them there. Those in the Enclave hadn't been so lucky.

Shots rang out as we crossed over the highway and approached the river. I radioed to Jonah, "What was that?"

Jonah's voice crackled through my earpiece. "It was a couple blocks west of here. Sounded like military or Fracture. I can't imagine the gangs having that heavy of weapons."

Delaware came in, "Do we wait or keep moving?"

Jonah waited for a moment, listening as more shots echoed across the neighborhood. "They're coming from north of the highway. We should be good. Just move quickly, could be a patrol."

I took a deep breath. *Keep going.* "Roger that." I motioned to the squad around me and kept pushing south through the snowy streets.

For the remainder of our trip we could hear the skirmish continuing, but it never came closer. Whoever was fighting seemed entrenched on the northern end of the neighborhood, likely near the wall separating Dayton's Bluff from the Downtown zone. If the Fracture and military were clashing there, then something had to be up, but I didn't have time to worry about that now. We had enough problems ahead of us already.

The first of those problems was right in front of us as we passed through a small line of trees: the Mississippi River. With the freezing temperatures, it had been iced over for months, but it was difficult to know how thick the ice was, and we didn't have time to find out.

Delaware and Snapback joined me along the riverbank. Snap had a smug look on his face as he looked to Del. "Darn. I forgot to bring my Delaware-saving swimsuit."

She smirked and punched his arm. "Shut up."

Still Del.

I climbed down the bank of the river and tested my weight on the ice. It groaned in response but didn't crack. "We should only go a couple at a time, otherwise it could send us all under."

Delaware raised her eyebrows and pointed forward with an open hand. "Ladies first."

I rolled my eyes. "Since I abandoned you last time, I guess it's more than fair."

Snapback smiled, waiting for the entertainment to begin.

I sighed and swung my rifle over my back. *Second time's the charm?* With a quick breath, I stepped onto the ice and began to shuffle my way across the river. The ice held firm despite the groaning noise it made with each step. *Just keep moving.*

I called back to the group. "Come on out, the water's a great temp!"

Delaware looked at Snap, who held her hand as they stepped onto the ice together, leading the crowd bit by bit. *Cute. Stupid, but cute.*

Progress was slow. Each step could mean the end of me and many others if the ice cracked. The kid in me loved that I was finally crossing the river successfully. The adult in me kept telling me how stupid this was. To be honest, it was not the greatest idea in the world, but we didn't have any other options. The Enclave had already become a ghost town, and the military had closed down every bridge leading into it to prevent Red attempts to re-settle it. We had no choice but to cross over the ice if we wanted to reach the vans that Julia had arranged to meet us on the other side.

After what felt like an eternity, I reached the bank and raised my arms in victory like an Olympic athlete winning the gold. Then I turned around. *Damn it...*

While Delaware, Snapback, and many of the Militia fighters were almost to the shore as well, a large fracture had been made in the ice. With each step those in the back took, smaller cracks spread along the ice around them. They were trapped.

I put my finger to my ear. "Talk to me, Jonah."

He instructed each of the fighters around him where to step before responding, "This definitely isn't an optimal situation."

"Is there anything we can do to help?"

"No, just stay off the ice. The less weight on here the better. We should be fine if nobody does anything stupid."

Delaware reached the shore with Snap and smirked at me. "Then Ivan should definitely stay off the ice."

I laughed. "Alright. Take your time. I'd rather delay things than lose you guys. The last thing I want to explain to Vera is how I managed to drown her chief of security."

Delaware cut in again, "If that happened, she might try to kill you. Oh wait..."

Jonah's laugh crackled intermittently over the radio. "Please don't make me laugh while I'm trying to be careful."

He was past the fracture in the ice now, and the rest of his group had nearly reached the shore. Jonah, though, was tailing the slowest of the group, just in case. They were making progress. It was just hard to tell if it was *enough* progress as the cracks expanded behind them.

Just when I thought they were clear, a large snapping noise cut across the river and the fighter next to Jonah slid through the ice, leaving a small hole behind. Jonah cried out and dove for the man's arm, trying to save him before the current pulled him downstream and away from the hole. He held on for dear life, gripping onto the fighter's arm underwater but was unable to pull him up. To make matters worse, he was slowly sliding towards the hole himself as the current pulled the fighter away.

Without thinking, I dropped my gear and sprinted back onto the ice, sliding my way towards Jonah. A few years ago, I had left Delaware behind on the ice. I wouldn't make the same mistake again.

Each step cracked the ice a little bit more as I closed in on the only royal guard who ever cared about me. He was always the real hero, and now his bravery had put his own life in danger. A few months before, he saved me. I needed to return the favor.

He leveraged himself on the other edge of the hole as half his body was now submerged. I slid over and grabbed onto him, trying to pull him out. He wouldn't budge, though, as the current continued to pull the fighter below the surface. I needed help, but any more people on the ice would risk a complete collapse. Finally, I gave up pulling. "Jonah, let go!"

He yelled in pain. "No! We have to save him."

"Jonah, trust me. Let go."

He looked at me, his face desperate, but he did what I said. In quick succession, he let go and pulled himself back onto the ice as I dove into the freezing water. My body screamed in pain the second my head hit the water. It was the coldest I had ever felt in my life, and it stabbed at my exposed skin, demanding my body give in. I refused.

The fighter was motionless. The current had carried him only a few yards away, but with his gear, he was being dragged towards the bottom. With all that extra weight, he never had a chance, and neither did Jonah. I swam after him, closing the distance as quickly as I could, but my lungs were already screaming for air when I reached him. I had never been the best swimmer, and this was far beyond anything I'd ever done before, but I had to try. I unclipped his backpack and forced the straps off his arms, still trying to fight the current.

The pack slid off his back and drifted towards the bottom. With my lungs emptier than they'd ever been, I grabbed a hold of him and kicked as hard as I could, pushing back towards the hole, which now felt like it was a mile away. My body was numbing to the cold, and each kick took everything I had. My head joined my lungs in the screams for air. The darkness began to close in on my vision. *This is not how I die.*

In the end, I was swimming blind, just hoping to reach the hole before my body gave in. Against all odds, my head broke through the surface, and Jonah cried out something that I couldn't understand. I was too busy gasping for air and trying to keep the fighter's head above the surface as Jonah tried to grab hold of him. Eventually, his hands managed to grip the fighter, and, together, we moved him back onto the ice.

Jonah quickly began CPR as I struggled to pull myself out of the water. There was nothing to grab on to, and I groaned in pain, sliding back down until something caught my arm. I looked up to see Delaware grinning down at me. "Didn't think I'd let you drown, did you?"

I shook my head and pulled myself out with her help. The cold air struck my wet skin and clothing like a wave. It felt worse than being stabbed or shot, and I'd felt both before. My body was overwhelmed, and I could feel it just struggling to hold on as Delaware helped me shuffle towards the shore.

Without the energy to look up, I could only sputter to Delaware, "Is he alive?"

Delaware looked back. "He's breathing."

I took a deep breath and shivered. "Thank God."

"What were you thinking?"

I groaned as my legs struggled forward. "That if I didn't do something, someone was going to die because of my plan to cross the river, and Jonah was going to die trying to save him. He's too brave to know when a cause like that is lost."

She scoffed. "Says the guy that dove into the frickin' freezing water."

I smiled. "It worked, didn't it?"

She shook her head. We were at the shoreline, and Snapback tried to take over for her, but I shrugged both of them off. "I'm fine."

I tried to take a step without either of their support, and Snapback had to catch me as I stumbled. "Yeah, you're doing great buddy."

I scowled at him. "One more word from your mouth and I'll throw that stupid hat into the river."

He laughed. "I'd like to see you try."

With Snap's help, I met up with the rest of the group at the vans while Delaware went back to make sure Jonah and the fighter made it to shore. He was in worse shape than I was. His eyes looked lost, and he coughed every couple seconds as his body spasmed. Jonah helped him into one of the vans before joining me in the leaders' one. "That was one of the most reckless things I've ever seen in my life."

I groaned as the hot air from the vents poured over me. It felt like my skin was fighting a war with the air temperature, and my mind spun. "You saved me when I was in over my head. Was just returning the favor."

He shook his head and chuckled. "You really are full of surprises, Ivan. I'm just glad you're alive."

I laughed, which was painful as my lungs were still angry with me, and I had a coughing fit before finally responding, "You're telling me Hell is worse than this? Shit."

He patted me on the back. "And I'm sure the princess will love to hear how you almost killed yourself."

I looked up at the roof of the van and groaned again. "Maybe you should just kill me."

Delaware turned around to look back at us. "Hell no. If I have to live through this shit, then you don't get to just die. You're going to suffer through it with me."

"Real friends keep each other alive to ensure the other one suffers just as much as they do."

She smiled cheekily. "Damn right!"

Snapback turned around too. "We've got probably two hours or so until we get to New Ulm. Take the time to recover now, Ivan, because we're going to need you."

I sighed and laid my head back. "At least if they shoot me it'll feel better than this."

Chapter 33

The New Ulm camp was different that the one we'd seen in Wisconsin. Instead of shoddily built tents in an open field to house the Reds, they were living in the remnants of a city that was destroyed during the Third Civil War. The buildings were nothing but ash foundations and the occasional half-a-roof. From a distance, we could see the snow-covered areas they were forced to sleep in. *It's a miracle they've survived this long.*

I scanned the camp with the long range scope on my rifle. There were also no sniper pedestals, unlike the Wisconsin camp, but machine gun nests had been setup on each side of the camp. Fortunately for us, though, the city was far from an open field, and there would be ways to avoid the machine gun fire if we were careful.

Delaware, Jonah, and I each took about a third of our fighters in an effort to surround the camp. An assault from the eastern side was impossible due to the Minnesota River running along the camp's eastern edge; none of us wanted to try walking across a frozen river more times than we had to.

My team was on the southern flank, which had a forest running right up to the barbed wire that surrounded the camp. The machine gunner was far from where we'd enter, and with the tree cover, it was unlikely they'd hit us anyway. Search lights constantly ran through the trees, but the forest was thick enough to cover us in the night.

Slowly, we advanced towards the barbed wire and reached the tree line. There was no going back now. "South flank in position."

Jonah radioed back. "Western flank in position."

We didn't hear anything from Delaware. "Del, what's your status."

After a few seconds, she came in with a whisper, "They're a couple yards away. We're not in position, but this will have to do until they pass."

I sighed. "Okay. Be careful everybody, and remember, the goal is to free the Reds, not to get caught up in a massive firefight. Good luck."

I nodded to my team, and we emerged from the woods one at a time, carefully making our way through the barbed wire. My body was still in shock from my plunge into the river, but now, adrenaline overpowered the pain. This was a moment I'd been waiting for, and I needed to be ready.

We scattered behind various buildings. I crouched near a central one, where my team could see my signals. I had a clear sight of the road in case any patrols came by, and I signaled to wait as two Green guards approached, their rough voices and heavy footsteps covering the shuffling of my team members taking their positions. We'd have to wait until they passed. Even with the military focused on the major cities, we were sure to be outnumbered, and any gunshots would bring the rest of the camp's guards down on us before we had time to escape.

The guard further away was speaking, "You hear about what's going down in St. Paul? Sarge says high command is getting antsy.

We're losing a lot of people for that shithole of a city, and they don't think it's worth it."

The closer one laughed. "If it's full of Reds like these, I'd just bomb the shit out of it. It'd make our jobs easier. Hell, hit those bastard royals while you're at it, but leave the princesses alive for us..."

My body tensed, and I almost broke my own orders and shot the guy on the spot for talking about Julia and her sisters like that. The mission came first, though. I couldn't let my personal feelings ruin our chance to save the Reds.

Soon, the patrol passed, and we snuck across the street. I shivered from both fear and the cold as I approached the next building. There were two sleeping Reds, huddled together for warmth with nothing more than a thin blanket wrapped around them.

My heart raced, but the camp remained silent as I woke them carefully. Their hollow eyes were wide as I held a finger to my lips and gestured for them to follow. They were slow, though, and I realized how weak they really were when they stepped into the moonlight. Their ragged, ripped clothing hung loosely on their bruised bodies. They shivered as I guided them back towards the safe point we'd established near where we'd entered the camp. We'd left a few of our fighters behind to cut the wire and guide the Reds through to the waiting buses.

The man was in his thirties at least, but it was impossible to tell for sure with the starvation. Based on the length of his unshaven beard, he'd been there since the beginning. After I checked for patrols, he and his wife followed me back across the street and to the safe point. When we reached it, I handed them over to the fighters, but as I turned to leave, I felt his bony hand grip my arm. I looked back at him. He whispered, his voice weak, "Save the children, please..."

From the sorrow in his eyes, I knew he was telling the truth, but there weren't supposed to be Blacks in there. The children had always been technically exempt from the worst punishments against the Reds. Had that changed?

I could only nod in response, and they scurried towards the exit. I felt an enormous weight on my chest as I watched them go. *That could have been me if it wasn't for Julia.* I shook the thought. There was no time to think about my luck. We still had a long way to go.

Each building I found had another group to take back. Every one of them was in the same awful condition as the first couple. With the food shortages across the country, apparently the Front had decided to barely feed them, if they were fed at all. Meanwhile, Bachton and his cronies sat in their fancy restaurants in Minneapolis and laughed as people starved in their "work cities." *We'll get our revenge.*

The groups we saved all gave me the same look and confirmed the stories about the kids. They were being kept together, deeper in the camp. We'd heard the rumors throughout St. Paul of the Black Tags taken from the Enclave and other areas, but we'd assumed they'd been taken to the orphanages, not here. I knew how bad those orphanages were, but they weren't the literal Hell that was these camps. *No child deserves this.*

I needed to pass the information along to Jonah and Delaware, so I paused after dropping off what could have been my tenth or fiftieth group. "Hey guys, you hearing this stuff about the kids?"

Jonah was the first to respond, "A few people have mentioned them being held near the center square. I thought they weren't taking Blacks?"

Delaware groaned. "Welcome to our life. Kids of Reds will always be Reds, even if their tag is Black."

I thought for a second about our strategy. "We need to make it a priority to gets those kids out, no matter what."

Jonah crackled through again. "Agreed. Ivan and my teams are the closest to the central strip, so we'll both work our way down there. Delaware, keep sweeping the north."

I nodded. "Roger that."

I let out a deep breath in a puff of fog. My body had already begun to numb to the snow and the wind. I felt like I stood on the edge of a dark void. There was no way to know what condition we'd find those kids in, and I didn't know if I was prepared for it. Someone had to save them, though. It didn't matter if I was ready or not.

After relaying the message to my team, I continued finding Reds and showing them back to the safe point. The patrols were occasional, but with the state the Reds were in, they didn't seem worried about them trying to escape. Most of the guards must have been back at the barracks near the center of camp, right where we were headed.

We were only a few blocks away from the center strip when the first shots rang across the camp, followed by a series of screams, shouting, and a blast. "What's going on? Guys?"

Coughing came over the radio as Delaware spoke, "They spotted us. We're in a shootout, and they're not afraid to use grenades with the Reds around."

It was inevitable that we'd be spotted eventually, but my heart still sunk when she said it. *The deaths are on them. We're saving everyone we can.* "Do you want back-up?"

"No, get out everyone you can. We'll hold them for now."

We did our best. Every moment was a blur, scrambling to escort anyone I could find to safety as we got closer and closer to the kids. I carried more people than I could count. I'd forgotten the pain from the frozen river. This was life or death; my sore muscles could wait.

As we went on, more and more shots rang out, and the screams became deafening. *What is happening?* Delaware's group was still pinned down on the northern edge, but their firefight had drawn almost all the guards from our area, so my team just pushed deeper, working in silence. Even if we could talk, I don't know what we could say. The horrors we saw that night scarred me for the rest of my life, and things only got worse.

The smell did not hang around the whole camp like it did in Wisconsin, but it hit us close to its center. The further in we went, the stronger the smell became, and I began to understand the screams. There were bodies everywhere. Their wounds were fresh, and some of the injured Reds were still alive, crying for help. I did everything I could to hold back a torrent of tears as I saw the carnage. The UPF had butchered these innocent people and left those who lived to suffer as they bled out.

I tried to bandage as many of their wounds as I could and carry them safety. For many of them, though, they were too weak and had lost too much blood. With shuddered breaths, they pleaded with me for help as the life slipped from their eyes. I was powerless to stop it. Everywhere I looked, there was another slaughtered Red, another life stolen by the UPF.

Sorrow and rage filled me at the same time, and my voice sounded distant when I called over the radio, "They're killing everyone. They're all dead."

Even when we thought we could surprise them, we'd fallen into the UPF's trap. They must have had orders to kill the Reds if a raid ever occurred, and when they realized what was going on, that's exactly what they did.

Delaware's voice came weakly over the radio. "We're pulling back. There's too many guards. We got a lot out, but there's bodies everywhere."

Jonah came next. "My team is pinned down too."

I shook my head. "No. There's still kids. We can't just leave them."

Jonah's voice was shaky. "My team has to pull back, but I'll try to find a way to meet you on the south side of the strip. Get your team to clear the rest of the area and escort the people out."

My whole body shook with rage. We had saved so many from this terrible fate, but I couldn't let so many more suffer. "Roger that."

I looked at the carnage in front of me. Buildings were on fire, and the rising smoke obscured the light from the moon. As the screams pierced through the night, I felt like I was in a horror movie. With a deep breath, I relayed the signal to my team before clenching my fists and charging forward. *Rage, rage against the dying of the light.*

Soon, I reached the edge of the central square and waited for Jonah behind a half-demolished brick wall, just high enough to hide me from the guards' sights. They were everywhere, shouting and shooting at fleeing Reds. The flames were all that exposed the figures that fled from them.

I wanted to stop them more than anything, but there were too many. With the obscured moonlight, though, it would be difficult for them to see me.

Jonah arrived soon, panting and groaning. "There's so many dead."

I closed my eyes, wincing as I pictured the bodies I'd passed. "I know. Hopefully, they haven't touched the kids."

Jonah nodded his head towards an old schoolhouse a block down. "They're in there."

I followed his gaze. The schoolhouse was one of the few buildings in half-way decent shape. Maybe there was hope for the kids. To get there, though, we'd have to sneak down the crowded street. Luckily, there were plenty of bombed walls we could hide behind.

With a quick breath, I leapt over the wall and snuck to the next building when the guards were turned away. Jonah joined me, but before we could continue, machine gun fire echoed from down the street. The whole world seemed to shake with each shot, rattling me to the bone.

I tapped my radio. "Del, everything alright?"

Her panicked voice flew through the static. "They're firing that damn machine gun at us. We're all out, but holy shit that thing is loud."

I breathed a sigh of relief. "Glad you're alright. Stay safe."

She forced a laugh. "Safe as I can be while being shot at."

Jonah nodded to me, and we crept between buildings as we approached the eerily quiet schoolhouse. *Please be alive.*

The street was clear at this end. The guards were busy fighting our teams as they tried to prevent the Reds from escaping. We took one last look down the street before vaulting over the last wall and sprinting towards the schoolhouse. I grabbed the door handle and pulled to no avail. *Locked.*

Jonah motioned for me to follow, and we crept along the brick schoolhouse wall to a side entrance that was cracked open. Pushing open the door, we entered a pitch black hall and flicked on our guns' flashlights. We moved slowly through the hall, checking behind all the doors. *Where are they?*

A tight feeling gripped my chest as we turned down the next hall. There was nothing there, but my gut told me to keep going. After checking all the doors, we reached the end of the hall, and I stopped as a sound caught my ear: a boot on the tile floor.

I grabbed Jonah and dove towards an open doorway as the hall exploded into gunfire. We forced ourselves to our feet inside the small classroom, trapped with who knows how many guards shooting at us. I took a shaky breath and pointed to the door connecting the classroom to the next one. If we could get there without them noticing, we could get around them as they tried to corner us.

Jonah understood what I meant and nodded before following

me through to the next room. It was the same layout to the one before it, and as the sound of the gunfire still filled the hallway outside, we locked the door between the rooms and piled as many things in the way as possible. It was our turn to trap them.

The shots died down as the guards moved closer to check if they'd gotten us. We hid on either side of the open hall door as they passed by, biding our time. There were four of them, two for each of us. I looked at Jonah and counted down with my fingers. On one, we spun through the open doorway and took them out from behind in quick succession. The shots echoed in the small hallway, and my ears rang from the noise.

I quickly spun to check there was no one else in the hall and could only breathe when I saw it was clear. "Now what?"

Jonah sighed. "They had to be guarding something. Likely back down that other hall. We're close."

I nodded, and we backtracked towards the first hallway, turning the other direction. With the attack before and the eerie darkness, goosebumps crept up my arms. We needed to find the kids and get out of there fast. The other guards would be closing in soon.

Jonah snapped to get my attention and pointed at the sign for the gym. We crept over to it, preparing for the worst as he tried to push open the door. It was locked. At this point, stealth was irrelevant after our shootout, so I shot the lock, and the door crept open.

Whimpers came from inside as we entered and shone our flashlights across the room. At least a hundred little faces stared back at us in fear, not understanding what was going on. There were no other guards; they must have just left the four behind to watch the kids.

I lowered my gun. "It's alright. We're here to get you guys out."

Smiles filled the kids' faces as they jumped to their feet and rushed towards us. It was obvious they hadn't been fed well as their bony bodies hugged my legs, but they were in much better shape than the adults outside. There was no excuse for what the UPF had done to them, but it was a massive relief to see them all alive.

A smile crossed my face for the first time that night, and I felt a tear slide down my cheek. These kids would be safe soon. We just had to get them out.

I held my finger to my lips, telling them to be quiet as we guided them through the halls and out of the schoolhouse. The older ones helped keep the younger ones in line as we stepped back into the freezing night. Gunshots still rang from the other end of the camp, but the street was as clear as it could be, so we sprinted across it and down a side path, heading back towards where we'd entered the camp.

I radioed to Delaware and Snapback, "We've got the kids and are on our way. How's the evac effort?"

Snapback crackled through. "We're cramming them into the buses, but so far so good. You need to hurry. We can't hold them off too much longer."

"Roger that. We're on our way."

As we winded through the side streets and empty buildings, I kept looking back to check that the kids were all still there. With the fighting pulling the guards away, there were no guards in sight, but we needed to be careful. If we were detected, every-thing we'd just done would have been for nothing, and over a hundred innocent kids would die.

I signaled to the rest of the group to stop as I heard a few guards' voices coming from around the corner. Taking a deep breath, I slid along the wall to the corner and peaked around it to see if I could count how many guards there were. From what I could tell, there were at least three of them, enough to cause a problem. They were huddled on the opposite end of the narrow street, firmly in range of my rifle, but I couldn't afford to make that much noise. The last thing we needed was more guards swarming the kids.

Jonah crept up next to me, glancing at the guards before mov-ing back into hiding. "What's the plan?"

I nodded back towards the Black Tags. "Watch the kids. There might be other guards."

"You sure?"

I smirked. "I'm better at handling guards than palace drama. I've got this."

While Jonah shuffled back towards the kids, I slid my rifle off my back and instead pulled two of my hidden knives. *Just like the good old days.* I counted down from three in my head, and on one, I bolted around the corner and aimed at the guard in the center, facing towards me. He quickly noticed me, but before he had time to do anything more than widen his eyes in surprise, I threw my knife threw his forehead, and his body slumped to the ground with a *thud.*

The other guards both reached for their guns as I lunged to-wards the one on my right, slicing at his wrist with my second knife before sweeping his leg and knocking him to the ground. Before I could turn to face the second guard, he grabbed me from behind and held his arm tight against my throat as he spat, "How many of you Red assholes do we have to kill before you get the point?"

"More than that," I said as the guard I'd knocked to the ground returned to his feet and pulled his gun. Using the weight of the guard holding me, I flung myself back and kicked at the gun, knocking it out of his hand. In his surprise, the one behind me loosened his grip, and I impaled my knife in this thigh before breaking free of his grasp. He cried out as I spun, pulled the knife from his thigh, and drove it into his head. *How many of you UPF assholes do we have to kill before you get the point?*

A gun cocked behind me as the guard fell to the ground. I raised my hands in surrender. *Maybe I'm a little rusty.*

The final guard said, "Turn around."

I did, still with my hands raised. He stood further away this time, having learned his lesson with my last kick. I thought I was doomed, but beyond his head, I saw a little figure making its way through the rubble and towards us. The boy was covered in ash, but I could see his sharp brown eyes focused solely on me. Slowly, I nodded to him as he approached.

The boy needed time that I didn't have, so I tried to stall. "Why do you guys do it? What do you gain from killing innocent peo-ple?"

A grin crossed the guard's face. "You don't look so innocent."

Glancing down at my bloodied clothes and the two bodies lying around me, I felt a twang of guilt. *Those kids just watched someone they considered a hero kill two people.* I wouldn't have killed them if I had a choice, but it scared me sometimes how easily I could do it when I had to.

The guard tightened his grip around the trigger. "Have fun in Hell."

Before he could shoot, the boy kicked him in the balls from behind, and I lunged at the guard as the gun wavered from my head. I fell on top of him and saw the boy watching as I struggled to hold my adversary down. For a moment, the boy disappeared as I delivered punch after punch, bloodying the guard's face before I looked up to see his small hand offering me the pistol. *You have a choice now.* I looked down at the guard and felt the raging fire within my chest. These men had starved and slaughtered innocent people, they'd ignored the cries of suffering children, and they felt no guilt for it. *Does he deserve to live?*

As I looked into that boy's eyes, though, I could only think of the future. The circle of death had to end somewhere. These kids needed to be taught mercy, or we would never be able to fix things.

I grabbed the gun and examined it for a second before checking the safety and sliding it into an empty holster. I said to the boy, "They might see us as murders and animals, but we're better than that, better than them."

The boy just gazed at me, studying my every move. I turned my head back towards the guard, now dazed on the ground, and delivered a knockout blow to his head. Even if I couldn't kill him, he needed to be out long enough for us to escape. We couldn't afford to let him alert another set of guards.

As I stood, Jonah approached with the rest of the Black Tags and handed me my rifle. "Nice work, though, I would not recommend using children to fight the Front in the future."

I rolled my eyes. "Point taken. Let's go. We're almost there."

Soon, we reached the barbed wire and helped the kids climb through the area we'd cut out before. Their little faces were a mix of fear and excitement. Many of them looked up at me with recognition but didn't speak. I had to laugh a little; I was a bit of a celebrity to these kids, but all that really mattered was that they were alive, and they'd be okay.

Delaware's face was contorted with emotion when we emerged from the forest. She and Snapback had waited for me as the rest of the buses drove the freed Reds to safety. "Just when I thought you'd used your reckless quota for the night..."

I wasn't in the mood for her sarcasm, and I helped the little Black Tags into the last bus before jumping into our van. Snapback signaled to the teams to return to the vans as the bus took off. The fighters hastily retreated towards the vans as the shots from the guards closed in, and once everyone was loaded up, we sped off, back towards St. Paul.

Jonah finally spoke as the van started moving. He smiled at me. "It was reckless, but brave."

I shut my eyes and leaned my head against the seat in front of me. "Brave, reckless, whatever. All those Reds, they're all dead because of us."

Delaware put her hand on my back. "No, they're dead because

the UPF decided power means more than life."

With all the rage I felt in my heart, I punched the seat in front of me and yelled, "Don't you get it? They massacred those people because we raided the camp. If it wasn't for us, they'd still be alive."

Jonah spoke softly from the front, "If it wasn't for us, every single person in those buses would still be trapped, both kids and adults doomed to starve or freeze to death. We cannot control what the Front does."

There was only silence in the van. When I looked up, everyone was crying. We all saw the horrors of the camp and the massacre that occurred in front of our eyes. This was only one of the camps, and now, the others would be prepared for an attack. So many innocent people suffered because of the Prism and Bachton's tyranny. I promised myself that we would make him pay.

There were no victory rallies or cheering crowds when we returned to St. Paul. Instead, the mood was somber as we resettled the freed Reds and Blacks in the Enclave. The UPF believed that, with the Enclave emptied and sealed off from St. Paul, there was no longer a reason to patrol the area. With thousands of Reds to resettle, it would have been impossible to shuttle them all across the Mississippi. Quietly moving them into the dilapidated houses on the southern edge of the Enclave was the best option we had for now.

Even if the freed Reds would now be separated from the Militia's new base in Payne-Phalen, supply runs to the Enclave would actually be easier. Instead of going through the gates at each neighborhood, we could go from the royal territory in western

Minneapolis, drive around the military's control of St. Paul, and enter the Enclave from the south.

If we could successfully repopulate the Enclave, the Militia would control two of the largest parts of the city, turning the chaos of the forced relocations into an opportunity to expand. It didn't fix the horrible suffering the government inflicted on those Reds, but it meant we could grow in power, hopefully preventing it from ever happening again. We had taken one step towards that goal with the raid, but there was a long way to go.

After everything that had happened that night, we were zombies. I wanted to feel proud for saving most of the people from the camp, but a heavy sorrow hung from my chest. Before, I had thought I'd seen horrors in my life, but nothing could match that camp. There was no reason for me to complain, though. I'd only seen one night. For those Reds, that had been the last few months of their lives. In their fight for survival, they were the heroes.

We found them places to sleep where we could. Like we did before the UPF forced everyone out of the Enclave, people shared the few real houses, and the rest made the best they could out of the dilapidated buildings. We brought fresh supplies of food that Julia had managed to smuggle away, and there was the closest thing Reds could have to a feast. For many of them, it was the first real meal they'd had in too long.

That night, or I guess that morning, was a meal that I will never forget. While we all felt the pain in our hearts, we were a community in that moment, reunited in our old home. With all the conflicts and divides, I'd forgotten what it felt like to be with a group that ignored our differences. The Reds were all outcasts, and that was enough to unite us despite everything else. We'd seen more than our fair share of death and suffering, but we were just grateful to be alive and to have each other, even if many of us had been complete strangers just hours before.

I was caught between two worlds: born to elite Purples and now living among the royals, but in my heart, I would always be a Red. My place was with the lost and the rejected, not with the rich and powerful. It was all a game to the Purples and royals, but here, in the slums, it was real life. It was dirty, dark, and hard, but it was real. Beyond Julia and only a few others, the Whites lived a lie behind their walls. While they drank and danced themselves into oblivion, the Reds starved and died in the slums and camps.

This was the appeal of the Fracture. Max's power fed off the anger the Reds felt towards the higher colors and the royals while promoting the idea of a community where it wasn't bad to be a Red. In a way, she was right about the country's problems, but her solution was to use the same brutal tactics against the oppressors, just repeating the cycle of crimson being spilled in the battle for power. I hated Bachton, but I pitied her and her followers. They had suffered like so many other Reds, and in blind rage, they sought to become the very thing they hated.

As I watched the rescued Reds and Blacks, I wondered what my parents would, or could, have done to stop this. *What would they think of me?* I needed to learn more about them: who they were, if they were working alone, where the rest of my family was, and what they believed could destroy the Prism and the UPF. We would never meet, but now that I knew who they were, there was a constant nagging in my head to finish what they started.

Delaware interrupted my thoughts by waving a hand in front of my face. "Yo, Ivan."

I chuckled. "Sorry, was just watching the little community you've built."

"Not just me, Ivan: *us*, all of us." She gazed down the street, towards the old house she'd shared with Pennsylvania before her roommate was killed during Operation Blackout. "I'm going to take a trip. Wanna come?"

Holding out my arm, I said, "Lead the way."

We started down the street, heading north. Each step I tried to avoid the cracks like I did when I was a kid. It was difficult, though, as the Enclave's awful state meant the street was more crack than road.

Delaware looked up at the stars as we walked. "Remember when this felt like a game? When you first started training me, I felt like a rebel from a storybook. It was fun and exciting when all the responsibility was on someone else's shoulders."

A smile forced its way across my face. "You've come a long way. From my mentee to Captain of the Militia." She blushed as I continued, "The Militia would have been destroyed if it wasn't for you. For so long we were just scraping by, trying to hold onto the little we had, but when we lost everything, you united people: the Reds, the Oranges, the Yellows, all of them."

"I don't feel like I've accomplished anything. Every day, all I think about is how we're going to survive and how many people we've lost. We lost twenty-one people during that raid, Ivan. That's twenty-one Militia members dead because I told them to raid the camp. Is this how you felt as a lieutenant?"

I sighed. She refused to realize all the good she'd done, but I wasn't feeling any better. We'd lost people, and the guards slaughtered too many Reds to count during our raid. We passed by my old house, and I hesitated for only a moment before moving on. "Every damn day. Whether it was a mission or whatever, I was worried about my team, about you."

She cut in front of me. "Adorable, but you don't need to worry about me anymore. I'm safe... and I've got Snap."

"Exactly why I'm worried." We both laughed. "I still worry about you, Del. You can unite the people hiding in the shadows, but I've seen how the kidnapping messed with you. Revenge won't fix it."

She turned and continued down the street as I followed. "You got revenge on Isaac. Besides, this is about more than revenge. If I don't do something, Max is going to take over St. Paul, our city, and kill everyone. You've seen her, she's insane."

She's got a point. I jogged to catch back up with her. "The military will stop them, and if they don't, we'll figure something out. Just promise me you won't do anything reckless."

Stopping quickly, she turned to face me with a smirk on her face. "Hey, if I do, I learned from the best."

I chuckled. *Everything has changed, except her sarcasm.* "Just know I'm proud of you, and I promise, we will beat the Fracture. For now, though, you've done everything you can for this city."

Her nose wrinkled. "How do you know if it's enough?"

I looked towards the old High Bridge and the St. Paul skyline. "You don't."

When I finally returned to the palace, it was almost noon, and I was exhausted from what had felt like the longest day of my life. After what I'd seen, though, I was humbled to have even my little closet bedroom to sleep in. Things had not been easy the past few months, but I had not slept out in the cold, starving to death as the UPF guards executed my friends and family.

I found myself not wanting to talk to anyone. I'd texted Julia that I was alive on the van ride back the night before, but I couldn't find the energy to explain the things I'd seen. How could I? She'd seen a camp from the distance, but there weren't words to describe to her the suffering and death we saw on the inside that night. The coup felt like a nice dream compared to that eternal nightmare.

Sleep found me quickly, but it did not last long. The images were burned into my brain. The silence of sleep just invited their return along with the screams and smells of death. When I awoke, I was breathing heavily and sweating like I'd been running for my life. *What is wrong with me?*

I heard someone breathing behind me, and I was suddenly aware of Julia holding me. I didn't know she'd come in or how long she'd been there, quietly trying to comfort me. No hug, even from the girl I loved, could fix the scar that had been left on my soul. Part of me was lost during the raid. I didn't know what part or how to get it back. All I knew was that I felt broken, lost. Her arm around my waist and warm breaths against the back of my neck were the only things grounding me to the real world. Everything else felt numb, lifeless.

Eventually, after I don't know how long, I worked up the energy to speak. "Tell me something happy, anything."

She thought for a moment. "Did you know that every snowflake is completely unique? If you look closely at each one, its pattern is not the same as any other snowflake in the world. They are each amazing and special on their own, but together they form the beautiful snow that covers everything."

I shifted, and the familiar smell of her soft wintergreen perfume flowed over me. For just a moment, I felt a small bit of joy again. "I didn't know that."

She softly kissed the back of my head and ran her finger up and down my neck. "We are the same way: each of us amazing and completely unique. Even if we look alike, there is no one else in the world exactly like us. We are all different, but together, we accomplish beautiful and previously thought to be impossible things. We build wonders, create music, laugh with friends, give each other hope, and find love."

I shut my eyes. As usual, I knew she was right, but I couldn't shake the dread inside me. "We also fight, murder, suffer, and control each other. I don't think snowflakes can do that."

She sniffled, and I was caught off guard at the sorrow she felt for me. For a moment, though, she chuckled and joked through her sadness. "I don't know. Have you seen Minneapolis recently?" I didn't want to, but I laughed and smiled as she continued, "Jonah told me everything."

I slowly rolled over to face her. Her eyes were red from crying. "Everything?"

She bit her lip, trying to hold back tears as she ran her hand along my cheek. "He told me about the people you saved and how terrible the camps were. He told me how they started killing the Reds you couldn't get to in time and how you refused to leave the kids behind. He even said you jumped into the Mississippi to save a man from drowning and almost drowned yourself."

I sniffled. "Jonah talks too much."

She smiled, but her eyes were still full of sorrow. "Ivan, you risked your life to save complete strangers. That is amazing. You are a hero."

I sighed. "It's not amazing. When I dove into that river, I wasn't thinking about the consequences or how I was going to make it out. I just knew I had to try. When I tried to save those Blacks, I wasn't thinking about survival or how I would do it. I was fueled by rage and fear for their survival. That's not heroism, it's recklessness, but I don't know anything else."

She whispered back, "You might not believe that you are a hero, but you saved thousands of Reds and hundreds of kids. To each of them, you are a hero. To me, you are a hero, and it is okay that this has messed with your head. No one should have to see that, let alone live like that."

I shut my eyes again and shifted so that our foreheads touched. There was nothing more I had to say. My chest still felt like it was in a knot, but even that little contact with her made the world feel a little better, safer.

She wrapped her arms around me and pulled me into a hug. "I'm so proud of you, my love. You will be an amazing king someday, because you care so deeply about people, even if you try to hide it from the rest of the world."

I kissed her cheek, still feeling shattered but grateful she was there, making me talk. "I'm glad I don't have to hide from you."

Chapter 34

We had all hoped for a bit of quiet after the raid, but it didn't come. Instead, both the Fracture and UPF had escalated their attacks in St. Paul. The capitol in Minneapolis remained safe, far away from the fighting, but whispers began among the royals that the military questioned whether they could hold St. Paul or not, echoing what we'd overheard from the guards in the camp.

Somehow, the Fracture had enough heavy weaponry to push the military out of the western neighborhood of Summit Hill and threaten the Green and Yellow controlled Downtown neighborhood, one of the military's last zones-of-control in the city. No one knew where they'd gotten RPGs, grenades, and anti-tank missiles that weren't available anywhere on the black market. The Fracture had them, though, and with the military split between holding the camps, protecting the country's other major cities against revolts, and fighting the various gangs that terrorized everywhere the Fractured didn't, they were stretched too thin to handle the Fracture's attacks.

Jonah and I spent days tracking the military and Fracture's troop movements with royal resources. We still couldn't figure out where the Fracture's weapons and supplies were coming from, but whoever it was had extensive resources. As information came in, we relayed the reports to Delaware and Snapback, who were trying to handle feeding both Payne-Phalen and areas outside of Militia control while avoiding conflicts. Both of us needed a way to be useful, and conveniently, this one allowed us to ignore the memories of the raid that still haunted us and allowed me to stay away from Vera. I didn't trust myself armed around her in my current state of mind, so I avoided her at all costs.

In the meantime, royal life went on for Julia, and along with it, her birthday. I'm not sure what I expected a princess's birthday party to be like, but it was a massive ball. Hundreds of royals and Blues were there, each bringing her some type of extravagant gift, hoping to outdo each other.

I stood at my usual security position to the side in the ballroom, watching with disdain. *St. Paul burns and the Reds starve in the camps while these ego-maniacs drink and flaunt their wealth.* Their gifts were eloquently wrapped, and some were massive. I thought about the blue box that I had in my room, waiting for the smaller party that was for Julia's closest friends only. I could never match the extravagance of the royals, but I knew her better than they did. None of their shiny gifts would impress their next queen.

With all the pain of the recent months, I was determined to ensure she had a good day. She deserved at least one. We didn't have much time in the morning before her handmaidens had to begin the intricate art of preparing a princess for a party, so I planned to take her for a walk in the woods after the parties. An eternity ago, we had our first kiss in that forest, and since then I'd fallen in love with her again and again. Even with the trials we faced in our relationship and beyond, we always came back to each other. That forest was an escape for both of us, one we so badly needed.

Now, as I stood, watching her flawlessly handle the crowd, I smiled to myself. We lived in a dark, crimson-stained world, but somehow I was the lucky one who could call the last pure light mine. Part of me was still missing after that horrific night. If anyone could help me find it, though, it was her.

Julia looked beautiful in her ice-blue gown as she danced, talked, and laughed with the guests. She smiled the most, though, when she crouched, listening to the little royal children telling her whatever they were excited about today. Her eyes met mine for a moment as the children rambled, and we both smiled. The kids were still too young to be caught in the chaos, and she always enjoyed her time with them, royal or not.

Even if the gifts were ridiculous, Julia enjoyed her time in the spotlight. She always wanted to be a good princess and an example for younger girls, and in that light she handled herself with the poise of a queen. She understood the efforts, though misguided, that the guests went through to try and impress her. For these people, there was little more to life than nice things and status. Somehow, Julia had remained so real, despite her life in that spotlight, and I loved her for that.

Eventually, the party began to draw to a close, and I drifted to my room to grab my gift. I grabbed the wide box and quickly climbed the stairs to the central room, where the small party would be held.

Julia was already there, along with Alex and many of the same friends that had been at the small party a few months ago. She was still in her dress but had let her hair down. Alex was telling some story, and Julia smiled and laughed as her sister talked. It meant the world to me to see her so happy, surrounded by her favorite people. She smiled at me as she noticed that I'd arrived, and I began to walk towards her.

I was interrupted, though, as Jonah's voice came through my earpiece. "Ivan, I've got bad news."

Please, not today. I tapped my radio. "What's up?"

"The Fracture bombed the old First National Bank building half-an-hour ago. The chief of the military has had enough. He just announced the immediate withdrawal of all military and civilian security forces from the city and ordered an evacuation."

They've given up on St. Paul. "The Fracture is going to slaughter everyone." There were still tens of thousands of Greens, Yellows, and Oranges who wouldn't have time to make it out of St. Paul, and the Fracture would kill all of them if somebody didn't do something.

One of Julia's friends had heard the news too and turned on the TV, which was showing footage of what was happening. From an aerial view, the camera showed the wreckage of the iconic First National Bank and its old "1st" sign cracked in the center of the debris. Fracture rioters were everywhere, and fires were spreading across the entirety of downtown as they threw Molotov-cocktails at every building they passed. It was obvious where they were headed: the old capitol building. If they could take that, they'd hold the symbolic seat of power in St. Paul.

The news anchor was reading the updates from his tele-prompter: "Video shows that the military has already pulled back in an effort to contain the threats within the city. It appears that the terrorists have seized complete control over the western and southern sections of the city, and General Secretary Bachton has declared that St. Paul is lost."

I dropped my eyes and whispered, "Crimson reigns." I shut my eyes and took a deep breath. *Why'd it have to be today?* I tapped my earpiece. "Jonah, I'm on my way. There's no one else that can stop this now."

Julia looked at me with sorrow from across the room, under-standing what was happening. She rushed over and pulled me down the hall. "I know you believe you have to stop them, but you can't Ivan, not alone."

It felt like a weight had been dropped on my chest as I looked into her eyes with a fire in my heart. "These are my people Julia, our people. I waited too long to do something about them, and now, they're burning down St. Paul and slaughtering innocent people. I might not be able to stop them, but I have to try."

Her hands shook as she took mine, but her voice was cold as ice. "Do what you have to do to protect our people, but promise you'll come back to me."

"I promise." I kissed her quickly, gave her hands one last squeeze, and ran towards the garage. *Why is nothing easy?*

Chapter 35

The V6 of the Minutemen car roared as I flew through the dying afternoon light. Once I'd cleared Minneapolis, the roads had become eerily empty beyond the fleeing military convoy. Nobody wanted to be anywhere near the chaos in St. Paul. No one except me.

I tried not to think about the impossible task in front of me as I drove. The UPF had desperately played their hand with the military to stop the Fracture, but now, the cowards would rather let thousands of innocent people die than actually defend the lower colors. St. Paul would burn while they sat back in their precious capital city. The Yellows and Oranges would suffer for their government's sins if I couldn't stop them.

The radio crackled as I tried to call Delaware, "Del. Del, you there?"

A few seconds passed before a blast of static and then her frantic voice came through my earpiece. "Ivan! They're burning the whole damn city down."

I groaned, pushing the gas pedal to the floor as I stormed down the highway. "I know. We need to stop them."

"There's no way."

I shook my head. "Listen to me, Del. I need you to gather everyone you can —everyone— and march them on the capitol building. They outgun us, but they don't outnumber us if we bring the other colors in on this. We need to show them we won't let them destroy the city."

She snapped, "This isn't the time for a stupid march, Ivan! We need to protect the territory we have, otherwise we're all going to die."

"No, Del. Listen to me. This is our only chance. Meet them at the capitol and show them what they're up against. You can have a hidden group of fighters, just in case, but don't bring weapons to the capitol. There's no way we can beat them in a fight. We need to prove to them that they're wrong."

She sighed. "Then what are you going to do?"

I took a reluctant breath. "I'm going to do the convincing."

It wasn't long before the destruction came into sight. The Summit Hill and Downtown zones were on fire. Smoke covered the sky as I drove, blocking what sunlight remained. I could see the expanding line of fire in the distance, slowly moving towards the heart of the city. *There's still time.*

The engine groaned as I pushed harder, skidding off the highway and onto the streets towards the old capitol, its white dome stabbing through the smoke in defiance as the flames closed in. There was no way to know if my plan would work, but I had to try. A battle would be the end of the fragile foundation we'd managed to rebuild for the Militia and the end of any hope to prevent a civil war. The country stood on the brink. It was up to us to save it.

The car skidded to a stop on the road to the side of the capitol. As I stepped out of the car, I was smacked by the smell of fire and the deafening noise of yells and explosions. *They're close.* I could only hope Delaware's people would arrive soon. Until then, I stood alone against the approaching wave of destruction.

To my right stretched the old capitol mall, and to my left were the steps to the capitol, flanked by two statues: Law and Obedience. I took a shaky breath and ran to the statue of Law. As I climbed its base, I gazed up at the scales of justice in her hand. With her blindfold, she couldn't see the tide of destruction approaching; I considered her lucky. Upon the elevated base of the statue, I stood above the approaching crowds and would have my chance to be heard.

The smoke shrouded the buildings in the distance, and out of it came the horde of Fracture rioters, armed with rifles, RPGs, and Molotov-cocktails. I could only watch as they approached, shouting and throwing the flaming bottles across the mall. At the head of the horde was Max herself, striding with pride as the city burned to the ground in her wake.

Delaware and her people were nowhere to be seen, and as Max approached, a devious grin crossed her face. She saw me, and she knew what I was about to do. The crowd behind her filled the mall as it was engulfed in flames, leaving nothing but smoke and ash where there had once stood green grass.

Soon, Max reached the edge of the mall and looked up at me before signaling for her crowd to halt. They followed her order without question, and for a moment, I stood in an eerie silence, the only person standing between the Fracture and control of St. Paul. After what felt like hours, Max sneered. "You stand alone against the winds of change, Ivan. There's no one to help you. Your princess and her corrupt family can't stop this."

I didn't respond for a few seconds. I just watched the fires burn in the distance, turning the blue sky to an ashy black. Eventually, I looked down at her. "You've changed nothing, Max. All you've done is shown everyone that they were right about us, that they were right about the Reds. The Prism divided us, and you embraced it. You destroyed everything the Fracture was supposed to be. It was supposed to unite us regardless of color, to fracture the Prism beyond repair, but instead, you fight to exploit its divide for your own gain."

A murmur rippled through the crowd, but it ceased when Max raised a closed fist. "It is bold for the one who abandoned his own people to speak of unity. Who are you united with, the Whites? The same people that allowed us to be chained in the first place? You're part of the rot, Ivan, and you'll burn with the rest of it."

I held my arm towards the burning city behind them and spoke, "I am trying to save this city, our home. I'm trying to change things without another civil war that will only lead to more innocent lives lost. I never abandoned our people. I have worked every moment to end the Prism. What were *you* doing while we saved those trapped in the New Ulm camp? Face it, Max, you're no better than them. You're no better than the people that put us in chains, because in the end, you want to do the same thing to the other colors. You're a maniac and a fraud, and if you go through with this, we will never be free."

A discontent murmur spread further among the crowd. Max raised her fist again. "It doesn't matter what you say, Ivan. You're alone, and you're not going to stop this." She dropped her arm and pointed forward. "Burn it down!"

A roar came from the crowd as they regained their resilience and marched forward. *This is the end.*

Just as they reached the edge of the mall, the sound thousands of footsteps echoed from around the building. I looked to the east as a wave of people pushed onto the path. In front was Delaware, leading the Reds, Oranges, Yellows, and even a couple Greens, all interlocking arms as they formed lines, blocking the rioters as they pushed towards me.

Max's eyes were wild as she watched the path to the capitol flood with people. *Delaware did it.* I'd never been prouder of my mentee than in that moment. Somehow, she'd brought so many people together so quickly, and they had stopped the Fracture dead in their tracks. Max screamed for her people to push forward and shoot anyone who stood in the way, but only a few of the rioters raised their guns. The rest wavered, unwilling to shoot at the unarmed crowd in front of them.

I stood tall on top of my statue and called down, "We can end the Prism, we can stop the oppression, and we can save this country, but we can only do it together. When we fight, they win. Lay down the guns, and let's work together for once. Ignore the color of your earring and realize we all want to be free."

The Fracture rioters lowered their guns slowly. Max shouted for them to fire, but they weren't listening. They saw the united group standing in front of them. They knew what it meant.

My joy was cut short, though, as Delaware stepped out of the front of the Militia's line. I couldn't see her face, but I knew what she was thinking. She shook as Max turned her head from the wavering rioters. Delaware raised a pistol towards her, and a crooked smile appeared on Max's face as she said, "Crimson must reign."

I cried out from the statue, trying to stop her, "Delaware! No!"

Bang! The shot echoed through the now deathly silent lawn, hanging in the air for what felt like hours as we tried to comprehend what just happened. *She got her revenge, but she destroyed everything else.*

Delaware stood, alone, between the two fronts. She breathed heavily, staring at Max's body slumped on the ground before her, a pool of crimson around her head. The pistol dropped from her hand and clattered against the cement pathway as she spoke, "Crimson must fall."

The rioters were enraged. We were no longer a non-violent group standing in front of them. Instead, we were the enemies that killed their leader, their demagogue. For one moment, it looked like we might have unity, but that moment had passed. They raised their guns, spurred on by their desire to avenge Max. I closed my eyes, waiting for the bullets to come, but they didn't.

A deafening roar filled the air, and I opened my eyes in shock. Planes screeched overhead so fast that the air around us shook with the force. A hush filled the crowd for only a moment before the world exploded into fire. My body screamed as the heat seared at my skin, and I was thrown off my podium and onto the steps beyond. The world turned red as I lay there, broken.

Through the pain, I turned my head to see the burning wreckage of where I'd stood moments before. The last thing I saw was the decapitated head of the statue of Law, illuminated by the light of the flames, before everything went black.

END OF BOOK TWO

A Word From The Author

Thank you for taking the time to read the second book of The Prism Files! I hope you have enjoyed reading it as much as I have enjoyed writing it. If you did, please consider giving it an honest review online.

To stay updated on my writing for the series, receive more insights into the world of The Prism Files, and have the chance to win free books, sign-up to receive my newsletter at: www.Brendan-Noble.com